Souvenir of Cold Springs

"Florey has a particular gift for characterization and imbues her protagonists' simplest moments of self-reflection with telling detail and startling awareness. The result is a smart and absorbing novel that rings true . . . Florey's forthright and witty prose buoyantly carries the tale." —*Publishers Weekly*

"The novel's achievement is that it presents several generations of the family with keen insight, tracing their specific eccentricities and shedding light on family dynamics in general . . . Readers might feel sorry to leave Florey's fictional family behind . . ." —*Newsday*

"It would be best if you just went and read the book now. It's a shame to spoil the pleasure Florey offers in her graceful revelations . . . These people seem real, and their secrets seem possible, fascinating . . . Florey has a knack for describing women in precarious mental states, women with skewed realities, women who seem capable of making anything possible . . ." —*Hartford Courant*

Vigil for a Stranger

"A chilling, eloquent novel that draws you in with mystery and holds you there with love, obsession, failure, insanity, and an enchanting hybrid of past and present . . . Florey infuses her typically irresistible characters with a depth and darkness that gives her newest work a coherent vision and lasting effect."

D0815121

Further praise for the novels of Kitty Burns Florey:

"An affectionately observed book, with a wholly female quality of brisk, amused resilience. Delightful is the word for it."
—*Cosmopolitan*

"Immensely appealing . . . Yeasty with bright recognitions and hard-won insights—indisputably heartwarming work."
—*Kirkus Reviews*

"[A] delicious book . . . Wit, imagination, inspired improvisation, and daring. Kitty Burns Florey has all of the above."
—*Los Angeles Herald Examiner*

Also by Kitty Burns Florey

Solos

soloS

Kitty Burns Florey

𝓑

BERKLEY BOOKS, NEW YORK

𝕭

A Berkley Book
Published by The Berkley Publishing Group
A division of Penguin Group (USA) Inc.
375 Hudson Street
New York, New York 10014

This book is an original publication of The Berkley Publishing Group.

PRINTING HISTORY
Berkley trade paperback edition / August 2004

Library of Congress Cataloging-in-Publication Data

Florey, Kitty Burns.
    Solos / Kitty Burns Florey.
        p. cm.
    ISBN 0-425-19599-6
    1. Williamsburg (New York, N.Y.)—Fiction. 2. Women photographers—
Fiction. 3. City and town life—Fiction. 4. Women pet owners—Fiction.
5. Divorced women—Fiction. 6. Dog walking—Fiction. I. Title

PS3556.L588S58 2004
813'.54—dc22

2004046282

PRINTED IN THE UNITED STATES OF AMERICA

10   9   8   7   6   5   4   3   2   1

This book is dedicated to
Ron Savage,
with love and thanks

Acknowledgments

Thanks to Katherine Florey for her very helpful early readings of the manuscript, and especially for the legal advice. To James Bloomfield for the migraine cure. To Williamsburgers Judith Maniatis for introducing me to 11211, Jane Schwartz for her continual inspiration, and Doug Safranek for the pickles. And of course to Noodles, Zipper, Eggy, Duster, Miko, and the incomparable Duke.

And thanks to the BARC (Brooklyn Animal Resource Coalition) shelter and to Peter Caine: the book owes a lot to them both.

I am also grateful to the following websites, of which I made liberal use for palindromes and other bits of wordplay. I recommend them all as delightful ways to while away far too many hours:

www.palindromes.org—*Jim Kalb's Palindrome Connection*
www.wordways.com—*Word Ways: The Journal of Recreational Linguistics*
http://realchange.org/pal/index2.htm—*The Palindromist*

Solos

soloS

Kitty Burns Florey

We shall not cease from exploration
And the end of all our exploring
Will be to arrive where we started . . .

—T. S. ELIOT,
FOUR QUARTETS: LITTLE GIDDING

By at the gallop he goes, and then
By he comes back at the gallop again.

—ROBERT LOUIS STEVENSON,
WINDY NIGHTS

1

Step on no petS

Step on no petS

(October 2002)

Emily Lime is walking up Bedford Avenue. She is wearing black jeans and a long-sleeved black T-shirt that just covers the blue zipper tattooed around her right wrist.

The tattoo is something she deeply regrets.

It doesn't seem right that because of a little Mexican weed and the incredible discount offered by Diane the Tattoo Monarch, she made a decision at age nineteen that resulted in a wrist zipper she will have to live with for the rest of her life. Someday she will be a doddering old crone in a nursing home with a zipper tattoo. Admittedly, it's a beautiful, deep blue zipper, the dainty tracks neatly done, the pull falling slightly to one side the way a real one might. No one would say Diane is not a genius. But hardly a day goes by when Emily doesn't wish it weren't there. On the subway, she always studies the ads for laser tattoo removal and wonders if having it taken off would be as painful as having it put on. She has decided it probably would, and instead has taken to wearing cuff bracelets over it. She has three—a beaded one she made herself, a leather one she found at a craft show in McCarren Park, and a silver one she bought when Dr. Demand gave her the check for her last BREAD photograph.

Today the sleeve of her T-shirt does the trick.

It's a warmish day at the end of October, as warm as June, but fall is in the air. Emily has just gotten over a bad cold, and it's her first day out. She still has the cough, but she finally feels normal after almost a week moping around her loft, drinking seltzer and looking out the window at the tugboats on the river and the puffy white clouds over Manhattan Island. The sky is brilliantly blue. Emily's dog Otto walks jauntily at the end of his red leash, his tags ringing like bells. They both love this walk up Bedford—a walk Emily has taken almost daily for eleven years and Otto for six.

They pass the sushi place, the Mexican restaurant, the video store, the Syrian deli, the Polish bakery (whose BREAD sign Emily has photographed a dozen times), the new baby shop that has a pair of studded black leather booties in the window, and Marta's Beauty Salon, whose faded pink-and-green sign has probably not been retouched since 1966. They pass Mr. Suarez, with his Chihuahua, Eddie, in his pocket and a shopping basket full of soda cans. They pass the Pink Pony Thrift Shop with the WHAT GOES AROUND COMES AROUND sign on the door, and the used-book store and its new café, where they can smell the hot apple cider all the way out on the sidewalk. The smell seems exactly right, a perfect match to the brown leaves on the ground and the V of geese overhead and the signs in the drugstore window advertising Halloween candy.

Emily is on her way to the park, where Otto can be let off his leash to run freely in the dog enclosure. This is the best part of Otto's day, and Emily is glad she can take him herself. All the time she's been sick, she's had to have Marcus take Otto out at ten dollars a run. Her cold cost her over fifty dollars in dog-walking fees. Plus another hefty chunk for the long-distance bills she racked up when she began to feel well enough to talk on the phone but not to go out. And eighty dollars for the tweedy sweater she shouldn't have ordered off the Web from Eddie Bauer to cheer herself up, but did. All that is nothing, of course, compared to the debt of gratitude she now owes to Anstice, her landlady and friend, who is much too good to her, and who knocked on her door every day with various practical gifts: Nyquil, more seltzer, a *New Yorker*, a DVD of *Watership Down*, a pint of home-made applesauce from the Greenmarket, and a pot of chicken soup she made herself from her late grandmother's late cook's recipe.

Emily also owes Anstice the rent.

As she hoped, Marcus is at the park with his Saturday morning crew: Rumpy, Chipper, Elvis, and Reba. Marcus beams when he sees her. "You have risen!"

"Yes," she says. "Still coughing, still a little stuffy, but basically I am healed." She inhales deeply through her nose. "See?"

"Impressive. When did you get better?"

"I began to feel almost okay last night. I had the most wonderful day yesterday. I curled up with Otto, and Izzy perched on my foot and unraveled one of my socks, and we all watched *Watership Down*."

"Sounds like heaven."

She smiles at him because she knows he means it literally: For Marcus, heaven is animals. Marcus looks not unlike a cute animal himself. He has just had his hair cut very short, and it's like soft suede against his narrow head. His ears, like his chin and his nose, are small and unassuming. Emily's friend Gene Rae once said, "There's something very *woodland creature* about Marcus," and she was right. Marcus has the face of a squirrel, or a chipmunk, including the luminous, watchful eyes, which are, however, the green of cats' eyes, and show a rim of white below the iris, giving him a misleadingly lazy, lustful look. Today he's wearing a T-shirt that was once olive but has faded so that his eyes and shirt almost match. Emily, who never tires of looking at people, regards him with delight.

"The world is a new and beautiful place." She means since her cold cleared up, but she also means that it just *is,* reliably, on a daily basis.

Marcus looks alternately at her and at the dogs in his charge. "Check out Elvis," he says. Elvis is leaping around friskily with a branch in his mouth. "Who would believe that dog is twelve years old?" Then he looks back at Emily. "Do you want to play Scrabble later?"

"I can't today. I really can't. It's so beautiful, I have to go out and shoot."

"Shoot where?"

"I don't know exactly. I thought I might drive out to Long Island. Northport, maybe. Or Centerport."

Marcus nods approvingly. "As long as it's a port."

"Yes, or a fort."

"Or a court."

"No, I really mean it. There's a town called Fort Salonga right near there."

"There is? On Long Island? There's a park in Africa called Salonga." Marcus always knows things like this.

"Isn't there an actress or somebody, too?"

"I don't know." He never knows things like that.

When Emily takes Otto off his leash, he rushes over to Elvis and Reba, whom he loves, and the three of them run around together, barking crazily. Emily and Marcus lean against the fence and watch the dogs. Mrs. Buzik is sitting on the broken bench with her ancient poodle, Trix, at her feet, and a man Emily doesn't know is there with a big rottweiler who keeps nudging Rumpy with his nose.

"Go on, Trix," Mrs. Buzik says. "Go on and play with your little pals. Get some exercise."

"How's she doing, Mrs. B.?" Marcus asks.

"We take it one day at a time, Marcus. One day at a time. Both of us."

"She looks good, though."

"She's a poodle. It's her job to look good." Mrs. Buzik takes a flowered handkerchief out of her pocket and holds it in her hand. "But she's been okay. No incidents lately." Her mouth opens wide, and she sneezes loudly and wipes her nose. As always, Emily is impressed with the perfection of Mrs. Buzik's dentures, which look better than any real teeth she has ever seen. "There. I knew I was going to do that."

Emily has recently stopped saying "God bless you" when people sneeze, but often feels bad about the skipped beat it leaves in the rhythm of the conversation. So she says, "I hope you're not getting a cold. I'm just getting over a real killer."

"There's something going around, I hear," says Mrs. Buzik. "I'm praying I don't get it. That's all I need." She leans down to the dog. "Go on, Trix. Get out there and play. It'll do you good. Get the bowels moving." Mrs. Buzik lives alone in a particularly dingy fake-brick-fronted house on Driggs Avenue, which she owns but on which, according to her tenants, she hasn't done any maintenance in at least ten years. No one can figure out if she's very rich or very poor. She is an unfathomably old woman who, like her house, must have once been stunning: deep-set dark eyes, a fine long nose. She still gets up every morning and puts on eyeliner and mascara and blue shadow and red lipstick, and winds up her sparse hair in a colorful scarf. "I'm just waiting until Miss Priss here does her business, then I'm off home. My daughter is coming over to take me to the market. My neighbor told me they got canned salmon on sale, ninety-nine a can. I like to mix it up with mayonnaise and those Greek pickles."

Rumpy and Chipper have found a stick, and Rumpy is trying to get it from Chipper. Marcus looks vigilant: Rumpy is unpredictable. Their struggle takes them close to Trix, and she gets up, looking offended, and moves under the bench, but the activity has apparently given her the idea because she squats and starts to do her business.

"There she goes, Mrs. B.," says Marcus.

"What a relief," Mrs. Buzik says. "I thought we'd be sitting here all day." She stows her hanky in one pocket and takes a plastic bag from another.

"Here, I'll get it."

"Oh, Marcus, you don't have to do that."

"I insist."

In one graceful motion, he takes the bag from her and scoops up Trix's business. Then he ties the ends together, pivots, and tosses the whole thing, underhanded, into the trash can.

"You're a saint, Marcus." Mrs. Buzik gets up stiffly. Trix looks suddenly animated, sniffing amiably at Reba, who has flopped down near her. "See? She feels better. Come on, then, Trix. Let's get going."

"So long, Mrs. Buzik," Emily says. "Don't get that cold."

"Have you ever tried those Greek pickles? They're a lot cheaper than the Polish. I get them at that deli up on Manhattan, by the church. I take the bus up there to shop, or my daughter drives me. They got the bargains. A dollar fifty-nine for a big jar. They're good with the salmon."

"Sounds delicious," Marcus says. "Though I'm not much of a pickle man."

"Just like my husband, may he rest in peace. If he ate three pickles a year, I'd be surprised." Mrs. Buzik winks at Emily, exposing a wrinkly oval of lavender-blue shadow. "Men!"

They watch her hobble away, her bright scarf bobbing, the dog plodding along beside her. The man with the rottweiler snaps his dog's leash back on and, wordlessly, they leave.

"Jeez. Friendly," Emily says.

"He's a friend of Lamont's."

"Is he a Tragedy Club person?"

"No, he's the guy who's subletting Jeanette's loft. I think he's probably just shy."

"You say that because you're a saint, Marcus. He didn't even talk to his dog. He's probably one of those guys who buys cheap generic dog food and forgets to keep the water bowl filled."

"Nah, Lamont said he's okay. I forget his name. Ted or

something. Bob. Jim." He pauses. "I wish I could remember. I hate forgetting people's names."

"You have such a thing about names."

Marcus nods soberly. "Yeah, I do."

Emily likes Marcus's obsessions because she shares so many of them—names, area codes, zip codes, anagrams, palindromes. She wonders if it can possibly be true that Marcus moved to Williamsburg for its palindromic 11211 zip code. She says, "Ask Lamont at the party tomorrow."

"I will." His face brightens. "I'm giving Lamont that picture of Daphne I took last summer when I was sitting for them. Remember? The one where she's curled up in the bathroom sink?"

"It's adorable."

"I put it in a frame."

"He'll love it." Emily jangles Otto's red leash. "Well, I should get cracking if I'm going to get to Fort Salonga." She has a brief coughing fit, during which Marcus looks at her with concern. She shakes her head and flaps her hand in the air the way coughing people do when they want to convey that they're all right even though they seem all wrong. Then she calls, a bit hoarsely, "Hey, Otto! Let's move on out of here."

"You sure you're okay?"

"I'm okay. I need a bottle of water."

"Good luck today. I hope they have a lot of bakeries and stuff. Watch repair shops."

"They will. It's amazing. Everyplace does. But of course they have to be right."

"Don't forget we have Trollope on Tuesday."

"As if I could forget. As if it's not the high point of my whole life. Come on, Otto! Let's beat it, boy." She coaxes Otto away from his friends and attaches his leash. "He's so in love with Reba."

"Too bad they're both fixed. They'd have cute puppies."

Emily looks dubious. Reba is a low-growing part-dachshund, Otto is a grayish-white mongrel mop with an underslung jaw. "Was that a joke?"

"Yes."

Marcus's mouth turns down into the little secret smile that Emily loves. She would like to hug him, but she just says, "Otto probably doesn't think it's funny."

"Otto needs to lighten up."

As she and Otto are crossing the park, Emily sees Susan Skolnick sitting on her usual bench. Susan Skolnick is given to taking long walks through the neighborhood after which she always ends up sitting on a bench by the dog run, silent and alone—a pariah—watching the dogs at play. She's a park regular, but she doesn't come with a dog. Susan is notorious for an incident involving her six-year-old daughter and the family dog, a border collie named Glenda, who had never shown a hint of bad behavior. In fact, Glenda never even barked except when someone sneezed—an endearing habit Susan and her husband, Murray, used to brag about at the park. But on a summer day just over a year ago, during some boisterous romping in their backyard, Glenda leapt up and bit the daughter, Vanna, on the lip. Within minutes, Murray was hustling Vanna in a car service to the emergency room (where she got two stitches), while Susan tossed the dog into the backseat of their Toyota, took her to the big animal hospital on Long Island, and demanded that she be put to sleep. The Skolnicks were regarded with contempt by the other park regulars. The sight of Susan, sitting stone-faced on a bench, watching the dogs play, only hardened their hearts further, though no one could figure out what she got out of sitting there.

And since no one ever talked to her, no one would ever know.

"As long as she suffers," Marcus always says. "I don't care why or how, I just want her to suffer. I want her to be eaten away with remorse. I want her to have nightmares about dogs."

Emily finds Susan's presence disturbing, even ominous, and she turns away from the woman's mysterious pain and continues back to Bedford Avenue. When she makes a brief stop at the Syrian deli for a bottle of water and a bag of chips for the car, Otto sits outside and whines. She knows he's tired; Elvis and Reba have worn him out. He's not a young dog; he wasn't young when she got him, and she's had him since her dog Harry died just before she split with Hart—more than six years. Otto wants his biscuit and a nap now as much as he wanted to play half an hour ago. But when they come to the corner of North Third Street—home—he gets a second wind and trots joyfully toward the sparkling river with its long gray strip of skyline and the bright blue sky above, pulling Emily along behind him.

2

Pa's a saP

Pa's a saP

Marcus is having Sunday brunch with his father, Tab Hartwell, known to everyone—except Marcus—as Hart.

Marcus insists on calling him Dad, because he knows Hart hates it.

Father and son are in SoHo at a sidewalk café on Wooster Street. Marcus dislikes sidewalk cafés. Why is it considered fun to eat food in the midst of exhaust fumes from traffic and stares from tourists? Tourism was down, but now it's up again, up higher than any city should have to tolerate. On a sunny autumn Sunday, the walk from the subway to the Bistro du Sud requires superior navigational skills, plus more rudeness and aggression than Marcus feels comfortable with, so he's feeling stressed by the time he gets there. Hart is hunched over the Arts and Leisure section, smoking. Hart likes sidewalk cafés because he can smoke, one more thing Marcus has against them.

"So, Dad," Marcus asks, sitting. "Who was I named after?"

"What?"

"Why was I named Marcus?" He waves away the cigarette smoke. "It's something I forgot to ask Summer."

Hart folds up his newspaper, looking disgusted. To Marcus's relief, he also butts out his cigarette. "She named you."

"Well, do you know where she got Marcus? I know Summer liked things to have *resonance*. She was very conscious of what things *mean*. So, like—Neiman Marcus? Marcus Garvey? Marcus Aurelius? Marcus Tullius Cicero? Marcus, Stanley, Dallas, & Polk?"

"What's that?"

"A law firm in Honesdale. I used to deliver their paper."

"You had a paper route?"

"After you left." *We needed the dough, asshole, of course I had a paper route,* he wants to say, but knows it would make Hart angry. He doesn't want to make Hart angry because he is hoping Hart will give him some money. "What I'm saying is, even that would be cool, to be named after some lawyer. I just want my name to mean something."

"It means your mother liked the sound of it. Who knows why? You're lucky she didn't name you Zeus, or Apollo."

"I wouldn't have minded."

"Or Fettuccine Alfredo. Or Compost Heap." Hart raises one hand as if hailing a cab and keeps it imperiously in the air until the waitress arrives. Without looking at the menu, they both order avocado omelettes.

Fascinating, Marcus thinks. Hart only lived with the family on and off until Marcus was ten, and then he left permanently. Yet he and his father share certain tastes, like this one. Has he inherited the taste for avocado omelettes, for unsalted peanuts, for the color brown, for Victorian novels, just as he inherited his father's strange greenish eyes? Or had these tastes simply rubbed off on him during those brief times together?

"I've been thinking lately about changing my last name to Summerson," Marcus says, after they have discussed the weather, Hart's arthritis, and Marcus's shirt, which Hart says looks like it came from the Salvation Army and Marcus says no, it's from a thrift shop on Bedford Avenue. "Like Esther in *Bleak House.* Marcus Mead sometimes sounds to me like the hero of a romance novel. I've also considered Marcus A. Sucram. Marcus Sacrum. Or Marcus Dame—how about that? Or Marcus Edam. Or Marcus Made. Does that sound cool or weird? I can never decide."

"Don't think so much, Marcus." His father leans back in his chair. "You're only twenty-one. Just relax and enjoy your life. Think when you get older."

"I do enjoy my life. I think I enjoy my life more than anyone else I know. Or almost," he says, thinking of Emily. Their omelettes arrive, and they both tuck in. "So come on, Dad, what would you have named me?"

"What?"

"Well, if you didn't like Marcus. I mean, what *did* you like?"

"I hate names," Hart says. "I hate the whole concept of names. So would you if your parents named you Tab. After some flaky movie star from the Fifties." He resumes eating, shaking his head sadly. "I've never really come to terms with my name."

Marcus read in the paper recently that five million Americans suffer from Narcissistic Personality Disorder. He wonders how they got that figure and if they counted his father.

"Movie star *and* recording artist, Dad. Don't forget *Young Love.*" Marcus thinks his father looks about as unlike a Tab as it is possible to look. He's more of a Thorndike, or a Wolfgang. A Heathcliff. Some saturnine, dark-haired, bushy-browed kind of name—not a blond one like Tab. "And Tab Hunter's real name was Andrew Arthur Kelm, anyway. AAK!"

"People should be called by their social security numbers," Hart says. "Just call me 067. Tell you what—drop the zero. I'm your father."

"Tab might come back into style, like Chad did after the election. They're both sort of paper names. I mean, names relating to paper. Though of course Tab also relates to typewriters and/or computers." He doesn't say it also could be short for *tabanid*, a horse fly, from the Latin *tabanus*. Or tabloid. Tab Lloyd. "Tab Hunter is kind of a funny name, when you think of it," he says. "You picture somebody who's a novice at the keyboard looking all over trying to find the tab key."

His father stares at him. "Are you serious?"

"No."

"I mean about Chad. Chad became a popular name after the election? Is that true? Do you know that for a fact?"

"I read it in the *Times*."

"Jesus." Hart sits shaking his head for a minute. Then he says, "Christ."

"What's this world coming to, eh, Pop?"

Dad and *Mom*, he often thinks: my first palindromes. *Pop. Sis.* Hah! Family life is crawling with them!

Hart signals the waitress for more coffee, and when it's poured, creamed, and stirred, he says, "I invited you to brunch for a reason."

"Because I'm your son."

Hart briefly closes his eyes, opens them. "Well, obviously,

Marcus, if you were a complete stranger I probably wouldn't have invited you. I wouldn't even have known your phone number. Also, I invited you because human beings have to eat food. If we were constructed differently, I might have invited you to gnaw tree bark in Central Park, or hook up to a hose at the gas station. But because you're my son, and because it's necessary to eat food periodically or die, I invited you to brunch."

"And yet, despite these two compelling reasons, there is apparently still another one."

"Correct."

Hart lifts his coffee cup and sips. Marcus hears from Hart three or four times a year. He hopes his father is about to—*finally*—say something about money. Hart used to be hard up, but now he has plenty of cash and Marcus could use some. His dog-walking and pet-sitting gigs don't pay badly, but everyone is cutting back on stuff like that. Luxuries, he thinks, and imagines the lonely unwalked dogs, the unpetted cats left for the weekend with a box of kibble and a filthy litter box. Even when he does bring in decent money—some months are better than others—it doesn't seem like much. He puts half of everything he earns into his account at the Greenpoint Savings Bank. Thirty thousand dollars is what he needs for what he intends to do, and the account is growing much too slowly.

He eats some more bits of avocado. He's tired of the egg part, but feels he could eat avocados forever. The avocado diet. Could man live by avocado alone? And why doesn't avocado add an *e* at the end when it turns plural, like tomato does? And potato? He remembers another article in the paper. A woman named Elvira Surito, of Los Altos, California, claimed she cured her arthritis by telekinetically transmitting her negative energy into the eggs of her neighbor's chickens. The neighbor was suing her. He would share this amusing anecdote, except that he's sure Hart's reaction would be to stare at him and then change the subject.

Hart sips, swallows, gazes absently at women who walk by. He is in no hurry to reveal why they're having brunch. Marcus admires his father's silky tweed jacket, which he wears with jeans over a blinding white T-shirt, and entertains himself by imagining Hart saying, *Son, you're twenty-one now, and it's time you had some responsibility for the family fortune.* The words *trust fund* dangle in his mind, with *stock portfolio* and *holdings* close behind. He waits, happily, while his father drinks coffee and looks pensive and ogles women. Finally, putting down his cup, Hart says, "I want you to do me a favor."

Accept this check, son . . .

"Okay. What is it?"

Hart purses his lips and looks down at the tablecloth. His face actually flushes, something Marcus has never witnessed before. He has the feeling Hart is giving himself a pep talk, steeling himself. "Well, the thing is, I've got a little problem. I'm flat broke."

"Broke?"

"Broke. As in no money."

"Broke."

"You've got it. I've had some business reversals, and I'm broke. And kind of in debt. A bit. You know how it is."

Neither of them speaks for a while. Hart continues to sip coffee and look at the people passing. A woman in a short and very tight skirt goes by, her ass swaying. She has very good legs. Marcus wonders why he doesn't respond to such things. Nor does he respond to the man with her, a smooth Latino dude with a chain bracelet on his hairy arm. He can see they're an attractive couple, easy to look at, but he has no desire to touch, kiss, stroke, fondle, unclothe, or fornicate with either one. He's wondered so often why this is that this time it flits quickly to the back of his mind, leaving the bulk of his brain free to process his father's news.

Hart has no money.

Hart had plenty of money when Marcus first looked him up two years ago. He was running a thriving art gallery. Some of Hart's money-making artists have since abandoned him, like Selma Rice, the wound woman, and Merlin Wolf, the dead bird guy; Marcus has seen notices of their shows at other galleries. But it's hard to believe Hart's little empire is *over*. Hasn't he been some kind of art big shot all his life? Or has he? Marcus has very little idea, really, what Hart has ever been or done. And why is Hart telling him this? He isn't the confiding type, and he doesn't like to admit failure. Things must be desperate. Marcus has a sudden horrible thought: Is Hart going to touch him up for a loan?

"Well, that's interesting, Dad."

Hart sets down his coffee cup and says, "I wondered if I could get you to kill Emily Lime."

"What?"

"My ex-wife. You know her—you said you walk her dog."

"Yeah, yeah, I know her. I mean, I don't know her well," Marcus fibs. *Kill Emily?*

"Presumably you have a key to her place."

"Well, yeah. I go in and out. I don't actually see *her* that often. I just pick up the dog and take him to the park when she's not there." He feels the need to keep talking so Hart won't. "I actually sort of forgot she's your ex-wife," he fibs further. "To me, she's just one of my customers."

"Good." Hart puts on a look Marcus recalls from his early childhood: the self-righteous smirk he wore whenever he told Marcus he was leaving but he'd be back real soon and they'd have some good times, they'd go fishing, they'd go to the zoo. "It's better that you don't know her very well. Then it won't bother you so much."

Marcus tries to take this calmly. His father has always been given to clumsy joking, making sarcastic, sometimes outrageous suggestions with no real intent behind them. He's going to assume this is a joke, too. "I have a few vices, Dad," he chuckles. "But I don't kill people."

"Even for money?"

Hart isn't looking at him, he's gazing across the street, he's lighting a cigarette, he's blowing smoke up toward the sky.

Of course it's a joke.

"Dad?"

Hart swivels his head slowly and looks at him. "Even for quite *a lot* of money, Marcus?"

"Emily Lime seems like a nice person . . ."

"Yes, but don't forget, she's also the reason I left your mother. So deep down you hate her. You can never forgive her for—"

"You didn't even *know* Emily when you left Summer."

"Not technically, but I left Summer so I could find the *kind* of woman Emily was in those days. Younger, smarter, thinner. Less of an oddball. I was looking for *an* Emily, and when I left Summer I found one."

This is a pack of lies. Marcus knows perfectly well why his father left his mother. But lying is one thing and paying someone to murder your ex-wife is another. Could Hart really be this despicable? Of course, the world is full of people who pay people to kill people. Well, not *full,* but certainly *well equipped.* It's in the paper all the time. There was just that case in Colorado. Montana? Someplace out west. If Hart is serious will he keep asking people until someone says yes?

"Are you serious, Dad?"

"I'm afraid I am, Marcus. It's not something I want, of course. In an ideal world. But I think we're pretty aware that this world is far from ideal."

His father is serious. He's either serious, or he's playing some sort of game. Or he's stark raving mad. Whatever the truth is, Marcus realizes he shouldn't alienate him. He studies his father's saturnine face and, to calm himself, obsesses on the word for a minute. *Saturnine* has nothing to do with Saturn the Roman god of agriculture, who has always sounded quite pleasant, even noble. A civilized god, married to Ops, the earth goddess— another nice one. *Summer could have named me Saturn,* he allows himself to further digress, and tries to picture himself with that name. *Saturn. Name of a car. Saturn Mead. Made as runt. Aunt dreams . . . Saturnine* refers to Saturn the planet. Which for some reason is supposed to be cold and distant—well, it is, of course, both those things. It's a planet, after all. Hart's saturnine face is handsome, though he's "not aging well," as people say. He's only forty-eight, but there are deep lines around his mouth, and they don't look good on him. His black hair is getting very gray, ditto. He squints. And he says, "What?" a lot, and turns his head so his left ear faces out, as if he's losing the hearing in his right.

"So why do you want Emily Lime to be dead?" Marcus asks.

"I'd rather not reveal that at this early stage of negotiation," his father says, like someone in a movie about hostages or the

Mafia. "You let me know how you feel about it, and then we can talk details."

"I see. Sure." It's important to say he'll think about it, so that Hart has to wait for an answer. But he needs to ask one question. "Can you just tell me this, Dad? How much money? What are we talking about here?"

"Hard to say, really, but I figure at least two hundred."

"Two hundred?"

"Thousand."

"Two hundred thousand." Marcus takes a deep breath and asks, cautiously, "Dad? Where are you going to get two hundred thousand dollars?"

"From Emily's death. It could be more. I'd give you twenty-five percent."

Marcus wonders if his father has lost his mind. Emily Lime pays six hundred dollars a month for a scruffy loft in Williamsburg, in a building that until recently housed a spice-importing firm. It still smells of mace and cinnamon on a warm day. It doesn't even have screens on the windows or a sink in the bathroom. Emily Lime sometimes has to make him wait a week for his dog-walking money because she's so strapped. She can't make a living from her photography, so in season she does manual labor for a gardener. She hauls pots and bags of soil and rosebushes and flats of perennials up to roof gardens in Brooklyn Heights. Marcus has lowered his dog-walking rate from fifteen dollars an hour to ten for Emily because she's so hard up.

And because he's so fond of her.

"Well, that kind of money is certainly tempting," Marcus says, cautiously, the way he might humor an escapee from an asylum before he tries to get him into the van.

"I thought it might be. That's why I asked you."

Marcus would like to reach across the table and stick a fork into his father's windpipe, a knife into his heart. His father wrecked his mother's life and—in a roundabout way—was responsible for her strange death. His father thinks his son is the kind of person who would murder someone for money.

"Do you understand me, Marcus? Are we on the same page here?"

"Yeah, Dad," Marcus says. His stomach lurches. "Basically, I think we are."

"And Marcus." Hart's face is cold, distant, grumpy, mean. And suspicious. "I have to see the body. You understand? I have to have evidence—"

"Wait, wait," Marcus holds up a hand. "You're getting ahead of me here. I need to *think* about this."

"What? Oh, right, think about it. Of course. I didn't expect an answer right this minute. But let me know by—let's say the weekend, will you? I'd like to set this in motion. It will take a while to realize the money."

"Do I get a deposit?"

"Ten."

"Thousand?"

"That's all I can lay my hands on right now."

"You're going to give me ten thousand dollars?"

"Yes."

"Well." There is no way this preposterous statement can be true, but Marcus raises his eyebrows and purses his lips in a look that says he believes it. "I'd sure like to buy a pick-up truck."

"That would just about do it. Get yourself a used Toyota or something."

"Right. Just what I was thinking."

"Or hold out for the big bucks—a couple of months, tops—and get yourself a fancy SUV." He smiles at Marcus across the table, showing yellow teeth. "Or whatever you like." The smile stays as is, but the eyes get a little plaintive at the corners. "I know I haven't been a good father, Marcus. Here's a chance to make it up to you."

"Gee, Dad."

"Better late than never."

In a flash of memory, Marcus sees his father's eyes welling up with tears as he explained that Marcus's dog Phoebe had been hit by a car and was now buried in the woods. Even then, in the midst of his grief, Marcus wondered how Hart managed the tears. Onion juice? "Well, I really appreciate this, it's definitely interesting," Marcus says.

Sad fatherliness is immediately overlaid with greedy hope. "How interesting?"

"I'll let you know by the weekend."

"Let's get out of here then." Hart pays with cash, and leaves a stingy tip.

Horribly, when they stand up, he holds out his hand, and Marcus has to shake it.

He watches his father cross Wooster Street, heading east toward his apartment on Crosby, holding his rolled-up *Times* like a club. He adds three bucks to the tip. Then he goes into the men's room and scrubs his hands with soap.

3

Egad! no bondagE!

Egad! no bondagE!

Emily pays six hundred dollars a month for fourteen hundred square feet on the fifth floor of her building on North Third Street. The slum floor, she calls it; the fifth floor is the South Bronx of 87 North Third, the sixth floor is Central Park West. The lofts on the sixth floor have been renovated into pristine white spaces with sanded floors and new combination windows and air-conditioning units and nice bathrooms.

Emily wouldn't live on the sixth floor if you paid her.

Actually, that's not true; she would *if* someone paid her.

But she wouldn't pay the two-thousand-dollar-plus rent to do so, even if she could afford it. She thinks the sixth-floor lofts are banal, boring, pretentious, untrue to the spirit of Brooklyn in general and Williamsburg in particular. What she covets, however, is the penthouse, which sits on the roof above the sixth floor like a treehouse. The penthouse is a gem. Anstice, her land-lady, whose vast loft takes up half of the sixth floor, got tired of rehabbing. So, like the lofts on Emily's floor, the penthouse has never been renovated. It was added on in the sixties and looks it. It has ancient faded linoleum in the kitchen and a cruddy little bathroom and a badly sloping floor in the bedroom and it's not even very big, about half the size of Emily's place.

But it's all windows and sunshine, or windows and darkness and city lights, or windows and rain and lightning. Nothing obstructs your view of the river, and you can have a garden on the roof. The place combines the grandeur that comes with the view—river, skyline, and the kind of sunsets only a seriously polluted city can provide—with a certain faded and rakish charm. Oliver Czerech lives in the penthouse, and he has no plans to move. But because Oliver's girlfriend is Pat Shapp, one of her best friends, Emily gets to visit it from time to time, which partly satisfies her—it's such a pleasure just to be there—and partly feeds her desire to possess it.

Emily is at the penthouse on Sunday afternoon, perched on the window seat that runs the length of the living room. Lying on the rug in front of her is Gus, the obese cat Oliver takes once a month, along with a shiitake mushroom, to the nursing home on North Sixth where the old folks chuckle over his powerful purr—when he really gets going, Gus can be heard two rooms away—and his legendary lust for mushrooms. Gus is purring now, though at muted volume, only revving into higher gear when Emily reaches out a foot to scratch his big belly. She is just finishing the Sunday *Times* crossword. If she looks up, which she does frequently, she can see the three bridges: Williamsburg, Manhattan, Brooklyn. The Brooklyn Bridge is very distant and beautiful. The Williamsburg, closer up, is massive and ugly. The Manhattan Bridge sits blahly in the middle. If she turned slightly to the right she would be able to see the Queensboro Bridge, but she has no particular desire to do this. She prefers the Brooklyn bridges and the view to the south.

Pat and Oliver are in the kitchen making a cake for Lamont's birthday party later that night. Pat Shapp is, oddly, as plain as the sound of her name. Her features are small and neat, as are her hats, her handwriting, her gestures, her hands and feet, and her studio apartment in Greenpoint. She is brisk and practical and teaches English in a private high school on the Upper East Side, where she is Ms. Shapp, hinting at erratic, even drunken wantonness. Emily pictures the headmaster at Pat's retirement dinner chuckling about how "We've had a li'l misshapp at our school."

Oliver is the other English teacher at Taggart, and he is as large and rumpled as Pat is small and neat. He is tall and over-weight, and his many-angled but somehow fleshy face reflects his complicated heritage, which encompasses Poland, France, Russia, England, and—Oliver claims—a far distant maverick great-grandmother who married a man named Juan Menchaca to provide a soupçon of Basque. A thin beard decorates Oliver's chin like pencil strokes, but his hair is thick and black, and straight as porcupine quills.

Both are writers: Pat occasionally writes a sharp, nasty essay on New York City politics for the *Village Voice*; Oliver publishes sonnets in an obscure literary magazine based in South Dakota. Emily can hear the two of them talking softly in the kitchen, but she can't hear what they are saying; there's loud big band music on the CD player. Pat and Oliver tend to talk about literature or current events: They are probably talking about Trollope or the Williamsburg rapist.

Emily is thinking about a different subject entirely. She's thinking about Tab Hartwell.

Her ex-husband is still occupying her head after coming into it the night before while she was cooking dinner. She cut up broccoli, put it in the steamer, and remembered that Hart would tolerate broccoli only if it had lemon juice squeezed on it. In her mind she said to herself, as she had so often said to him, "Damn it, I forgot to pick up a lemon." Emily is mulling over the night Hart left. It was a warm September night, and he went out to pick up Thai food. Both terrible cooks, she and Hart took their take-out seriously, especially Thai. They discussed for quite a while—ten minutes, maybe even as many as fifteen—whether to call Thai Café or Planet Thailand. Finally they decided Thai Café had better chicken peanut curry. Hart preferred to phone in the order and then go pick it up to avoid tipping a delivery-man. It was seven thirty when he left, not yet dark.

"Get that table set, Roderick, I'll be right back," he said as he went out the door.

Roderick was their imaginary butler.

They'd ordered the curry, some vegetarian panang, and a couple of spring rolls. By eight thirty, Emily had found the chopsticks, set the table, poured herself a beer, and stared out the window for a while at the dark green river. The sky was turning rosy pink, laced with shards of purple. She skipped through the *Times* crossword puzzle (the Tuesday puzzle, so easy it was hardly worth doing), finished her beer, looked at the clock, and called the restaurant.

No, the order for Hartwell had not yet been picked up, a Thai voice said, sounding harassed, over crowd noises in the background.

"Well, he's on his way," Emily said. "Don't do anything with it."

"Getting cold," the voice said. "You can heat up?"

"Yes, don't worry, we can heat up. I'm sorry. Thank you."

He had run into someone. Lamont or Luther. Saul Smith. Or Gene Rae and Kurt. He could still be downstairs in Saul's studio, yakking with him about Saul's newest digital doo-dad or what they did over Labor Day weekend. (Hart and Emily had barbecued chicken up on the roof with Oliver and Pat and a few other people, which hadn't gone well partly because Hart drank too much sangria and became alternately mean and maudlin.) She could call Saul and ask him. She could take the elevator down and check. Or she could just wait and not interfere, let Hart lead his mysterious messy life, which is what she did until nine thirty, and then she called Thai Café again.

"No, sorry, no pick up yet. You want we hold it?"

"No, no, I guess not, I'm really sorry, no, don't hold it, something must have happened, sorry, thank you."

She stared at the river for another half-hour, wishing she had someone to hug and wondering if she should call the police. She finally called Saul, who hadn't seen Hart, and he and Luther drove around the neighborhood in Saul's truck looking for him, while she stayed home in case he tried to get in touch. Finally, at eleven o'clock, she went to the phone to call 911, and as she reached for it, it rang. It was Hart saying he wasn't coming back, he thought they should separate, he was sorry he couldn't tell her to her face but she knew what a shit he was, what did she expect?

What stunned her was not that he had left—their life together had been mediocre for a long time, and she was not under the illusion that he was faithful to her—but that he had actually called the Thai Café, ordered the food, and forced her to be embarrassed and to make excuses about why they didn't pick it up.

And he'd stuck those nice people at the café with an un-claimed order.

Also, she was shocked that he had taken nothing with him, which was distinctly unlike Hart, who ("I'm a *thing* person") liked his possessions. Especially his clothes. After his call, on a hunch, she went into the bedroom to check, and discovered the drawers of his dresser contained only the shabbiest remnants of his T-shirt collection and a pair of socks with holes in them. His shirts were missing from the closet, except for the old stained denim one that she always borrowed. His suitcase was no longer under the bed. She looked in the closet in the hall: His tweed overcoat was gone, and his leather jacket, and his plaid hunting cap, and his cowboy hat. There were gaps in the shelf where his jazz CDs had been. He must have been spiriting his stuff away for days.

Well.

When Luther and Saul rang the doorbell, Hart-less of course, and she told them about the call, they confirmed that he was indeed a shit. A mega-shit. A world-class shit and a grade-A shit. Then Oliver came down from the penthouse and confirmed that Hart was a top-of-the-line shit. Oliver called Pat, and when he put Emily on the phone Pat said she always knew Hart was a premium peerless deluxe shit. And though Emily agreed with them all, she buried her face in the denim shirt and cried. He had abandoned her. Over the years she had learned to work around his shittiness, and now, suddenly, he was gone. In some awful way she didn't want to admit, she knew she would miss him.

It is at that point, as she is recalling the humiliating comfort of having her friends around her when the husband they all disliked deserted her, that Pat and Oliver come out of the kitchen. "Safely in the oven," Pat says. She sits down on the couch opposite Emily. "I just hope it will be cool enough to frost by the time we have to leave."

"We could eat it warm," Oliver says. "The frosting would melt, but we could pretend we intended it that way and tell Lamont it's a sauce."

"Sounds delicious," Emily says. "Is it chocolate?"

"Yep. Deep dark chocolate butter cream, and the cake is marble."

"Over the top."

"Way, way over."

"We're worried about you," Pat says.

"What?" Weren't they talking about cake?

"Worried. And we decided we should tell you."

Oliver sits down beside Pat and they confront her like a pair of upset parents. Emily feels like a teenager who's failing algebra or hanging with the wrong crowd. Or did they find the joint she hid in her underwear drawer? It worries her that Pat and Oliver are worried. She is the least worrisome creature on the planet. If Pat and Oliver are worried about her, maybe she should worry about them?

"So tell me," she says.

Oliver says, "Well," and looks at Pat, and Pat says, "Well," and pauses. And then she says, "Since you and Hart split up you haven't gotten involved with anyone else."

There is a silence while they look at her.

"So?"

"So are you still, like, grieving or something? I mean, not grieving, of course, but—I don't know." Pat shrugs and looks at Oliver, as if she's just realized her concern is absurd. Then she frowns and recovers. "I don't know, Em. It's been six years. Are you permanently alienated from the whole male sex?"

"I haven't met anyone I like."

"But—" Pat leans forward, her elbows on her thighs and her hands clasped before her. She is wearing dark green knee socks, loafers, and a plaid skirt. Only Pat can get away with outfits like that. In fact, she can't get away with anything else. "Why is that, do you think?"

Emily stares at her. "Pat, have you forgotten that before you met Oliver all you talked about was how the world is full of men who don't like animals, or who wear gold chains around their necks? Or corporate guys who think the most important thing is thinking outside the box 24/7 so they can hit the ground running? Guys who go to the gym at six A.M. and yak about their therapy all the time and buy forty-dollar T-shirts with designer logos? All that is still true." She looks down at her puzzle. The upper right-hand corner is pesky. *Dartmouth founder Wheelock. Shrub of the heath family.* She looks up again. "And now it's even worse. They're older, they're more set in their ways, and they have Palm Pilots and cell phones and Web logs."

"Well, we thought—" Oliver says, and falters.

Pat takes it up. "We have this person we thought you might like to meet."

"Why would I want to meet him?" Emily asks. She keeps looking at the puzzle, but she is, in fact, interested. She is mildly tired of not meeting men she likes. The only man she likes is Marcus Mead, and he's not only fifteen years younger than she is but he's Hart's son. He also seems to be asexual. But for over a year she has been in something approaching love with him, which she knows is crazy. If she could meet someone who would detach her from her feelings for Marcus, she might be grateful. . . .

"He's a guy named Hugh Lang," Pat says. "The father of one of my students. Divorced. Joint custody. Journalist. Very nice guy."

They're waiting. She can sense Pat and Oliver glancing at each other, raising their eyebrows, maybe even shrugging. *What's with her? Doesn't she want to be happy?*

"Yeah? So?"

"So we think you'd like him."

Shrubs of the heath family. The blasted heath.

"I have his daughter Heather in my class, and his son Josh is in Oliver's sophomore Shakespeare class."

Emily stares at her. "Heather?" Is heath related to heather? *Heather* is seven letters, but it only fits if *allium* and *tempura* and *harmony* are wrong. Besides, it would be so tacky to make *heather* the answer to a *heath* clue. Also, it's not plural.

"Cute little thing, and quite gifted as a writer. She wrote a snappy poem about her hamster, named Dirty Gertie."

Azaleas, Emily thinks, with relief, and writes it in. Not *heather.* Still, it was a bizarre moment. She writes *azaleas* with the maroon-and-white TAGGART SCHOOL pen Oliver lent her. And so it must be *Eleazar.* Is that really a name? Eleazar Wheelock. And that's it. She sighs and puts down the *Times* magazine. Out the window, a flock of pigeons wheels over Wythe Avenue, turns somewhere down around Metropolitan, and heads back. *The view,* she thinks, *the view.* You can see the whole world from here. A spasm of longing pierces her heart. Oh, how she wants this penthouse!

"Isn't that sweet, Em? Dirty Gertie?"

"It's a poker game," Emily says. "Dirty Gertie."

"Maybe that means Hugh is a poker player. You'd like that," Oliver says encouragingly.

"And it means they have pets," says Pat. "That Hugh is not an animal-hater like Hart."

"It means the kids talked him into a hamster. Why don't they have a normal pet, like a dog or a cat?"

Pat and Oliver are silent. Emily brings her attention gradually back from the view—the birds, the slate-colored river, the blue sky soft with clouds, and gray Manhattan with the two tall blanks in it that no one will never get used to—and focuses on Oliver and Pat. She smiles. "I'm sorry," she says. "He sounds nice. I actually think hamsters are sweet. I'm sure I'd like him."

Pat seizes on this. "Should we invite you both for dinner? Or would you rather go out? What would make you feel least uncomfortable? What would be the most fun?"

Marcus, Emily thinks. He will be at the party tonight. Will he wear his beautiful hemp shirt?

"Hey! We could all play poker," Pat goes on. "You could teach us."

Emily smiles, shakes her head. "I'm sorry. I really am." She stretches out her foot to rub Gus's tummy, and he wraps his paws around her moccasin and bites it. "I don't mean to be difficult or ungrateful, but I don't want to meet him."

"You said you thought you'd like him!"

"I probably would like him if I met him."

"So?"

She can't bear Pat's earnest, affectionate, puzzled, getting-irritated face. Gus drops her foot and lies back, sated and fat, purring. Emily leans her cheek against the cold glass, looking out the window at the sky and its scrapers. From seven flights down, a car alarm starts up. The pigeons swoop by again.

"I just don't want to. Thanks."

4

Flee to me, remote elF!

Flee to me, remote elF!

"Did you do the puzzle?"

"It was too easy."

"I had a small upper-right-hand-corner problem."

"Eleazar?"

"What a silly name."

"Ridiculous. What were his parents thinking?"

They are eating cake and drinking brandy at Luther and Lamont's place on Grand Street. It's the loft Emily lived in when she first came to New York, but it has been, to severely understate the case, fixed up. The party is a success. First a lot of beer, then presents, then more beer. Then Lamont's famous vegetarian chili and Luther's hush puppies and somebody's cole slaw and somebody else's garlic bread—superfluous but delicious—and then "Happy Birthday to You" and candles and Pat and Oliver's chocolate cake, which cooled and so has regular frosting, not warm sauce. Lamont believes in serving dessert not with coffee or tea but with brandy: it's V.S.O.P., but a brand Marcus doesn't recognize, which is how he knows it's really good.

Now the party is winding down. Even Gene Rae and Kurt have left—Gene Rae, famous for partying, has changed since she became pregnant and now goes to bed by midnight. Even the intrepid Tragedy Club staff—Fiona and Zelda and Carey the bartender—are on their way out.

"You're not eating that cake," Emily says. "You're pushing it around on your plate like a kid does with spinach."

"I'll take it home." Marcus wonders if his appetite will ever return. He sees Emily studying his face, and knows it must have a strange look on it. The look of someone who has brunched with a monster. He says, "You never told me about Fort Salonga. How did it go?"

"It was a bust. I got a nice TIME from a billboard, but I'd really hoped to find a BREAD or two."

"Not a good bakery town?"

"Nope. And not a single DOG, either."

"Well, damn. Did you have fun, though?"

"I did have fun," Emily says, as Marcus knew she would. He watches her slow smile assemble itself: the little puckers in her pouty bottom lip smooth out and disappear, the bow in her top lip flattens and stretches, and a deep dimple appears in her left cheek as if she'd slept on a button. Her lips are very pink. She picks up her plastic glass of brandy and sips. "So did Izzy and Otto. Izzy chirped along with my Pretenders tape, and Otto sat next to me and looked out the window."

"Dog is your co-pilot."

"Exactly. And somewhere around Cold Spring Harbor my

cough departed for good. Isn't that strange? My cold sprang away!"

"You're making that up."

"Yes, sort of, I am. I wish it were true. But I actually felt completely better by the time I got on the expressway. Hey, Marcus, there's the rottweiler guy."

Marcus turns and sees that the rottweiler guy has just come in, he is hugging Lamont, he is being given brandy and a piece of cake. "Yeah, I knew he was a friend of Lamont's."

"He's pretty late."

"Elliot. That's his name. I remember now. Elliot something that begins with a C."

Emily finishes her cake. "I'm going to go over there and get another piece. Maybe I can find out why he doesn't talk to his dog."

"Wait. Emily. Do you have any . . . insurance, or anything?" Marcus asks.

"Do I have any *insurance* or anything? Like—health? Yeah, I have health. I pay three hundred a month for it. I have a huge deductible. Why?"

"You don't have any, like, life insurance or anything?"

"Are you crazy?" Emily smiles again, her fast one this time: a flash of small white teeth, slightly crooked. "Of course not. Why on earth are you asking?"

Marcus is ready. "I was thinking I should maybe get some insurance, and I just wondered if—you know. I thought I'd ask around."

She stops smiling. "Is something wrong? Are you ill?"

"I was just thinking."

"Dog-walkers don't just go out and buy life insurance! What are you telling me? What's the matter?"

"Emily, nothing is the matter." Marcus feels as exasperated as he would if he were telling the truth. "Life insurance is an *investment*. It doesn't mean you're terminally ill. If you're terminally ill, they won't even sell you a policy."

"Suicide."

"What?"

"Are you going to kill yourself?"

"I'm sorry I even brought this up." He takes her plate from her. "It was an idle question. It didn't mean anything. I'm not sick, I'm not going to kill myself. I *am* going to get you another piece of cake, so that you'll forget I asked. Okay?"

She nods warily. He can feel her eyes on him as he makes his way to the cake.

Lamont and Elliot C. are standing near the dining room table, eating cake and talking. Behind them is the fish tank, populated by a flock of delicate black mollies and two muscular catfish—femmes and butches, Lamont and Luther call them. Over the tank is a sign printed out in thirty-six-point Garamond, which says:

"I KNOW THE HUMAN BEING AND FISH CAN COEXIST PEACEFULLY."
GEORGE W. BUSH, SEPT. 29, 2000

Lamont is wearing a shirt of blinding whiteness and a blue tie, tied loosely around his neck. The tie, a birthday gift, has extremely tiny Betty Boops printed on it. He is also wearing a gold paper crown with BIRTHDAY BOY in glitter. Elliot C. is short and chunky, wearing a black polo shirt and black pants and black shoes. He has dyed blond hair, buzz-cut and in need of a touch-up. He wears a gold hoop in each ear.

"Marco, I'm so drunk," Lamont says. Lamont is very tall, with a saintly, bovine face that Marcus has to tilt his head back to see.

"Now that you're forty you can get drunk whenever you want," Marcus says. "No one can tell you not to, you're an official grown-up."

"That's why I'm getting drunk," Lamont says, being cute, putting his head to one side like a puppy. His glass is half full of brandy, and after he takes a gulp it's only about three-eighths full. "I don't *want* to be a grown-up."

Marcus doesn't feel like encouraging him. Sometimes it seems Lamont is coming on to him, especially when he calls him Marco. Lamont says he does this because the ablative case is so sexy. Not without difficulty, Marcus pictures a threesome—himself with Luther and Lamont, two staggeringly handsome men, one black and one white. He tries to picture them all in Luther and Lamont's extremely cool bedroom with the gray walls and the platform bed and the windows looking out on the back garden, still lush in late October, where, somehow, they manage to grow something that looks like a palm tree. He feels nothing but a slightly repelled neutrality. "Emily needs more cake," he says.

"Cut her a nice big piece, Marco." Lamont manages to make this sound suggestive. "You know Elliot Cobb, don't you?"

"I don't think we've actually met." They shake hands. Elliot Cobb's hand is unpleasantly damp, and there is a moustache of sweat on his upper lip. "You moved into Jeanette's place, didn't you?"

"Subletting just for this year."

"Lucky Jeanette. London for a year."

Elliot Cobb makes a face. "I can't stand London."

"You from around here?"

"Kind of."

"I met Elliot at the Tragedy Club," Lamont says helpfully. "He was looking for a sublet, and I hooked him up with Jeanette. Right, Elliot?"

"That's it."

It's not just his dog. Marcus cuts a piece of cake and flops it onto the plate, where it falls to pieces. *Elliot doesn't have much to say to anyone.* "So what do you do, Elliot?" He doesn't really know why he's asking these questions. Just a vague feeling that it would be good to know things about Elliot Cobb. And for Emily's sake, because she'll ask.

"I'm a writer." Elliot forks in a bite of cake, looking at Marcus challengingly, as if expecting to be disbelieved.

Marcus can't stop himself. "What do you write?"

"Pornography, actually. I'm a professional pornographer. I write dirty graphic novels for an outfit called Wanker Press."

"Wow," Marcus says, feeling the nausea he's been fighting all day threaten to rise. "Is that a dream job or what?"

"Graphic graphic novels, eh, Elliot?" Lamont chuckles drunkenly at his own joke.

"Yep, they're pretty graphic, all right. That's the point. I do the Master Bedroom series," Elliot elaborates, not looking embarrassed or even ironic. He could be talking about an article on otters for the *Times* Science Section. "Maybe you've heard of them? Master Bedroom is basically an S&M guy, but—you know—I try to diversify a little. Keeps it interesting for me."

"I'll bet," Marcus says. Grudgingly, he admits that Elliot is attractive in a sleazy, pimpish way. But he doesn't like looking at him; he concentrates on the catfish, who are brisking around the floor of the tank and waggling their whiskers, while the mollies do their complicated dance up above.

"Maybe you could move on to Master Bath if you get sick of it," Lamont says. "He could do stuff in the tub."

"Yeah, I've already thought of that."

Lamont beams. "Elliot's in Williamsburg to do *research*."

"You could put it that way." Elliot Cobb's smile is bunched up and small, showing sharp teeth. If you photographed it, and took it out of context, you wouldn't know if it was a smile or the grin of a rabid animal.

"I won't grow up," Lamont sings over the sound system, which is playing an early Alison Krauss album. "Ida wanna go to school."

"I'd better get this cake over to Emily," Marcus says.

"Ida wanna something something. And obey the golden rule. Who knows the missing line?"

"So maybe I'll see you around, Mark," Elliot says.

"No, that's not it. That doesn't even scan. It's 'I don't want to wear a something . . .' But what?" Lamont gulps more brandy, humming.

"I've seen you in the park with your rottweiler a couple of times," Marcus feels compelled to say.

"Huh." Elliot nods.

He doesn't volunteer anything else. Emily will want to know about the dog more than she'll want to know about Master Bedroom, but Marcus needs to get away. He has the same feeling he had after brunch with his father: He would really like to wash his hands. He decides, right then, as he makes his way back across the room, not to call Hart. Not by the weekend, not at all. Let his father call him. Is that wise? What if Hart gives up and finds someone else? Some creep like Elliot C.? He wonders why he finds Elliot C. so creepy. But Hart won't get someone else. He'll call. Definitely. Hart will call. And he'll be able to judge from how long it takes just how serious his father is.

But it had to be a joke.

Emily is leaning against the mantel, looking dazed. She has made heavy inroads into her plastic glass of brandy. He hands her the cake. "Ew, it's all crumbled."

"Yeah. Sorry, Em."

They look at each other and then away, blushing.

The first time Marcus called her *Em*, she said, "Wow, Marcus. Em! That sounds like we're an old married couple or something." They both remember this. The usual sequence goes through Marcus's head: *I wish she wasn't thirty-six, I wish I wanted to go out with her, I wish I wanted to go out with anybody.*

Emily attacks her cake. "Who would have suspected that chocolate cake and brandy go so well together?"

"Lamont."

"Lamont is such a genius. So what's with Mr. Rottweiler?"

"He's just some guy who's here for a year. Some kind of writer."

"What kind?"

"I don't know. He was pretty vague."

"What's his dog's name?"

"We didn't get to the dog."

"Oh well." Emily gazes off into space, maybe grooving on Alison Krauss's fiddle. They both look in the direction of the music system, which is housed in a custom-made bird's-eye-maple Shaker-style unit. Daphne, Lamont's orange cat, is asleep on top of it in a basket, only the top of her head and her ears visible. Luther is leaning against it, drinking brandy and brooding. He has recently started shaving his head, and his beautiful skull is as smooth and gleaming as a piece of expensive chocolate. Luther is—Marcus realizes—watching Lamont and Elliot C. Alison's piercing soprano floats above the noisy room: *"I've got that old feeling that you're leaving."*

"I like those earrings," Marcus says, then blushes again.

Emily's earrings are silver, dangly, glinting in the light from the incredibly tasteful recessed ceiling lighting system. She looks at him in surprise. "Thanks."

"You have a lot of jewelry. It seems."

"It does?"

"Well—don't you?"

"I guess." Emily smiles. "Earrings, mostly. All cheap. Bought on the street. Or at the Indian place on Mulberry. I always find great earrings there. You know that woman? The batik lady?"

"I do, actually. I've bought batik from her. That pillow I made?"

"I love that pillow."

"I like talking to her. She has very radical politics."

"She has very radical earrings."

"You don't have any valuable stuff, do you?"

"Nope. Just junk." She takes a bite of cake. "Why do you ask?"

"Well, there have been a lot of robberies lately. I wondered."

"Robberies? I thought we were just having rapes."

"Oh well. I don't know." The nausea now feels like it will

never pass. He can still drink, but his glass is empty. "Excuse me," he says, and sprints into the kitchen, finds the bottle, splashes some into a plastic glass, takes a gulp, returns. "You're still here."

"I go nowhere until I get enough cake. Almost there. Coming down the home stretch."

Luther's black cat, also named Daphne, is rubbing around Emily's legs, and Marcus stoops to pet her. The change in altitude and the pressure on his gut make him feel, suddenly, even sicker. Out of the noise in the room, his mind constructs the echo of his father's voice. He has to abandon the cat and stand upright. Black Daphne, fat and indignant, waddles away from him. Marcus stares after her glumly, listening to the pulse beating in his head, hoping he won't throw up. "Marcus?" He realizes Emily has been watching him.

"Yeah."

"Why are you being so weird tonight?"

"I don't think I'm being weird." He has a sip of brandy, then another. "Let's change the subject. Did I tell you about this guy I met once in a bar? Who would do anything for a joke? Like he went to some dinky college in Gettysburg, Pennsylvania, so he could have a Gettysburg address?"

She looks at him skeptically. "Oh yeah?"

"I swear."

"What was his name?"

"Mark Romano. He was six feet two, and he was born in San Diego. His father was a professor of biology, his mother sold real estate. His social security number was 093-57-7882."

"What was the name of the bar?"

"Cappy's Bar, in Minneapolis. They had a little sign in the

window. It said YOUR BEST DAYS BEGIN AND END AT CAPPY'S BAR. It was either an optimistic sentiment or a pessimistic one. Depending on your mood."

Emily's eyes narrow. "What were you doing in Minneapolis?"

"Drinking beer in Cappy's Bar. My best days began there."

Unexpectedly, she puts her hand on his arm. "Marcus," she says, and gets the half-maternal, half-something-else look in her eyes Marcus both dreads and loves. "Don't lie to me."

"I'm not."

"You are my dog-and-bird-sitter. Never lie to me."

"I am your dog-and-bird-sitter. I will never lie to you," Marcus lies.

"Okay. Good. Thank you." Emily picks up her brandy glass and drains it. "I can leave now."

"I'll walk you home."

"That would be great."

They make their farewells, but Luther is in a mood, and Lamont is so drunk he doesn't respond very well. "Am I going to hate myself in the morning? Am I going to begin my forties with a bad attitude? Low self-esteem? A hangover?"

"Kingsley Amis says the best hangover cure is *Paradise Lost,*" Emily tells him. "Book 12, lines 606 to the end."

"Who's Kingsley Amis?" Lamont asks. "What's *Paradise Lost?*"

Oliver, who is standing nearby, gives Marcus a despairing look. Pat hugs him and Emily. "Did you like the cake?"

"We did a job on the cake," Marcus says, even though he hid his on the mantel behind one of Luther's pigeon sculptures.

"The cake was sublime," Emily says. "Awesome. Mega-outta-sight." She hugs Lamont and tells him he doesn't look forty but happy birthday anyway. Marcus shakes his hand. They all say, "See you at the Trollope meeting," and then Emily and Marcus leave.

Outside, it's chilly. Emily has worn a red sweater and sensible shoes, but Marcus is in sandals and his light brown hemp shirt. "You're cold," Emily says, and laces her arm through his. "You should have your own dog. Or cat."

Marcus knows this is not a non sequitur: Emily is imagining him going home and sleeping alone, uncuddled, cold. He has never told her about the dog of his childhood, his beloved Phoebe, for whom he still grieves. He remembers his grandmother's house up near Rochester, and the railroad tracks that ran behind it at the end of a field of blueberries. How he used to count the cars of the freight train that went by once a day, making bets with himself on how many there might be. Hobos sometimes hung around down by the tracks. The hobos rode the trains, Grandma said. *Going where? Anywhere. Out west. Up to Canada. Further east to the coast.* Marcus had been impressed by the romance of it, the delectable queerness of living on the road, being always on the move, sleeping always alone. He has no plans to become a hobo, but he does know that, seductive though it is, 11211 will not be his zip code forever.

"One of these days," he says, "I'll get a dog."

"Or a cat."

"Or a bird."

They have had this conversation more than once.

When they come to Emily's building, Marcus frees his arm. Emily says, "Marcus."

"Emily."

"Thank you for walking me home."

"Well, our rapist is out there somewhere."

"I know. But I still appreciate it. It's so old-fashioned. Isn't it? Walking someone home. Like an old song."

"I guess." He looks at her. Her curly hair, her blue eyes, her mouth curving into its smile. "You have to walk Otto now, right?"

"Nope. I walked him before I left. He'll be okay until morning."

"Sure?"

"Sure."

He pauses and looks at her in the light from the street lamp. He doesn't know if she's pretty, or if she just looks exactly the way he thinks people should look. Both, probably. He could go upstairs with her, he knows that. He could say he'd like a cup of tea, would she make him a cup of nice hot tea? He knows her smile means they could do more than drink tea. He tries to imagine something they might do. Instead, he has a sudden memory of one of the word games he used to love when he was a kid. *Mead to Lime,* he thinks, and then, concentrating, *Mead-mend-mind-mine-mime-Lime.* He smiles. "Okay, then. I'll say good night."

"Good night, Marcus." She is slightly taller than he, and she leans down, as she always does, to press her lips to his forehead.

He watches while she goes in. Then he puts his cheek to the big metal door so that, against his face, he can feel her key turn in the lock. Then he walks back to his apartment on North Sixth Street near Roebling. Even when he is at his most distraught, Marcus can't walk past Roebling Street without remembering that John Roebling—who invented the steel cable and used it in his design of the Brooklyn Bridge—died of lockjaw. This fact he finds as amazingly ironic as Al Capone's arrest not for racketeering but for income tax evasion. Roebling should have died gloriously, falling from one of the bridge's towers into the depths of the East River, not sadly in his bed. Like Marcus's mother, whose name was Summer but who froze to death in the middle of an upstate winter.

At 222 North Sixth Street, an address that provides a little jolt of pleasure every time he contemplates it, Marcus takes off his clothes, showers for the third time that day, and puts on a pair of clean striped pajamas. What he wants to do is go to bed and have his favorite dream, that he's gone for a walk in the woods and fallen asleep with his head pillowed on his backpack, and gradually the gentle animals of the forest gather in a circle around him. But he's still agitated from seeing Hart, and he knows he won't sleep. He turns on his fifth-hand tape player and puts on a Welsh rock band. He can't understand a word, and the music is now so familiar he doesn't even hear it, which is what he likes.

He makes himself a cup of herbal tea, hoping to settle his stomach, then sits in his favorite chair. On the wall opposite is something Emily gave him: the neatly framed front page of the *Daily News* on a day last June. The big headline, DOG DAYS FOR DONNA, is about ex-Mayor Giuliani's almost-ex-wife, who wants but isn't going to get $1,140 a month for the upkeep of their dog, Goalie. The small headline, SEAMUS IS MY NEW BUDDY, SAYS BILL, is about the new dog ex-President Clinton's wife gave him as a replacement for Buddy, who was killed by a car a year before. The first time in history, Emily said, that two dogs have ever shared billing on the front page of a newspaper. Emily read him the article inside about Seamus. Bill Clinton said Buddy's death was the worst thing that had happened to him since he left office. Emily had said, "I find that deeply affecting." He had thought of his dog Phoebe and wanted, as always, to tell Emily about her, but didn't.

When he finishes his tea, he takes from his file cabinet a thin folder neatly labeled MY LIFE, and removes a fading color photograph. It's a picture of himself and his father and his mother taken in early fall, 1991, when Hart was living with them for the last time. They are standing on the bridge over the Delaware River at Callicoon, New York. Marcus is dressed in a striped T-shirt and baggy knee-length shorts. His skinny legs give him an avian look. Summer is wearing a cotton dress and looks large and pretty, with the aura of strangeness that she never lost, not even during the brief period when she worked at the drugstore in Jeffersonville and wore a maroon blazer and put her hair up in a neat bun. In the photograph, her hair is waist-length and messy, blown back by a breeze that also ruffles Hart's hair, which hangs long and stringy above his shoulders. Hart has his left arm around Summer and his right hand on the shoulder of Marcus, who stands between and a little in front of them. In the background, the river is shirred—blue and sparkly.

The photo was taken at a picnic they'd had with their neighbors, the Estradas—it was his mother's romantic but unrealistic idea. Hart got drunk, as usual, and was sarcastic. Summer took a long walk, came back crying, and didn't really cheer up all afternoon. Marcus and Jessica and Rosie and little Rafaelito, who still drank from a bottle, were all the wrong ages and sexes to play together successfully, and they could sense that their parents weren't having a good time, so they spent the afternoon being crabby.

Marcus remembers wanting to glide down the river in one of the canoes for rent by the bridge, and he asked Hart if they could rent one, and Hart said nastily, sure. They could rent one, he sneered, and the kids could come for a ride. Then he said with a chuckle, "Don't be surprised if I push you all over the side, one by one, at the deepest part of the river." Jessica Estrada burst into tears. Her father—who was called Big Rafe and didn't like Hart any more than Hart liked him, maybe less—took his daughter on his lap and said, "I don't think that was funny." Hart said, "Who's joking?" Then Mrs. Estrada said, "Maybe it's time to head home, they said we might get a storm." They all packed up to go, squinting at the bright, cloudless sky, and then before they left she took pictures. Somehow this one ended up in Marcus's possession. It's the only picture he has from his childhood.

Marcus stares at the photo thinking, *Anyone who didn't know us would think we were a happy family.* The overweight but radiantly blonde mother, and the tall, slightly bohemian father, maybe an artist or musician. Looks like the kind of guy who relocates from the city to the country because it's a more wholesome place to raise a kid. And the kid in question is weedy and knock-kneed but his smile is pretty cute; the tilt of his head and a certain sharpness around his eyes indicate intelligence or at least curiosity.

It's Hart Marcus stares at most particularly, though.

Hart's hand on his shoulder looks imprisoning, not fatherly.

When he looks at his father's face, he tries to fathom what's going on behind the false smile. When he was ten years old he couldn't decide whether Hart was crazy or evil.

It's eleven years later, and he still doesn't know.

5

Swap for a pair of paws

Swap for a pair of pawS

(1991)

Emily moved to the Williamsburg section of Brooklyn because that's where her friend Gene Rae Foster went to be with her boyfriend Kurt. It was only one subway stop across the river from Manhattan, and Gene Rae said the neighborhood was cheap and eccentric and full of artists and other interesting people. So it proved to be: Williamsburg was an urban wilderness of warehouses and factories, desolate streets, and crumbling, asphalt-fronted row houses you could see had been pretty once, with grand cornices and intricate iron fences, but were now ratty little boxes. The streets were almost bare of both the delights of nature and the amenities of civilization. There was the occasional ailanthus, some sycamores, a few linden trees with their starry spring blossoms, and the vast but barren park. There were two delis, a dubious natural foods store, a Polish restaurant and a Polish bakery, a café near the subway entrance, two stores catering to the neighborhood pigeon flyers, and rumors that an art gallery was planning to open on North Ninth. Someday. You wouldn't know you were in New York City if the maddening, magnificent towers of Manhattan hadn't glittered just across the river.

Gene Rae found Emily a place to live, the corner of a cavernous loft on Grand Street, which Emily rented for almost nothing from two gay sculptors, one of whom was Luther in his pre-fame, pre-Lamont days. Emily's space was boxed in with tall bookcases. She had a square of splintery wooden floor, a mattress, one window, access to the kitchen and the startlingly squalid bathroom, and a key to the roof. During that first summer, she would go to the roof in the evenings and photograph the sky and the skyline as the sun went down across the river. It was a scene that, like the Lake District sunsets Dorothy Wordsworth described in her diary in the early 1800s, was never the same no matter how many times she witnessed it. Then she would sit on the warm tar until dark, her arms wrapped around her knees, thinking about, among other things, her words.

It was always words that interested Emily, and so it was words she wanted to photograph. Though she majored in literature in college, only taking photography courses as electives, she became as enthralled with taking pictures as she was with reading English poetry and French novels. Her two passions coexisted very nicely—by day, she roamed the streets taking photographs; by night, she curled up in bed with a book—and she knew, without being able to explain it, that she was a better photographer because she loved words. At first, they were BREAD, MEMORY, and TIME. It wasn't long, though, before she realized not only that MEMORY and TIME were too closely related, but that MEMORY was almost impossible to find.

She narrowed her focus down to BREAD and TIME.

That was satisfactory for a while, but she knew she had to have three words: she was like a woman with two children who just knows—*knows*—she was meant to have three. She devoted many hours of thought to choosing a new word, but didn't come up with one she liked until, at the combination animal shelter and pet-food store called the Pet Pound on Metropolitan Avenue, she fell in love with Harry.

She had never meant to love a dog, much less own one. Her life was to be devoted to art, not to a pet or a husband or a child or any other living creature. Her life was about her Hasselblad and her Nikon and her two, soon to be three, words. But she would visit the Pet Pound sometimes, the way she visited the Polish bakery or Marta's beauty shop, with no intention of eating the doughy pastries or getting her hair cut, but because she liked to chat. Gaby and Hattie, who ran the Pet Pound, were a long-time couple, friends of Gene Rae's boyfriend, Kurt, who had gotten his dog from them. They also knew Luther—in fact, Hattie introduced Luther and Lamont a few years later when she found out they both had cats named Daphne. Everyone went to the Pet Pound because it was an entertainment—like going to the theater, only it was free and you didn't have to get on the subway. The Doggie Dorm was out in back, with a run attached, but the shop itself was small—too small—and full of what Emily thought of as free-range cats. They perched on windowsills, on the counter, on the stacked bags of litter and kibble, and on top of the cages in which a few of the dogs waited, noisily, to be adopted. One dog, old half-blind Babyface, missing half a tail and most of one ear, had lived there for years, unadopted for obvious reasons, roaming the place by radar, mingling with the cats, who accepted him as they might accept a walking tree stump. A parrot named Bugsy screeched his own name from time to time, and wouldn't stop until someone gave him a piece of celery or scratched his head. For a while they had a miniature goat, and for another while a pot-bellied pig, and one afternoon when Emily stopped in just to check things out they had Harry in a cage with two cats draped across it, asleep.

She wouldn't have noticed the dog, she sometimes thought, if she hadn't stopped to pet the cats, two sleek and beautiful mackerel-tabby brothers in the process of being adopted. The cats didn't wake up when she petted them, just purred and stretched in their sleep. When Emily looked down to see whose cage they were lying on, the sad brown eyes of a true mutt looked back up at her.

"Well, hi there, cutie pie," she said, and he whined with joy.

Harry was an older dog, with, Gaby told her frankly, bad teeth that needed seeing to. He wasn't pretty: a little foxy fellow with short, rough, tan fur that leapt out in long, inexplicable wisps here and there. He had short ears and a long muzzle and a solid, piggy body.

"He's obviously part terrier," Hattie said.

"And maybe part toilet brush," Gaby added. When she opened the cage door, Harry shook himself and emerged. He sat on the floor looking up at Emily with an expectant grin. A black cat came over and sniffed him disdainfully.

"You have to admit he's a really silly-looking dog."

"For Harry every day is a bad-hair day."

Gaby and Hattie stood over him, chuckling. They knew they could say anything. They had been in the pet placement business long enough to recognize love at first sight when they saw it.

Emily bent to pet him, and he licked her hand once, politely, then freaked out and tried to lick her face. He smelled good, she thought: He smelled like a dog, with an overlaying smell that reminded her of pancakes. Pancakes? How could a dog smell of pancakes?

"Harry, get down," Gaby said. "Don't be disgusting."

Emily found she had the beginning of tears in her eyes. She didn't mind if the dog licked her face. She hugged him, and he quivered all over, then tried to jump up on her again. His head knocked against her chin, jarring her teeth together. How long had it been since she had loved anyone so intensely?

"I really want him," she said. "Am I crazy?"

"If you're not, it's okay. Harry is."

Harry had belonged to a textile designer from Greenpoint with the wonderful name of Malaysia Morales—they knew Emily would want to know this—until she moved to Baltimore with her boyfriend, who was allergic to dogs. Malaysia was broken-hearted, but Gaby and Hattie were delighted that she entrusted Harry to them. "We knew he'd be adopted in a week," Gaby said.

"So how long has he been here?" Emily asked.

"Six months," Gaby said, and giggled. Then she said, "Just kidding. Four days. We've had lots of inquiries."

Four days, Emily thought. What if she hadn't come in? What if someone else had adopted him? Harry was gazing at her with a sort of calculated enthusiasm—comparing her, Emily figured, with his lost Malaysia. Well, who could blame him? Her job was to measure up. He looked like the frisky kind of dog who enjoyed having a ball thrown for him, so she bought a red ball with a bell inside it. She also bought a red leather collar with a brass plate where she could have his name engraved, and a red leash and a box of dog biscuits, size small. She arranged to have a sack of Science Diet (for Older Dogs) delivered. She filled out the adoption forms, wrote a check, and got the name of a veterinarian who could do something about Harry's teeth.

"Good luck," Gaby said, snapping on the leash. She scratched Harry's head, and Harry closed his eyes and put his ears back in pleasure. "He's pretty needy. If he doesn't drive you nuts, you're going to love him."

The parrot screeched "Bugsy!" as they left, but Harry never looked back.

DOG, Emily thought as she and Harry walked down Metropolitan. BREAD. TIME. DOG. "Dog," she said to Harry, who paid no attention, just kept walking toward the corner, where he turned left as if he had lived on Grand Street all his life.

Luther was happy about Harry, though Daphne the cat wasn't—she skulked under the bed, then moved to the top of the refrigerator, blinking her yellow eyes and hissing. But Stephen, the other sculptor, said, apologetically, "I'm just not a dog person," and told Emily she'd have to move. She'd just sold two BREAD photographs to Dr. Demand for two thousand dollars and a cleaning. She had planned to use the money to travel around Italy, where she had never been, photographing PANE and TEMPO signs, but the check was also the equivalent of half a year's rent for her own place, provided the place was cheap enough. The loft in Anstice Mullen's building on North Third Street was advertised on a hand-printed flyer attached to the wall outside the natural foods store:

LARGE LOFT FOR RENT $300.

NO FREAKS.

PREFER PET-OWNER.

Emily Lime was twenty-five, she had an old dog named Harry, and she thought she was on her way to being a real photographer, one who could make a living at it. She moved into the loft, which smelled strongly of cinnamon from the spice factory and had an ancient, dangerous freight elevator that required brute strength and extreme bravery to operate. She painted the floors battleship gray and each wall a different color. The ceilings were eighteen feet high, and to paint the upper parts she had to borrow an extension ladder from Anstice and, terrified, lean out and up and down to slap on the paint with a giant brush. It took her most of a week, at the end of which she was exhausted. She spent a whole day sacked out on her mattress with Harry. He didn't smell of pancakes any more, he just smelled of Harry, which was fine with her. Harry slept nicely at her side when she slept, and woke up instantly when she stirred, and began alternately begging for breakfast and looking for his ball. She remembered part of an Ogden Nash poem she had learned as a child:

I envy oft my faithful pup.
He has no trouble getting up.

Harry's playfulness energized her, and she felt the exercise of chasing a ball was good for him, at his age. She would throw the ball for him from the mattress end of the loft to the kitchen end where she had a mini-stove and mini-refrigerator. The second she let it go, Harry would let out a joyful yip and take off. Sometimes he would catch it in midair, a dazzlingly graceful maneuver that turned her ridiculous little dog into a ballerina.

She doted on Harry, and within a week he was doting back, not wanting Emily out of his sight, and howling—her neighbors reported to her, sourly, in the elevator—like a soul in hell when she left him alone. She had to leave him alone pretty regularly; within three months, Dr. Demand's money was gone—Harry's teeth alone cost four hundred dollars—and she hadn't sold anything else. She couldn't get a grant or a gallery, or even a spot in a group show in a restaurant in Greenwich Village where she knew one of the waiters, so she took a job working three days a week as the assistant to a gardener named Sophie Lopez.

Sophie lived in Emily's building, two floors down. She was English, tall, blonde, fortyish, and classy, divorced from a Mexican painter. She didn't look like someone who dug in the dirt for a living: She looked like a glossy socialite gotten up in jeans, muddy boots, and knee pads to raise money for the Central Park Conservancy. She specialized in the roof gardens of the wealthy who lived near the Promenade in Brooklyn Heights. Emily had almost no gardening experience—as a child, she had, under protest, helped her parents in the yard with weeding and deadheading—but they got along. Emily was strong and willing to learn, and Sophie was easy-going and willing to teach.

It was on a rooftop terrace on Pineapple Street—the kind of immaculately pastoral place where no wildlife ventured, unless it was the family cat—that Emily encountered Izzy. She and Sophie were working at the home of Victor and Tilda Ramsey, doing the fall cleanup and bulb planting on their fourth-floor terrace. The terrace looked out to the river and to Lower Manhattan on the river's other shore, the towers of the World Trade Center rising up from the shimmering village at their feet like the twin spires of a strange cathedral. It was a blue-sky day in November, unexpectedly warm. Emily dug a trench and prepared to set some tulip bulbs. She stuck her shovel into the dirt, turned to scoop a handful of bone meal out of a sack, and there sitting on the sack was a pale yellow bird.

Emily stopped stone-still and stared at it.

It put its head to one side and stared back with its round black eye.

Emily didn't move, but the bird swiveled its head around, first one side and then the other, as if trying to figure her out. Then it said something like "Tk." Emily replied, gingerly, "Tk." The bird gave a squawk—"Erk"—and Emily said "Erk" in return. They looked at each other for another half minute, and then Emily, very slowly, raised her arm and stuck out a finger. The bird cocked its head and stared, but when she moved her finger closer to the vicinity of its round ivory breast, it hopped on. Emily stood very quietly with her arm held out straight, making soft "tk" and "erk" noises. The bird's feet on her finger were dry, with sharp claws that dug in and almost but not quite hurt. Gradually, she bent her arm and brought the bird closer. When it was six inches from her face, it flew suddenly to her head and perched there. Emily said, warily, "Sophie."

Sophie looked up from the rosebushes she was tying and said, "Oh sweet Jesus, what the bloody hell is that on your head?"

"I. Don't. Know." Emily spoke between clenched teeth. She was afraid to move anything, even her lip muscles.

"I think it's a cockatiel," Sophie said. "Cockatoo? Whatever. It's certainly cute."

Emily could feel the little claws on her scalp. She said, "Tk." The bird didn't answer at first. Then it said, "Tk tk tk tk," a soft, contented mumble. Carefully, she raised her finger again. The bird hopped on, and Emily, feeling more confident, brought it down to look at. It was a creamy yellow bird and on its head was a tall tuft that went up and came down at random. It had a spot of orange on each cheek and a long, stiff tail. Its legs and feet were pale pink. It looked her in the eye. It said "Tk" again, and "Erk."

"I wonder whose it is," Sophie said. "The Ramseys don't have one. Maybe it belongs to a neighbor?"

"It belongs to me," Emily said.

"I think it crapped on your head," Sophie said. "It's claimed you for its own."

Tilda Ramsey gave her a cardboard box with holes punched in it, and it settled in quietly. Tilda didn't know anyone with a cockatiel, but Sophie made Emily put up signs in the neighborhood. On the way home in Sophie's truck, on which was painted: A TREE GROWS IN BROOKLYN GARDEN DESIGN SOPHIE LOPEZ, PROP, Emily held Izzy's box on her lap, making noises at it. The bird was quieter, but now and then it would let out a loud "Tk" and once a shrill "Eek."

"You don't have a cage."

"I'll get one at Pet Pound."

"Do you have any money?"

"Sort of."

Sophie reached into her wallet, pulled out a twenty and handed it to Emily. "Bird seed," she said. "Cuttle bone. A little mirror with a bell on it. Sandpaper thingies that fit over the perches."

"Thank you, Sophie."

"What if someone calls and says it's theirs?"

Emily didn't answer immediately. Then Izzy let out a quiet, pensive "Tk" and Emily shot back a reassuring "Erk."

"Tough shit," she said.

6

Live not on evil, madam, live not on evil.

Live not on evil, madam, live not on evil.

Every time Hart returned, Summer believed against all odds that this time they were going to settle down and be a family, like the Estradas next door. The year Marcus turned ten his father came to live with them again. Hart had left two years before, claiming he couldn't compete with Zeus and Apollo. "It's all Greek to me!" he'd said at the door. No one laughed. Outside, his friend Joe Whack had waited in a car with the motor running. Summer was weeping, and Marcus, who was eight and had never gotten used to seeing his mother's tears, was staring down at his shoes, afraid that if he looked at his father he would have to kick him.

Marcus understood the joke: Summer was too weird and fat and out of it for Hart.

But Summer took Hart's words literally, and renounced her beloved pantheon of gods and goddesses in favor of a milder form of nature worship. Her new religion didn't involve much more than putting in a vegetable garden—beans and lettuce that were mostly eaten by the raccoons and rabbits—and occasionally dancing on the lawn in her bare feet. She sent weekly letters to Hart at his apartment on West 196th Street, reporting on the progress of the garden, her latest cooking triumphs, and Marcus. The address seemed phony to Marcus; even a big city like New York couldn't really have 196 streets. Hart seldom answered the letters, but after two years he called to say he missed them both and was returning.

Summer's friend Tamarind said that, more likely, whatever scam he had going in the city was dried up.

Summer said she didn't care. She loved him, and—here her voice got hard and stubborn—the important thing was they'd all be together again. Like the Huxtables on TV. "Okay, he's not perfect, but he's Marcus's father, and we need him," she said to Tamarind. Marcus couldn't comprehend the third part of her statement: They needed him for *what?* Another time he heard her say, "This time I think we're actually going to get married," her voice wobbly with excitement, which is how he'd found out his parents weren't married. But the *needing* part was the bigger mystery, because Marcus knew that Hart had nothing to do with their lives in any practical way, and that it was his grandmother who supported them.

Grandma Mead was the widow of a long-dead man who had been a minor official on the New York Central Railroad. The tracks of an ancient branch line ran east and west behind the old farmhouse outside Rochester, where the old lady lived modestly on her husband's pension. Every month she sent Summer, her only child, a check made out to Janet Parsons Mead, which was Summer's name before she changed it during her freshman year in college.

Their little gray house at the edge of Honesdale had been built by Grandma Mead's parents in 1912, and Great-Grandma Parsons had died there at the age of ninety-six, leaving the house conveniently available for Summer to move into when she became pregnant with Marcus and quit college. Marcus was born there in the upstairs back bedroom, an event at which Tamarind and a woman named Songbird were present. They had invoked the Roman goddesses of childbirth, Hera and Artemis (and their lesser counterparts Cynosura and Adamanthea), to encourage Marcus's emergence from the womb. Where Hart had been, Marcus never learned, though he once heard Grandma Mead say, "Leave it to the weasel to slink off the day his son is born." His grandmother routinely called his father "the weasel," so he figured Hart's record of disappearing from their lives without warning had begun with his own birth.

After Hart called to say he was coming back—*coming home,* Summer called it, though Hart never did—she cooked and baked for days. There were two pies and Hart's favorite fig tart lined up on the kitchen counter, a coconut cake on a stand, and two kinds of homemade ice cream in the freezer—and those were only the desserts. She also made guacamole and a Provençal beef stew and a big kettle of a soup that always charmed Marcus: a rich broth with fluffy little dumplings in it, each one wrapped neatly around a crouton. When she was finished with all this, she had some time left, so she roasted a pork loin and made a batch of mango-lemon chutney and a loaf of potato bread. What Summer cooked didn't always go together, but it was always good.

Hart arrived in his own car this time, a beat-up Volvo wagon, and he was hungry, which pleased Summer. He looked handsome as ever, but skinny and haunted. He carried one suitcase, his computer in a leather case, and a shopping bag with BARNEY'S NEW YORK printed on it. From the suitcase, in addition to his usual collection of natty shirts and Italian shoes, he pulled a gray pin-striped Armani suit. He called it his art-dealer costume as he shook it out and hung it up in the closet. In the shopping bag there were presents. For Summer, a large box of Godiva chocolates and a painting done by Hart's friend Joe Whack: a still life of a broken cup, a piece of burned toast, and a safety pin. "Joe's new direction," Hart commented, and said he'd chosen it because it was the only painting that was food-related. For Marcus, he brought a book of *New York Times* crossword puzzles and a Manhattan phone book containing a zip-code map of the city confirming that New York had many, many more than 196 streets. These were perfect presents.

The three of them sat amicably around the kitchen table eating roast pork and chutney and fig tart and apricot-almond ice cream and the chocolates, and Marcus decided to think more kindly of his father.

It wasn't easy.

Hart was more of a disciplinarian than Summer, who let Marcus do pretty much what he wanted. Hart made him take out the garbage, and go to his room when he talked back, and eat his goddamned beets or he couldn't have dessert. Marcus could live with that. He figured out early on that his father's disciplinary efforts had nothing to do with Marcus's behavior but were only about a need to dominate him, and so he knew that they would be erratic, contradictory, and not to be taken seriously. As for his father's remoteness and sloppiness and boozing, they didn't bother him either. He was almost glad Hart was such a slob, because cleaning up after him gave Summer something to do.

But what got to him was the way Hart hated everything. His commonest facial expression was a sneer—his lip curled up on one side to expose a yellow canine.

Hart approved of a few artists, and he liked pro football, old movies, and pre-1960 jazz. But he had only scorn for a long and eclectic list of items, including pop music, opera, junk food, what he called "yuppie food," Indian food, Chinese food, baseball, lawyers, doctors, accountants, banks, the checkout clerks at the supermarket, supermarkets, the neighbors, and his own apparently immense and underachieving family back in Wisconsin, whom he brought into the conversation only to denounce as "bourgeois cretins." He hated politicians, scientists, academics, and critics. He claimed that most writers were illiterate, journalists were corrupt toadies, and activists were phonies, no matter what cause they worked for. He seemed to get the most fun out of sneering at the TV shows Summer liked, providing a running commentary about people's clothes, hair, and weight problems. When he said, "They should shoot people who look like Roseanne and put them out of their misery," his malevolent glee was like a bad smell, as though he had farted instead of sneering.

Not that Hart's objections to TV kept him from watching. He never missed a Jets game, and he was also partial to late-night talk shows and black-and-white movies. While Hart was in residence, Marcus didn't like watching TV, even the game shows. In the evenings, instead of curling up on the couch against Summer's friendly bulk, Marcus would leave the two of them in front of the set—Summer with popcorn, Hart with a tumbler of Jack Daniels—and go upstairs with his dog to do crossword puzzles or page through a phone book.

Regularity, number sequences, certain words and combinations of letters, puns, anagrams, lipograms, pangrams, palindromes, word games, crosswords, the rhythms of poetry—these things gave Marcus a deep sense of peace and contentment that he achieved otherwise only in the company of animals. With people, he tended to be friendly and curious, even nosy, but people often disappointed him, and he became glum and silent very quickly when they turned out to be boring or uncommunicative. With his dog, or at the dairy farm down the road where he went to watch the cows, or in the woods surrounded by invisible wildlife—*wildlife,* how he loved that word—then he was happy, and himself, and free. Once Hart arrived, all this became more important to him than ever.

The year he was ten, Marcus was preoccupied with three things in particular: crossword puzzles, phone books, and his puppy, Phoebe. Crossword puzzles were a fairly recent discovery. With a quarter in his pocket he walked down the road every morning to the Honesdale CVS to buy the *New York Times.* He noticed right away that the puzzles got harder as the week went on—they didn't get at all interesting until Thursday. He still did the Monday through Wednesday puzzles, but on those days speed was the important factor. His record was ten minutes for a Tuesday puzzle; it was so easy his pen could hardly keep up with his brain. He had a small stack of Friday and Saturday puzzles that were unfinished, and that he would go back to from time to time. If he plugged away long enough, he always finished them.

As for the Sunday puzzle, it was basically just a big Thursday one, and he could usually polish it off with his breakfast.

The phone books went way back to when, bored one rainy day while visiting his grandmother, he opened the Rochester directory and discovered there were fourteen Meads in it, and only one was his grandmother. Then he found eighty-seven Smiths and almost as many Diazes and Rodriguezes and Cohens and Chins. He was entranced. Now he had the Manhattan phone book. It was a revelation, a brave new world. Incredibly, it contained over a thousand pages of names. Five pages of Smiths! Four of Rodriguezes! People named Leszek Zymerloshaj and Ping Me Ming and Lillian Lux and Sable Brown! He liked chanting the names of all fifty-one Meads: "Amber, Beth, Bruce, Charles, Charles, Chatwin, Elaine, Eugene," he would say to his dog. "Gerard, John, John, John, John B., John F., Jonathan, Karen, Kevin," and Phoebe would look at him with bright eyes, wagging tail, and single-minded attention.

He acquired Phoebe when the Estradas' dog Connie had puppies the previous June. He had missed seeing them being born. When Jessica Estrada stood on her front porch that morning screeching to the world, "Hey everybody! Come on over! The puppies are coming," Summer was in the shower, and Marcus was still in bed with the covers over his head, memorizing a poem by Robert Louis Stevenson as a present for her birthday. "Windy Nights," it was called—inadequately, Marcus thought— and it contained the lines:

By, on the highway, low and loud,
By at the gallop goes he.
By at the gallop he goes, and then
By he comes back at the gallop again.

Marcus mumbled the lines over and over to himself, enjoying the way they began to sound exactly like what they were describing. (He didn't yet know the word *onomatopoeia,* though when he learned there was an actual Greek word for what the poem did, he was thrilled.) After he recited the poem and Summer had applauded and hugged him, they went over to see the puppies, four of them: two mostly black, one mostly white, one spotted.

Summer was immediately entranced, and flopped down on the floor beside their basket, crooning to Connie at eye level about the beauty of her babies. Jessica Estrada told Marcus excitedly about the birth, how they came out slimy and had to be cleaned up by Connie, who not only licked off all the crud but ate a big pile of what looked like guts, something called the afterbirth, that also came out of her thing. Marcus was glad he'd been under the covers when it happened.

All the puppies but the white one, which the Estradas named Queso, were available for adoption, and when Summer decided she had to have one, Marcus was thunderstruck. He had always longed for a pet, but assumed they were too odd to have one. But Summer said a puppy born on·her twenty-ninth birthday would be the most perfect present she could give herself, and before she could change her mind, Marcus made a case for the spotted black-and-white, floppy-eared female. Summer agreed immediately. She wanted to name the puppy Gemini, after her sign, but Marcus persuaded her in favor of Phoebe, the name of the imaginary sister he invented years ago. He loved it that *Phoebe* was pronounced nothing like the way it looked. So different from most names, which were perfectly straightforward. "It's like a magic word, it's as if Marcus was pronounced Magoo or something like that," he explained to Summer, and she chuckled and ruffled his hair and gave in.

One thing he liked about Phoebe (one thing of many) was that if you ever did anything so crazy as to shave off her hair and sort it into two piles, one black and one white, the piles would be the same size. Not that she was symmetrical. Just that, if you studied her closely, her allotment of black and white fur, however randomly scattered across her compact puppy body, seemed equal. This he noticed as soon as he picked her out of Connie's litter. He also liked that Phoebe enjoyed hearing him recite names from the phone book or—even more—poetry.

> *By at the gallop he goes, and then*
> *By he comes back at the gallop again.*

When Marcus recited, Phoebe would gaze at him raptly, and when he paused, she always gave the little bark that, otherwise, she used only when she was dancing around the kitchen waiting for him to shake kibble into her bowl. Marcus deduced that poetry pleased Phoebe the way food did, and that she understood it in her own way. He grew to love Phoebe more than he loved anyone else, maybe even his mother, a thought that caused him some guilt. And he bonded with Phoebe as he never had with a human being.

Not that he had bonded with anyone very often.

He did have one important friend for an entire summer when he was almost nine, a boy named Donnie Ryan. Donnie lived near the bakery, and they met when their mothers were in the same short-lived organic-gardening-and-nature-worship group. They liked to ride their bikes all over Honesdale, ending up at the little park between Ninth and Tenth to sit on the bench in front of the Civil War monument. There they'd make up limericks and knock-knock jokes, anagrams and palindromes. Once Donnie came up with "Dennis sinned," which Marcus refined into "Dennis, I sinned." Their favorite game they called simply the *word-wore-fore-fare-fame-game,* and they called each other *Mar-bar-bat-but-bus-cus* and *Don-doe-die-nie.*

They also liked to hang around Donnie's house playing a computer game called Numerabilis that involved arranging numbers in sequences in order to destroy the entire planet, country by country. Numerabilis was very difficult. Donnie was two years older than Marcus, and the sequences that led to world destruction came somewhat easier to him, so when one hot day in July Marcus destroyed, in rapid succession, Australia, New Zealand, and most of the islands in the Indonesian archipelago, he screamed so loudly Mrs. Ryan dashed upstairs in terror, ready to call 911.

At the end of that summer, Donnie's family moved to Jeffersonville. It was only twenty miles away, across the river in New York State, but the friendship was essentially over. Donnie and his mother did come to visit once, during Christmas vacation, but it was a wet, snowy day and, without bikes and Numerabilis, the boys couldn't find much to say or do. Marcus got upset when Donnie insisted he had made up a brilliant new palindrome ("Go hang a salami, I'm a lasagna hog"), even though Marcus had heard it on TV two days before. They ended up spending the afternoon combing halfheartedly through Marcus's collection of phone books looking for odd names, a pastime that fascinated Marcus but bored Donnie, who at his new school had become interested in MTV, the different makes of cars, and girls.

Marcus missed Donnie, but Phoebe soon became indispensable to him, a friend who never let him down and whose main interest was always the same: Marcus. Phoebe also kept him home. Since he was seven or eight, on warm summer days Marcus had taken to disappearing. There was a field behind the house that was pink and white with clover and daisies all summer, and behind it a woods that went on and on until it joined up with a state forest somewhere near Route 191. Marcus would pack a book and a notebook into his Nelson School backpack, along with a sweatshirt and heavy socks and a bottle of water and whatever he could find in the kitchen—crackers, a box of cereal, once a bag of frozen peas—and he would walk across the field, go deep into the woods, and sit quietly under a tree reading or figuring things out in a notebook. He'd watch as the little creatures who lived there gradually returned, realizing he was no threat to their turf. Once, a squirrel had actually run right over his leg. Another time a flicker perched in a tree a few feet above him and pecked out a rhythm. One evening at dusk, a solemn-eyed raccoon family stared at him through the brush for a long minute before they turned and vanished. His ambition was to see a fox.

When it got too dark to read he would put on his warm shirt and socks, pee into the bushes, and go to sleep, using the backpack for a pillow. He liked sleeping in the rustling silence of the woods, and waking up in the morning, not moving, opening his eyes slowly, bit by bit, in hopes of finding himself surrounded by animals. This never happened, though the birds were always noisy above him, and several times he saw deer, delicate and unexpectedly small, who would stand motionless until some subtle movement or shift in the wind would mobilize them and, white tails flashing, they would disappear into the trees. It was in the woods with a flashlight that, amazed at the beauty of the *w*'s and *l*'s, and the truth of what they said, he memorized the lines:

> *What would the world be, once bereft*
> *Of wet and wildness? Let them be left,*
> *O let them be left, wildness and wet;*
> *Long live the weeds and the wilderness yet.*

Summer had stopped calling Marcus's habit "running away," and also stopped getting Big Rafe or the volunteer fire department to come and find him. She took it for granted that Marcus would come back.

Phoebe didn't like the woods. She liked the big, open field, and would run through the clover, away from Marcus and then back, leaping on him joyfully. But once they entered the woods, she would whine and look over her shoulder and want to go home, like a banished child in a fairy tale. Eventually, she'd start barking, and a barking dog meant his disappearing days were over. *She's only a puppy,* he told himself, *she'll be braver when she gets older and bigger.*

Marcus wasn't going to school that year, so come September, he was looking forward to spending time at home with his books and charts and puzzles and games. The Nelson School for

Gifted Children, for which Grandma Mead paid the tuition, hadn't worked out. After two months, the headmaster explained to Summer that Marcus was certainly gifted but not in ways the school was equipped to deal with, and suggested home-schooling. Summer, who spent almost three years at Oswego State Teachers' College as an early education major before she dropped out, petitioned the Board of Education and got permission to teach Marcus at home, which meant he was left on his own to do whatever he liked while Summer baked pies and did her big, swooping dances on the lawn. An arithmetic tutor came on Saturday mornings, but after a while she stopped showing up. It didn't seem to matter.

When Hart came back, though, Marcus knew he'd be forced to get on a school bus every day and go to a real school again. He was cooperative about it, as part of his campaign to get along with his father, and he was enrolled in the fifth grade at the middle school in Honesdale. He approached it with optimism, hoping fifth grade wouldn't seem like a waste of his time, as fourth grade had, and that he'd find a friend. But it did and he didn't, and everything was over before Halloween.

It was the same story: *Marcus needs special attention, he shows no interest in regular schoolwork, his test scores are out of sight, but he's not thriving in the atmosphere of school.* Translated, this meant that the only arithmetic Marcus would participate in was the recitation of the multiplication tables, which he did with noisy enthusiasm. That he spent a good portion of his time working on Self-Descriptive Numbers, which he found out about in a library book. That he came up with a variant he called Meaningful Numbers, by which he figured out that his zip code corresponded to his house number, and that he announced his discovery joyfully to Miss Bright, disrupting a discussion of the principal products of Uruguay. That at recess he stayed alone with his pencil and notebook, refusing to play two-square or tag. And that in the lunchroom he wouldn't sit at a table with other kids. He preferred to take his carefully packed lunch box and sit on the floor.

Marcus couldn't eat at a noisy, crowded table, and so the sitting-on-the-floor-in-the-lunch-room thing was something he devised out of desperation. This, of course, wasn't allowed ("Why on earth not?" Summer asked, with her little laugh, which didn't help), so Marcus was amazed when it actually turned things in his favor. His classmates ignored him when they saw he was impervious to anything they said, and the school was very nice about what the guidance counselor called Marcus's *highly individualized coping skills*. Marcus is a sweet child, they said, polite and respectful, but desperately, irretrievably, bewilderingly *different*. If he kept on as he was going, he would end up repeating fifth grade. One stumped teacher ventured the words *autistic* and *retarded*, yet there was no denying Marcus tested far above his grade level in both arithmetic and reading. The Board of Education said there was no reason Summer couldn't go back to teaching him at home, though she and his father might want to pay more attention to socialization skills.

Hart, of course, did not go to this school conference, and when Summer broke the news, he took it rather well, only asking Marcus, rhetorically, why he had to be such a weird little twerp. He also said Marcus should join a Cub Scout troop, or take piano lessons, or go away to summer camp next year, or at least play more with the Estrada kids next door. But he and Marcus both knew that none of these things would come to pass.

No matter what Summer might wish, they were an odd family.

Hart did claim to be working. When he wasn't watching football or working his way through the fifty-four novels of Anthony Trollope, he spent much of his time in closed-door phone conversations with people in New York or tapping the keys on his off-limits-to-Marcus laptop. Checks arrived in the mail from time to time, and once or twice he had to drive to Allentown. "To see my main man," he said with a smirk, and when Marcus asked Summer who that was, she said, vaguely, "Maybe a car mechanic?" Hart was still, apparently, an art dealer, even though he now lived in a small Pennsylvania town, far from the galleries and the artists and the need to wear his Armani suit, "the whole sick fucking art market," as he called it. When Marcus asked what an art dealer was, exactly, his father replied, "An idiot, son. A mad dreamer. I suggest you become a sanitation worker when you grow up."

While Hart holed up in the spare bedroom he'd commandeered as an office, Summer looked at cookbooks and puttered around the house, running the vacuum cleaner, scrubbing sinks, imposing her obsessive order on everything. Marcus's socks (in the bureau drawer labeled SOCKS AND UNDERWEAR) were rolled into neat bundles and sorted by color. The pasta in the cupboard was alphabetized: angel-hair to ziti. At four every afternoon she would begin banging things around in the kitchen; they would finally eat at eight or nine. The smells would start wafting up to Marcus's room by five, and he would sit with his stomach rumbling, losing himself in games and numbers, until finally, when he knew he would faint if he didn't eat soon, Summer's voice would float up the stairs on two notes: "Dinnnnnn-errrrrr!"

Marcus was a small-boned, skinny boy with a limited appetite that could disappear entirely when he was upset or excited, and he was a continual disappointment to his mother when it came to food. It wasn't that he didn't appreciate her cooking, just that he could appreciate it only in small portions. Sometimes he would eat his first helping, then rest up, maybe take the dog out or go watch a little TV before he returned for more food, finding Summer still sitting at the table, calmly putting away another slice of roast pork and her third mound of mashed potatoes, reading an article in *Gourmet* about a restaurant in Zurich or the perfect cheese soufflé.

Hart managed to eat everything Summer put on the table and not gain an ounce.

On his nasty days, he also kept up a running commentary about her weight and her appetite, calling her "Some more" or "Chubber," which got Marcus so angry he lost his appetite entirely.

But sometimes Hart was nice, and then Marcus believed his resolution to like his father better was something that could actually work. Hart and Summer would be friendly and affectionate with each other: Marcus would come across them embracing, and once he looked out the window to see them kissing on the lawn—he clocked one kiss at ninety-six seconds, which astonished him. He knew what it meant, vaguely, when in the night he'd hear the rhythmic bed-banging noise from their room, and next morning Summer would look exhausted but cheerful, and even Hart would be in a better mood, slapping her on the bottom and calling her "Babe" or "Pumpkin."

Occasionally, Hart would put on one of his jazz CDs and sit Marcus down with him to listen. He could talk entertainingly about Trollope's convoluted plots: blackmailing viscounts, crooked members of Parliament, lovesick maidens living on country estates, impoverished younger sons driven to reckless gambling. Once or twice Marcus and his father even drove to the mall in Scranton, where Hart would buy him a sweatshirt, a pair of sneakers, a new crossword puzzle book—it didn't matter what, Marcus was always impressed when Hart, who was famously stingy, not only noticed his existence but shelled out money to confirm it. And that they had done something together that was normal.

Then Grandma Mead died suddenly, and Summer drove to Rochester alone for the funeral. There was no question of Hart (the Weasel) accompanying her, and Summer said Marcus, at ten, was too young. When she kissed him good-bye, he could feel her wet eyelashes on his cheek. Marcus had never been without his mother, and he had never been alone with his father for more than a few hours.

Summer was gone for nearly a week.

It wasn't quite winter yet—the oak trees bordering the yard still held on to their stiff brown leaves but the days were grim, chilly, and sunless. Hart, as always, remained in his study all day, smoking and talking on the phone. Marcus stayed in his room with Phoebe, reading, doing puzzles, slipping down to the kitchen to make himself a piece of toast or a bowl of cereal. For dinner on their first night, Hart thawed some chicken parts and boiled them, and they ate them with gummy rice in front of the TV. On the second night, Marcus tried his hand at making spaghetti with tomato sauce but burned the sauce so badly they had to throw the pan away. On the third night—*Home Improvement* was on, one of Hart's favorite shows to make fun of—they had fish sticks from the supermarket. On the next night, they ate leathery fried-egg sandwiches. Finally, on the last night, after Hart quit cursing and blaming Summer for not leaving them food, the two of them drove to Mario's Olde Italian Inn in Honesdale. "What the hell," Hart said recklessly, as if he were contemplating a dive off a cliff. "What the hell, let's live it up, kid." They would go to a restaurant and stuff their faces, to hell with the cost. It would be a chance to spend a little quality time together.

All his life Marcus would remember this strange evening.

He sat across the table from his father, with a Coke and a plate of lasagna. Hart drank one double Jack Daniels before dinner and two with. He began talking about his pet topics: the joys of Trollope, the tediousness of baseball, the tribulations of the New York Jets, and the moronic lyrics of pop music. Then he talked about his friend Joe Whack and the venality, stupidity, and shortsightedness of the art business and the mass of idiots known as "the public." The only person who really appreciated Whack's work, Hart said, was a Polish dentist in Brooklyn, who had actually bought one of his paintings. Marcus listened to this with interest—Joe Whack fascinated him because of his strange name and his strange paintings, and because he was an actual friend of his strange father. Then the conversation turned.

"I want to tell you something," Hart began. "Something you're probably too young to have observed for yourself." Hart was deep into his second Jack Daniels, and it was a moment before he went on. Marcus watched him expectantly. Finally, with the air of a sage uttering a profound truth, Hart pointed his index finger into the air and said, "There is something very wrong with almost everyone in the world."

Marcus didn't think he was too young for such an observation. When he was at Honesdale Middle School, in fact, he would have agreed with this statement, but now that he was home again he was inclined to dispute it. He had an idea he didn't quite know how to express, which was that, if you weren't happy, you were more inclined to think there was something wrong with almost everyone in the world, but if you were happy, then you figured other people were probably okay. Also, he didn't know if this sounded stupid or not.

Hart didn't expect a comment. He went on. "I've been observing for a long time the fact that, although people seem diverse—you know, their opinions and their interests and their values—basically they're all very similar. They operate on mechanical reflexes and primitive thought patterns. All six billion of them, or whatever it is. Probably seven billion by now. Eight."

"I think it's still just about six billion," Marcus said helpfully.

"Well, whatever. A hell of a lot of people." Hart picked a large green olive out of a dish on their table and took a bite, shaking his head as he chewed, as if the taste of the olive illustrated what he was talking about. "And yet, it's funny," he said, with a half-snicker and a near-smile. "The ideas that populate those people's minds, ideas about religion, morality, freedom, happiness—they're like germs that infect and spread. They have no point or purpose. They exist without any logical foundation." He set the olive down on the tablecloth and leaned toward Marcus.

Marcus noticed that his father's eyes were bloodshot, he needed a shave, and his longish hair was unwashed.

"Do you understand what I mean?"

Marcus nodded and said, "I guess so."

"Good. Keep listening." Hart sat back in his chair with his drink. "These ideas are of course idiotic, and yet people are completely controlled by them and can't see beyond them. But here's my point, son. The important thing is not to let yourself give in to them. Don't let them fuck you over." He jabbed his finger in the air in Marcus's direction. "And it takes more than just realizing they exist. You've got to *resist* them. You've got to *question* things that have no point. Illogical ideas. And never, Marcus—" Hart lurched forward suddenly and slammed his glass down on the table; it contained only ice, which rattled. "Never accept imperfection or compromise, and *never*—this is the important part—*never* forget that you are the emperor of your own life."

The emperor of your own life. Marcus liked the idea. "Cool," he said. But then he wondered, what did it mean, anyway? Life wasn't a kingdom. And if it was, how could there be six billion emperors?

"Your life is yours, your decisions are yours, and what seems right to you, son—that's what's right. If you get your mind oriented the right way. If you get your head screwed on right, you can never be wrong. Do you understand?"

Marcus squirmed. "Sure."

"I hope so," Hart said. "Because if you don't, and if you don't stay eternally vigilant, you'll always be nothing but a product of random evolution. You will not be an important person, Marcus. You'll be nothing."

His father kept talking. Hart's voice was harsh and gravelly, punctuated by smoker's coughs. Marcus tuned out for a while. He looked around the room, cataloging things, while still trying to look like he was paying attention. In his line of vision, there were ten tables, six booths, a total of forty-two chairs not counting a high chair against the wall, six scenes of (he assumed) Italy framed in gold on the wall. He noticed there was a tank of fish behind his father's chair, under the window. Why would a restaurant have a tank of fish? Was it an old Italian custom? Were they raising them to put on the menu when they got bigger? He counted five goldfish, including one with mottled black markings, like a calico cat, and four or five triangular gray fish and maybe a dozen little darting guys that seemed—could it be?—to be lit up by a long bluish neon streak. He would have liked to get up and look more closely, but he didn't. He picked at his lasagna and looked at his father and nodded often enough to show he was listening, knowing that if he accompanied the nod with a frown now and then, or the rise of an eyebrow, it was more convincing: This was something he had learned in the guidance counselor's office at Honesdale Middle School.

But he tuned in again when Hart said, "I worry about you, Marcus. I worry that you and I haven't been closer. I worry that your major influence has been your mother." Marcus saw a look on Hart's face he didn't recall seeing before: a sort of sickly-sweet smile. "Not that Summer's not a great girl."

Marcus nodded. "Summer is the best."

"Agreed. You'd have to go a long way to find a—" He paused. "A nicer person than your mother. Right?"

"Right," Marcus said warily. He had a feeling something terrible was coming, and braced himself.

"But you have to admit she's a little out of it."

"What do you mean?"

"You know. The Roman gods. The food. The crazy nature

stuff. The labels. The—well, doesn't it ever occur to you that your mother isn't like other people?"

This had occurred to Marcus many times, but he didn't like it when his father said it. "I thought that was good."

"What?"

"I thought it was important to be different from other people. The six billion. Isn't that what you said?"

"Hey—Marcus? Let me put it this way: There's different, and then there's *different*. There's different, and then there's your mother!"

Hart genuinely cracked up at this, and Marcus noticed how handsome his father was when the expression on his face was humorous and genuine. Anyone looking at them would think Hart was sharing a moment of winsome humor with his son, not making fun of his mother.

"I like her the way she is," Marcus said, refusing to smile. "I love her."

"Well, of course. Right. I hope so."

Marcus waited for his father to say, "So do I," but Hart just sighed and signaled the waitress for another drink. They sat in silence for a moment. Marcus had made only a small dent in his lasagna. He looked down at his plate, thinking how the lasagna looked like a tiny version of one of those Indian villages in Colorado that was dug into a canyon wall, made of flat layers of stone. He wished they could leave. He knew Hart wasn't through talking, and he knew he didn't want to hear what else the gravelly voice would say. He thought about going home in the cold, then entering the warm house where a warm dog awaited him. He thought about being up in his cozy room under the roof with Phoebe under the covers beside him and yesterday's crossword puzzle to be done. Wednesday, and pretty easy, but still . . . . Or maybe Summer would call from Rochester.

"Of course you love your mother," Hart said finally. "But you know, Marcus, she's pretty much a slave to a set of wacky ideas and preferences that—well, if you were to be too influenced by them, they would not stand you in good stead out in the real world."

"Isn't this the real world?" Marcus asked, knowing as soon as he uttered the question that his father would crack up again.

"*Honesdale?*" Hart asked when his laughter subsided. "Honesdale, *Pennsylvania*? Crossword puzzles and phone books? Your mother's pie? Big Rafe Estrada? Is that the real world? Give me a break, kid."

Marcus said nothing, just poked his fork into his lasagna. He felt a vague anger beginning to stir in him. He wanted to get up and go—but go where?

"I've got just one piece of advice," Hart said, serious again. Now, if anyone looked at them, they might think this handsome, earnest father was impressing upon his small son the importance of studying hard and doing well in school so he could get into a good college someday. "Get out as soon as you can. I'm serious. Summer's a nice person, and there was a time when she wasn't so—" He twisted a hand back and forth in the air as if the gesture would tell Marcus everything. "Let me just say that things were different. But now, frankly, all I've got to say is—well, you're my only son, my only child. At least so far. And I want you to take this seriously, what I'm about to say." He tapped Marcus on the arm three times, as if he were casting some sort of spell. Marcus drew his arm back. "Leave," Hart said. "Don't let Honesdale be your downfall. Don't be like the kids I see down on Main Street, hanging out at the pizza parlor talking about the sex lives of rappers and movie stars."

Marcus had never been to the pizza parlor on Main Street. "Okay," he said.

"Get out as soon as you can, and go as far away as you can go. Do you understand me? It's important."

"Yeah," Marcus said, rubbing his blue sweater where his father had touched it.

Hart stared at him a moment. Then, narrowing his eyes, he said, "I think you do, sonny. I think you do. You're a smart kid. But somehow—" His voice slowed down, and he nodded his head a little with each word, a habit he had. "I just. Don't. Have. A lot of confidence—" Here he changed direction, and shook his head from side to side. "That you'll do that."

Marcus shrugged. He wished his father would become so disgusted with him he'd just go away—leave, leave, *leave*. He noticed Hart's half-chewed olive was still on the tablecloth, looking gross, and his gaze drifted past it and back to the fish tank. He could feel Hart looking at him, then heard him give another loud sigh. "Well, it's your life." Hart drained his glass and wiped his mouth with his napkin, which he threw on his plate among the grease and tomato sauce. Marcus wondered how the restaurant would get the red stains out of the white napkin. Then he asked, "Can we go now?"

The next day, Friday, the weather suddenly warmed up, the sun came out, and Marcus asked for a quarter so he could walk into town and get the *Times*. Hart gave him a ten and asked him to pick up some shaving cream and a quart of orange juice, and then stop at the bakery and get half a dozen cupcakes—a surprise for Summer when she got home later. And keep the change, he said.

Marcus would always remember how beautiful the day was, and how pleased he was that his father took the time to think Summer would like cupcakes. How he had walked to Honesdale in a Summer-ish haze of sentimental optimism. Maybe his father, for all his strange talk, wasn't such a bad egg. Maybe he even regretted last night, wanted to make it up. He'd been drunk and a little weird, is all. Maybe the cupcakes showed Hart wasn't bothered any more by Summer's weight. Maybe the shaving cream meant he wanted to shave before she got home. And maybe the gift of the change from the ten meant he did have confidence in Marcus as a responsible boy, that maybe he didn't consider him the jerkoff weirdo he always said he was.

Marcus did the errands in a leisurely way, picking out a blue gel shaving cream he thought his father would like, and checking the date on the orange juice. He chose three chocolate and three white cupcakes, all of them with stand-up frosting and colored sprinkles, and enjoyed the way the bakery woman put the cupcakes into the box, alternating brown and white in a checkerboard pattern. He smiled at her, and she said, "Well, aren't *you* a nice boy!" The sun was so warm that on his way home he sat on a bench basking in it and looking at the headlines on the front page of the newspaper: DEMS CHALLENGE BUSH ON HEALTH CARE. NEW HAMPSHIRE VITAL TO CLINTON, AIDES SAY. DID INTERNET KILLER LEAVE PAPER TRAIL?

In a way, he understood what his father had meant—he knew there was another world out there. He told himself he would start reading the paper like a conscientious home-schooler, and discover for himself what that world was all about, instead of just diving into the crossword puzzle and tossing the rest in the recycle bin. *DID INTERNET KILLER LEAVE PAPER TRAIL?* He said it over to himself. He had not the tiniest idea what it meant.

Walking home, he wondered if his mother had arrived yet. He wanted to hear about Grandma Mead's funeral. He would have liked to go—partly out of a morbid desire to see what a dead body looked like, but more because Grandma Mead's death was unreal to him. He had a hazy idea that his mother's tears, the details of the death and burial, would help him believe it, and that that was a necessary thing—your grandmother's death shouldn't be something that passed over you without consequence, like winter sunlight or a newspaper headline. And at the back of his mind was a worry that, with her death, Grandma Mead's checks would stop coming, and they would have to depend on Hart to take care of them.

Summer's car was in the driveway. Marcus hurried up the road, humming a little, skipping on every fourth step as was his habit, and when he neared the house he could hear his mother's voice raised in what sounded like hysteria. "You're lying!" she said, and then said it again, and then she cried out what sounded like, "Dig her up, damn you! Just go and dig her up!"

Marcus stopped in his tracks.

"Dig up the fucking dog, damn you! Dig her up, you lying son of a bitch!"

He dropped the bag and began to run.

When he entered the kitchen, Hart was standing on one side of the table, Summer on the other gripping a carving knife in her clenched fist. She was still wearing her black winter coat, and her hair was tied back. Her face was distorted and red. She looked like no one he knew.

"I want to know what you did with her," she said, raising the knife. "You dig her up and let me see her, or get out of here."

Hart backed away, his hands palm out in front of him. "Hey hey hey—calm down, Summer. Just calm down. If you don't believe me, that's your business, but I am not digging up a dog I just spent half an hour digging a hole to bury. Are you crazy?"

"Show me where you did it! Show me the grave! I'll dig her up myself."

"You're out of control! Calm down and just accept it. It was a terrible accident. These things happen."

Marcus's voice split the air. *"Where's my dog?"*

They turned and saw him, and Summer's face crumpled. She put down the knife and held out her arms. "Oh, Marcus. Oh, my baby. She's gone, sweetie. Phoebe is dead."

Marcus didn't move. He stared at his father until Hart ducked his head, waved his hand uneasily, and said, "It was an accident. It happened just after you left, Marcus. She ran into the road, and a car hit her. Didn't even stop, the bastard. It was over in a second." Something resembling tears came to his eyes, making them brighten. "She didn't suffer, son," he said, blinking. "I buried her out in the woods. I didn't—well, I didn't think you should see her."

"The woods." Marcus's mind stuck at the words. "The woods. She hated the woods."

"It seemed the best thing."

Summer's face returned to its mask of rage. She gave what sounded like a strangled scream. "You're lying," she said to Hart through gritted teeth. "Do you think I don't know when you're lying?" She picked up the knife again. "Take me to where you buried her or get out of here and don't ever come back."

Marcus didn't feel queasy as he always did when his parents argued or his mother cried. His mind was empty of everything but Phoebe. *Phoebe*. Her spotted fur and floppy ears and polite little bark and muddy paws and big laughing grin with teeth like a tiny ivory mountain range. What had she been doing when he last saw her? Dancing around the door, wanting to go with him. "I can't take you with me into town," he had said. "We'll go out when I get back." And his father had smiled at them both and said, "It's a beautiful day out there," and then Marcus had left, basking in his father's niceness and gloating over the stupid ten-dollar bill from which he would get to keep the change.

He turned and walked outside. Behind him, he could hear his mother's voice—shrill and out of control, but tough, unwavering. The sun was still shining; he stood for a moment, feeling it warm his face. He saw that the carton of juice he dropped had opened up and spilled, an orange smear against the dirty snow, but it had missed the newspaper and the cupcakes. He picked them up, and went inside as his father was backing out of the kitchen. "All right," Hart was saying in a placating, singsong voice. "Whatever you say, Summer. I'm out of here. Like I really need a fat, hysterical madwoman in my life."

Marcus put the box down and went to his mother, and stood with his face pressed to her soft front, her arms around him, until they heard Hart stomp back downstairs with his suitcase and his computer bag. Then he came down again, grunting, with a box of his books. Marcus went to the window and looked out. His parents' cars—the blue Volvo wagon, the white Toyota—rested side by side, like shabby old friends.

Hart went through the back door and walked down the steps. He was wearing his Armani suit. He put his stuff in the trunk, lit a cigarette, and stood in the sun, smoking. He didn't look back at the house. Finally, he tossed the cigarette into the snow and got into the car. Marcus watched him drive off, and when the Volvo was out of sight he remained at the window thinking maybe Hart was joking, or lying, and when he went up to his room Phoebe would be there, curled up asleep on the bed.

But he decided not to go upstairs just yet, because maybe she wouldn't.

Marcus made his mother a cup of coffee and set it in front of her with two cupcakes on a plate—one white, one chocolate. Then he sat down at the kitchen table. His mother was a stone. She sat across from Marcus in silence, staring at nothing, her eyes hot and burning, for many long minutes, before she drank the coffee and ate the cupcakes.

7

!Ah, Satan sees NatashA!

!Ah, Satan sees NatashA!

Near the end of 1991, the gardening year over, Emily was happily collecting unemployment as a seasonal worker. Her boss, Sophie, always traveled in the off season, this year to Bali. Dr. Demand had bought another photograph, a fairly new TIME, as a Christmas gift for his partner, Dr. Wrzeszczynski. Emily's pictures were being considered by a gallery in the Village—she expected a verdict soon after New Year's—and she was busy taking more pictures, teaching Izzy to say "pretty boy" and Harry to come, sit, and stay. She had flown out to Berkeley to have Thanksgiving with her mother and sister and brother, leaving Harry and Izzy in the care of Anstice; in return she had agreed to stay in Williamsburg for Christmas and look after Anstice's six cats.

As the days grew shorter and colder, she began to wish she had a nice warm boyfriend to share the mattress with her and Harry.

It always surprised people who knew Emily that she had trouble with men. When she was younger, she had assumed maybe it was her big feet or her funny-looking ears that were the problem, but she had begun to suspect maybe it was something about her attitude.

"I think he got discouraged," Gene Rae told her when her last boyfriend, a law student named Peter with melting brown eyes and a dog named Louie, broke up with her. "He told Kurt that sometimes you seemed to forget his existence."

"I really liked Peter," Emily said mournfully. "Of course I forgot his existence sometimes! But just on a situational basis, like when I was in the darkroom or reading. In a *cosmic* way, I loved him."

"I'm not sure that was clear to Peter."

"And anyway, I thought women were supposed to play hard to get."

"Is that what you were doing?"

"No—I was just being normal! But if he *thought* I was neglecting him, why didn't he see that as a challenge?"

"Maybe he did," Gene Rae said. "At first. But nothing changed, and so he got discouraged."

Emily sensed behind these comments a long heart-to-heart with Peter, and sighed to disguise the fact that she resented this. "Well then, I'm glad he's gone, Gene Rae. He could have tried harder."

"Emily! He did try harder! But you didn't try at all."

"But I didn't know anything was wrong!"

She called Peter and explained to him that if he had had a problem with her attention span or her reading habits or something, he should have let her know instead of writing her a stuffy letter saying, "I have needs that are not being met, and so frankly, although I really respect and admire you, I just don't see a future for us." On the phone he told her that maybe she was right, he could have handled it better, but it was a pointless discussion anyway because, actually, he had found someone else.

"Does she meet your needs?"

"She adores me."

"Peter, I adored you!" Emily wailed.

"Oh, Emily," he sighed. "No you didn't, sweetie. You really didn't."

Emily had no idea what it all meant. She had had a boyfriend with beautiful brown eyes who made her laugh and was fun in bed and whose dog got along with her dog, and then suddenly she had an ex-boyfriend who respected and admired her.

"You probably need to meet someone as self-sufficient as you are," Gene Rae said.

"Do you really mean self-absorbed?" Emily asked.

"No, that's not it. You're not self-absorbed at all, you're the opposite. You're more interested in other people than anyone I've ever met. You just don't really focus—you know? And the things that do absorb you . . . well, it's hard to define exactly what I mean. You're—" Gene Rae gestured helplessly. "You're just—"

Emily found she was on the verge of tears. "I sense the word *oblivious* struggling to come out." She struggled to keep in control. "Or *clueless*. Some word like that."

"That's not *quite* it," Gene Rae sat for another minute, lost in thought. Then she said, "But it's close, baby. You know I love you to death, but—it's pretty close."

Emily resolved to be less clueless, to focus better on her next boyfriend. *Focus* . . . meaning what? She had a general idea, but when it came to particulars she drew a blank.

Christmas in Williamsburg would be quiet and solitary; most of the people she knew were going out of town. It would be just her and Harry and Izzy making their own holiday cheer in the loft, phone calls to Mom and Milo and Laurie on Christmas day, a quart of eggnog with some rum in it.

In preparation, she arranged twinkly lights around the windows. She bought a four-foot blue spruce from a young couple who came all the way from Vermont to set up outside the subway entrance on North Seventh Street. She decorated the tree with strings of popcorn, paper cutouts, and, on top, a star she made from cardboard, gold paint, and the spangles from a broken bracelet she'd never been able to fix. To her mother and siblings she sent photographs of the Manhattan skyline at three different times of day. She gave Gene Rae and Kurt a picture of their dog that she took secretly and put into a homemade frame. She made cranberry bread for Anstice to find on her return, and painted a little picture of Harry with Izzy sitting on his head (not a real-life situation) for Luther. She baked dozens of Christmas cookies to take around to people in the neighborhood, like Gaby and Hattie and Marta and Mrs. Buzik and the guys in the pigeon-feed store.

On the late afternoon of Christmas Eve, as she was coming home from the deli, she ran into Joe Whack in the elevator. She was looking forward with pleasure to her dinner, which was going to be a simple and early one of rum-and-eggnog, along with slices of the fruitcake her mother had sent. The fruitcake was the good kind, dark and moist and mysterious, full of dried fruits and nuts but *sans* citron. Her mother made a dozen of them weeks ahead, doused them with booze, and left them to stew in their juices, then packed them up and mailed them to her far-flung children and relatives and friends. Emily had been eating this fruitcake as long as she could remember, but it was only recently that she had discovered the delights of washing it down with rum-laced eggnog. The combination, she thought, not only required no cooking but would console her for being alone on Christmas Eve.

Then in the elevator Joe Whack invited her to a party.

He was a painter, and that was nearly all she knew about him. Except that he was the only person in the building who didn't have at least one dog or cat. Anstice preferred to rent to what she called "animal people"; they were more honest, reliable, kind hearted, and generally lovable, she said. Joe Whack had a beagle named Bouncer when he moved in, then it turned out he had just borrowed Bouncer to get the loft. Anstice had no way of proving that or, indeed, of getting rid of him even if it was true. She had asked him to get at least one small cat, but he said he was allergic to cats, and he couldn't have a dog because he was living on the edge and he couldn't afford dog food.

He did seem, even to Emily, to be living on the edge.

His clothes weren't ragged, exactly, but they seemed old, cruddy, and few. He had a scraggly beard to match his patchy reddish hair. It was said that he painted compulsively, and his loft was stacked with canvases, but either he never tried to show his work or no one would take it on. Anstice had seen some of his paintings and said they were weird, monochrome still-lifes of oddly assorted objects. The one Anstice remembered depicted the edge of a frayed carpet with a crumpled candy wrapper and a milk bottle. "He doesn't seem to get out much," she said. Anstice didn't like Joe Whack, and would love it if he became a success and moved to Tribeca or SoHo. Emily had no opinion about him, except that, observing his emaciated frame and bad complexion, she wondered if he was entirely well. And she noticed that whenever he was in the elevator with her and Harry, he kept his distance, smiling nervously, as if Harry was a piranha. Otherwise he was wanly friendly. But today he was almost effusive.

"It'll just be a bunch of people from the neighborhood who are stuck in the city for the holidays," he said. "You know—the rejects and weirdos and sociopaths."

"Well sure, if you put it that way, I'd love to come," Emily said. "I guess I'm a little lonely."

"Well." Joe Whack smiled uncomfortably. "Great. I mean— okay, then. Whatever."

"What time? And what shall I bring?"

"Don't bring a thing. We're having a big spread, food and drink." Joe looked momentarily disoriented, as if food and drink were outlandish foreign ideas. "I've got an old friend staying with me—just moved here from upstate. Maybe you've met him in the elevator? A tall guy with long hair? My friend Hart. Anyway, he's organizing the whole thing. We're expecting about twenty people, maybe. Or more. Or possibly less. Hard to say."

"I see."

"So plan to come around nine." The elevator door opened, and he pointed down the hall. "Right down there. 4-B."

Joe got off, giving her another awkward smile, and Emily

ascended to the fifth floor thoughtfully. She had told two lies to a man she hardly knew: She wouldn't *love to go to the party,* she would *sort of like to go, maybe.* And she wasn't *a little lonely,* she was *very lonely.* She had spoken as if the party would somehow cancel out the loneliness, but in her heart she doubted that was the case.

In fact, it would probably reinforce it, as parties do.

She let herself into her own apartment, made herself an eggnog-and-rum, sliced a piece of fruitcake, and sat down with Harry and Izzy and a book. After a while, Hattie called to thank her for the cookies, and her brother Milo called, and Gene Rae called from Kurt's parents' place in Vermont. All this cheered her up so much that when nine o'clock finally rolled around, she put on her good black dress and her sparkly red earrings, and walked down the two flights to 4-B.

8

Was it a rat i saW?

Was it a rat i saW?

(October–November 2002)

Lamont opened the Tragedy Club on Berry Street at the moment 1999 flipped over and became 2000. It was conceived originally as a place that would present what Lamont whimsically called *stand-up tragics* who would "make people cry, make them think, make them *feel*." But early into the new century, Lamont realized there just weren't a lot of stand-up tragics in New York who could make people weep into their beer. The Tragedy Club evolved into a comfortable bar serving cheap drinks and snacks with, occasionally, a poet or storyteller sitting on a stool under the spotlight.

But the name stuck, and nearly two years later, it is a huge success. The place has become a curiosity that people from New Jersey and Germany and Japan include on their tour of the sights of Williamsburg, and it is packed every Saturday night.

The Trollope group meets there on the last Tuesday of each month, and they usually sit at a large table in back because, even midweek, the bar area is crowded. When Emily and Marcus get there, they see Elliot C. sitting at one end of the bar with a cigarette and a bottle of Bud in front of him. Although the night is chilly, he is wearing a short-sleeved black T-shirt that shows his bulging biceps. He doesn't look at Marcus, so Marcus doesn't have to say hello to him.

"Jeez," Emily says as they make their way to the back. "Crowded."

"I used to hate crowds," Marcus says. "But I stopped when I realized you can't live here if you hate crowds.

"Yes, you could," Emily says. "You could live here in a state of constant loathing."

Marcus thinks of his father, who loathes everything no matter where he lives. He wonders if Emily is thinking of him, too; he knows, of course, that she is his father's ex-wife. He also knows about the Thai food because Saul Smith told him the whole story. What he doesn't know is why on earth someone like Emily married someone like Hart in the first place. *I think she was lonely,* Saul said. *Sick of being alone. And Hart's not a bad-looking guy.*

This wasn't enough for Marcus. He imagines an actual shotgun wedding, Hart and Emily at City Hall with Hart poking a gun in her ribs as she says the vows. Or did he slip some drug into her English Breakfast tea? He wishes he could ask her, but he won't. He believes their friendship would be over if she knew he was related to Tab Hartwell, even though when Emily mentions his father—which she doesn't do often—it's not with loathing and revulsion but with a sort of detached amusement. "My ex was a Trollope fan," she said once at a meeting, and snorted. "Possibly the world's most uncivilized person, obsessed with possibly the world's most civilized novels." Marcus wanted to hear more, but the group immediately got into a discussion of what exactly she meant by *civilized* (in regard to Trollope, not Hart), then lost itself in a consideration of the ways in which Trollope tried to reconcile the outward stability of Victorian life with its underlying violence and social chaos.

This month, the group is discussing *Dr. Wortle's School,* Trollope's fortieth novel, which he famously wrote in twenty-two days in 1879. " 'I do not know that the history of fiction affords another instance of a novel of real merit having been written in twenty-two days,' " Emily quotes a critic as saying.

"Not to mention a novel of real merit about bigamy," says Gene Rae.

"Well, it's not really bigamy, it's suspected bigamy," says Oliver.

"But isn't it interesting that Peacocke wants to stick with Ella even if it turns out she's a bigamist?" asks Gene Rae, and the discussion turns to the changes that were happening in Victorian society in the late 1870s.

The Trollope group, which Marcus joined over a year ago, still seems to him—Is he crazy? Can this be true of anything but animals?—to be *intrinsically good*. Individually, its members may be foolish, venal, thoughtless, angst-ridden, but when they're at the meeting, they are changed, all of them. And why? Because the books are greater than they are, and some of the greatness rubs off. Maybe it's like religion, Marcus thinks, religion the way it's supposed to be but hardly ever is. It brings the lot of them together, joined in a devotion to the novels that comes from deep in the heart, a place where Marcus has so often found it hard to dwell. He knows some people consider Trollope a lightweight—Saul, for example, refuses to join a group that reads about, as he puts it, fox-hunting and parsons. Saul belongs to a Kafka group in the Village. And it's true, Marcus admits, that Trollope doesn't exactly take an ax to the frozen sea inside. . . . Maybe he's more of a lamp-lighter than an ax-wielder, melting the ice a little, shedding a nice little glow. . . .

He looks over at Emily—curly hair, new tweed sweater she ordered off the Web, yellow notebook, special kind of marker (Pentel, black, fine), peep of funny blue zipper under her sweater sleeve. He wants to talk to her about Trollope versus Kafka, so that he'll know if his image is apt and interesting or a load of crap. "That's so true, Marcus," she will say, and her blue eyes will beam at him like Trollope's lamp. "What a wonderful way to express it." Or she'll wrinkle her nose and bunch up her lips and ask him why he's so weird lately. As he watches her, she looks up from her notebook and says, "I think it's time to talk about the dog," and there is a little chorus of agreement, in which Marcus joins.

Near the beginning of the novel, Dr. Wortle's wife and daughter take a walk by the river with Neptune, the family dog, and a couple of small boys from the school. Imagine "a pretty little woman," as Trollope describes her, and her even prettier teenage daughter, Mary, both in pastel dresses, carrying parasols to keep off the sun; the boys in knee britches and loose shirts; and the big shaggy Newfoundland who loves to "romp"—Trollope's word.

One of the boys is a young baronet, heir to a fabulous fortune.

As the children (clearly a little out of control; Mrs. Wortle is always telling them to slow down) run up the hill that overlooks the river, the dog leaps playfully on the baronet and pushes him over the cliff and straight into the river—a sort of reverse Lassie. Mrs. Wortle promptly faints, but fortunately Mr. Peacocke—the same man who will soon be faced with the apparent bigamy of his wife—happens to be walking near the river, jumps in, and pulls the young heir out of the water with no harm done.

Luther says, "Well, it seems to me that the first question is, why did that blasted woman faint? And the second is, what was Mary Wortle doing?"

"Luther, the answers are obvious," Gene Rae says crisply. "In those days, women didn't *do anything* in emergencies. They expected some man to fix things, while they either screamed or fainted."

"I wonder if that's really true or if it's just true in the novels of the period," says Luther.

"Haven't we decided that Trollope is a pretty realistic writer?" Pat interjects. "I mean, in terms of depicting the times?"

"Sure, but he still had his own hang-ups. He was into the whole chivalry thing, which basically means he liked women to keep their place." Gene Rae can always be expected to raise the question of Trollope's depiction of women. "You know how he went on and on in *The Small House at Allington* about how women have to be the weaker sex."

"Yeah, but look at the women around him," says Luther. "His wife was a hot ticket who wouldn't take any shit from Anthony or anybody else. And his mother was—well, we all know about Fanny! Plus, he was pals with George Eliot, for Christ's sake. Now *there* was a formidable woman."

"But even the great George Eliot could be meek and super-respectful," Oliver says. "Always kind of deferring to men even though she was such a giant intellectually."

"Well, Mrs. Wortle is no George Eliot," Luther insists. "She's a good-hearted lady but basically out of it. When the going gets tough and the kid falls into the river, she faints, like a good Victorian wife. And then they put the kid to bed for two days! He falls into the water, he gets pulled out, they feed him—what?" Lamont finds it and reads: "Sherry negus and sweet jelly." He looks up. "What the hell's that? Wine and Jell-o?"

"Negus is a sort of sweet punch," Pat says. Pat is fascinated with the domestic minutiae in the novels. When they read *Orley Farm,* she invited everyone over to her tiny Greenpoint apartment for a reproduction of Mrs. Mason's Christmas feast, which included turkey with the trimmings, plum pudding, and mince pie, even though in Mrs. Mason's opinion (overridden by her husband) it's vulgar to serve plum pudding and mince pie together. "And sweet jelly is probably just jelly," she said. "Like on bread. It was considered a nutritious food for children."

"Okay, they give him the goodies and then make the little fucker stay in bed two days? What's *with* these dudes?"

"Ma Wortle probably took to her bed for *three* days."

Emily sighs. "Look, we're getting way off the track. Who cares what Mrs. Wortle did? The important thing in the scene is *the dog.*"

They all agree, somewhat raucously. Glasses are raised to Neptune the Newfoundland.

"Isn't it great," Marcus says, "that they didn't *blame* the dog? I mean, nobody seems to have whacked him or anything for almost killing a baronet. In another kind of novel, that dog could have been shot."

"Trollope loved dogs," Kurt says. "You should read that essay, what's it called, 'A Walk in the Woods,' where he says he always walks with his dog, and if he wants to think he doesn't bring the dog because it's too distracting. Can't you just imagine Anthony out there throwing sticks for his big old Newfie?"

"How do you know it was a Newfie?"

"All the dogs in his books are Newfies."

"Except the hunting dogs."

"*Hounds,* please. They're not dogs, they're hounds! Remember when the American senator looked like such a bozo when he called them *dogs?*"

"And don't forget the poodle in *Framley Parsonage.* What's-her-name's dog?"

"What was her name?"

They all try to think of the name of the poodle's owner. Emily, who is the group's unofficial secretary, flips back through her notebook. "Oh, what is it, what is it, this is so maddening, it's right on the tip of my—hah! Dunstable! Miss Dunstable!"

They toast Miss Dunstable, who had a poodle and who, they remind Gene Rae, is one of Trollope's smartest and feistiest female characters.

"But let's get back to Neptune."

"Fanny Trollope's dog was named Neptune, by the way."

"A Newfoundland?"

"Dunno." Emily makes a note. "I'll find out."

They discuss the Wortles' dog: his function in the scene as a way to demonstrate Peacocke's excellence, his three other appearances in the novel. Then they discuss his probable age and size, and his importance to the happiness of the boys boarding at Dr. Wortle's school, with whom, Trollope says, Neptune was on friendly terms.

"Those poor little boys were torn away from their families at *much* too young an age," Gene Rae comments. "Such a barbaric practice." Protectively, she lays a hand on the mound of her stomach that houses Roland, the six-month-old fetus. "And most of them probably had dogs at home—not just parents and siblings. Can you imagine being separated from your beloved dog at, like, seven? Eight? I'll bet they worshiped that Neptune. He was probably spoiled rotten."

"I still wonder about cats," Kurt says, not irrelevantly. They have searched in vain for a cat in all the novels they've read so far. "I thought one might turn up in a school novel."

"But no."

"Not a one."

"Could it be Anthony was not a cat-lover?"

It is a question they have raised before, but they have been able to find no evidence one way or another. They prefer to believe that cats were such a taken-for-granted part of life *chez* Trollope that he felt no need to mention them in his books.

The group always ends with a reading from the novel, so that they can savor the famous "Trollopian cadences" spoken aloud. This month it's Marcus's turn, and he reads a page or two from the last chapter, when the Peacocke crisis has been resolved and young Mary Wortle seems to have found the right man in Lord Carstairs:

I cannot pretend that the reader shall know, as he ought to be made to know, the future fate and fortunes of our personages.

They must be left still struggling. But then is not such always in truth the case, even when the happy marriage has been celebrated? Even when, in the course of two rapid years, two normal children make their appearance to gladden the hearts of their parents?

When he is done, Lamont yells out, "Say it, brother," as if it's a prayer meeting, and everyone intones, "Amen."

For next time, they decide to read *Miss Mackenzie*. "Outside of a dog, a book is man's best friend," Lamont says.

"And inside of a dog, it's too dark to read," Luther replies.

The old Groucho joke is their ritual break-up, and they drain their glasses and gather their books and pens and notebooks. As always, they argue with Lamont, who insists the drinks are on the house. He won't budge, so they leave Fiona the waitress an extra-large tip—as always.

Emily and Marcus go out through the bar together. Elliot C. is still sitting there, still alone, still not looking in their direction. Carey the bartender is energetically mixing up a pitcher of margaritas for a raucous party at the other end of the bar. Marcus says, "Hi there, Elliot."

Elliot turns with an elaborate look of surprise, and Marcus realizes that he has already seen them but pretended not to. "Oh, hey there, Mark. Marcus?"

"Yeah. And this is Emily."

"Right. From the party."

"And the park."

"How's your dog?" Emily asks.

"He's fine." Elliot takes a drag on his cigarette, tough-guy style, holding it between thumb and forefinger. "Why wouldn't he be?" The margarita-drinkers let out sudden loud whoops of laughter and start slapping each other on the back. Elliot C. glares at them, exhaling smoke from the corners of his mean little mouth.

"Just asking."

"My dog is fine."

"Does he have a name?"

Elliot C. shrugs. "Of course he has a name. What kind of question is that?" Showing his sharp teeth, he laughs like a man providing canned laughter for a sitcom sound track. Elliot's laugh makes Marcus remember his damp handshake.

When they get out into the cold, Emily says, "I love the Trollope group so much," and Marcus knows she doesn't want to speak of Elliot C. "Don't you?"

"They're a great bunch." Marcus has a hard time saying he "loves" things. "I thought we had a good discussion about Neptune."

"Neptune the wonder dog." Emily takes his arm. "Didn't you ever have a dog, Marcus? Not even when you were a kid?"

Marcus hesitates. When Gene Rae said, "Imagine being separated from your beloved dog when you were seven or eight," he amended, "Or ten," and thought of Phoebe. The memory of Phoebe is still vivid—her beautiful ivory teeth, her complicated arrangement of black and white fur, her big puppyish paws—and still hurts him. He is horrified to find that tears are stinging the corners of his eyes. He has a sudden image of himself back in Honesdale, walking through the woods where Phoebe is buried and where his mother died. He remembers the smell of the woods, the feel of the spongy earth under his feet, the absolute dark when he curled himself up to sleep at night. *Long live the weeds and the wilderness yet.* He blinks, and the tears, which for one bad moment had threatened to fall, are held back. "Yeah, I had a dog for a while when I was ten. She got run over."

"Oh, shit, Marcus, I'm sorry. What was her name?"

He takes a breath. "Phoebe was her name." He hasn't said it aloud in years. "Phoebe."

"Damn it. What a terrible thing. You must have been devastated."

"Yeah. My—uh—my father was home when it happened. I wasn't even there. I didn't even get to—you know—"

"Say good-bye to her."

"Yeah. She was just—by the time I got home—just gone."

Emily stops under a street lamp and looks at him. "What do you mean, *gone,* Marcus?"

"Oh well, you know, he—she was buried. He buried her right away. Because—you know." He broke off. "Anyway, that's the only dog I ever had."

Emily is silent, frowning at the sidewalk, before she takes his arm again and they resume walking down Bedford. Across the street, the figure of Susan Skolnick emerges from the deli carrying a plastic bag of groceries, and passes out of sight like a wraith. They pass Dolan's Bar & Grill, the bookstore and café, the record shop, the weird windowless club that used to be a pigeon-feed store before Williamsburg became chic. When they get to the WHAT COMES AROUND GOES AROUND sign, Marcus remembers something he read once: that a human being naturally walks in a slow curve, so that eventually he will return to where he was.

> *By at the gallop he goes, and then*
> *By he comes back at the gallop again . . .*

"Well," Emily says finally. "One of these days you'll get another dog."

"Or a cat."

"Or a bird."

Emily squeezes his arm.

9

Desserts i stresseD

Desserts i stresseD

When Emily goes to her landlady's door on Wednesday evening, she hears the Lou Reed album Anstice plays when she has one of her migraines, so she knocks extra loudly. Anstice likes company when she has a migraine: "Anything to distract me from the pain." Loud music, she says, creates a wall of sound that the pain can't get through; a visit from a friend creates something else, "an aura of goodness that's the opposite of the headache," is the best she can explain. Anstice believes her headaches are evil, and that she must resist them the way her New England ancestors resisted Satan. She is the descendant of a famous witch-burner, Judge Jedediah Mullen, of Salem, Massachusetts, where most of her family still lives, inhabiting historically significant houses and indulging in lifestyles that Judge Mullen would surely have considered the work of Beelzebub.

But it is the Mullen money that enabled Anstice to buy the

old spice factory, divide it into rentals, and furnish her loft on the sixth floor.

Everything Anstice has is perfect. This is a fact that strikes Emily whenever she knocks on the door, because the perfection begins there: The door is aubergine, and it is painted perfectly; the surface is like deep purply-brown glass. There is a brass plaque with *Anstice Mullen* engraved on it, and in front of the door is a woven mat of bright pink straw that Anstice found in Spain and a black-and-white striped ceramic umbrella stand she had made to order at a place in the Village. Even the little box into which she punches the code that deactivates her state-of-the-art alarm system is beautifully designed.

Emily surveys all this while she waits. The music stops abruptly, and Anstice opens the door a crack, showing her right eye, which is light blue and suffering. "Well, look what the cat dragged in."

"I've been working like a dog in my darkroom, and I thought I'd take a break and pay my rent," Emily says. "How are you?"

"These damned migraines really get my goat, but aside from that I'm fine."

Emily and Anstice have an unspoken agreement to trade a few animal clichés when they get together. "It's a dog's life."

"You said it." Anstice opens the door wider. "Come on in. The damned thing is winding down, actually. They're so predictable. They're like farmers—up with the birds, to bed with the chickens."

Emily holds out the rent check. "It's late, of course. Sorry to be so hare-brained."

"Late? It's early. It's only the end of October, ducky."

"This is the October rent, Anstice." She wonders what it must be like not to bother keeping track of such things—*six hundred here, six hundred there, late, early, what did it matter.* She says, "Now I'm going to owe you November. But I promise it won't take me so long."

"I'm okay with it, Emily," Anstice says. "I always get it eventually."

She takes the check over to her desk, which is a dainty antique with a white cat asleep on it. Anstice tucks the check into one of the pigeonholes and scratches the cat behind the ears. Emily sits in the striped wing chair, Anstice stretches out on the overstuffed couch by the window and sighs. "I haven't been out of this damned house all day."

"Well, it wasn't very nice out. Chilly. Damp. It wanted to rain all afternoon but it could only squeeze out a bit of a drizzle."

Emily is embarrassed at having to pay her rent so late, and she is, as always, a little intimidated by the tasteful luxury of Anstice's loft. The chair she is sitting on probably cost the equivalent of two Dr. Demand sales, maybe three. The cashmere robe in which Anstice endures her migraines cost at least one. The cute little mug on the coffee table, which Emily knows holds the dregs of the one kind of herbal tea that doesn't aggravate the headache, was probably a cool twenty bucks at one of those design places on Mercer Street. Emily hates herself for thinking about such things, but she has been more broke than usual lately, and money is on her mind. She looks out the window and sees that it's almost dark, and that the overcast sky is beginning, belatedly, to break up, with a narrow window of rosy light between two gray clouds.

"So talk to me," Anstice says. "What's new in the world? Had any photography adventures?"

Emily tells her about the trip to Long Island with dog and bird. "I found a beautiful TIME on a billboard."

"Context?"

"THIS IS A GOOD TIME TO CONSOLIDATE YOUR DEBTS. I cropped it to GOOD TIME TO CON. It looks wonderful."

"I can't wait to see it."

Anstice always checks out Emily's photographs with enthusiasm, but she has yet to buy one. Emily is hoping Anstice is afraid if she buys one she'll get addicted, like Dr. Demand, and she awaits the day Anstice succumbs to a TIME or a DOG and will be unable to stop, and then the money will flow in. Anstice doesn't like BREAD: she says the BREAD photographs make her crave carbohydrates, which she is always trying, and failing, to avoid. She calls herself "unpleasantly plump," but her plumpness is actually very pleasant. She has a thin face surrounded by a straight bob of hair with the color and shine of an onion skin, but the rest of her is as rounded and soft-looking as the sofa she sits on, right down to her fluffy red slippers. Anstice always wears a touch of red, even when she has a migraine.

"Maybe Dr. Demand will buy it," Anstice says. "I ran into him yesterday. He was having lunch at the Busy Corner."

"Don't tell me. A container of those little mozzarella balls with parsley and stuff?"

"*Bocconcini!* Right."

"And a Dr. Pepper."

"How well you know the dear man."

"Was he wearing his divine dentist whites?"

"He certainly was. Over a pale blue shirt with a red plaid tie. Gorgeous."

"What's new with him?"

"He said, 'Hi Anstice, you're due for a cleaning.' How does he know that? I mean, he has like twenty million patients."

"He follows your teeth closely. He's got a crush on you."

"He does not."

"Does too. He thinks you're the cat's pajamas."

"Jeez, Em. Puppy love?"

"Exactly."

"How do you know this?"

"Um—a little bird told me?"

"You're making this up to distract me from my migraine."

"Maybe," Emily says, "and maybe not."

"Well, it's working. I feel a whole lot better. Want some real tea? A cookie? I made Grandma's molasses ones yesterday. I can't seem to stop baking, don't ask me why."

"You don't have to make excuses for molasses cookies," Emily says. "Lay 'em on me."

Anstice's late Grandma Mullen's late cook, Agnes, is legendary throughout the building for her recipes, which Anstice executes frequently and which tend toward the homey: hearty soups and flaky piecrusts and big fat cookies. The molasses ones are the best, and with them Anstice serves tea the proper way: a loose English blend in the Mullen family pot, with a supply of extra hot water on the side and a silver pitcher of cold milk.

With their second round of tea and cookies, they reach the subject of Marcus, as Emily was pretty sure they would. Anstice is the only person in the world to whom she has ever confided her inconvenient love for Marcus Mead. She told Anstice because she had to tell someone, and Anstice is safe because she is not in the Trollope group, nor does she hire Marcus to sit her cats, so she and he don't know each other very well. Anstice is fascinated by Emily's passion for a twenty-one-year-old. Emily hasn't told Anstice that Marcus is Hart's son, however. She hasn't told anyone that, and she wasn't really sure of it herself until the night of the last Trollope meeting.

Until then, her only evidence was the envelope Hart left behind.

He'd been gone a week when she found it. It was in the big closet, on what used to be Hart's side, where Emily was moving some of her clothes. On the closet floor there was a pair of his old sneakers that she threw into the trash, and when she stood on a chair to check the shelf, she saw an ancient Jets T-shirt and a manila envelope. In four years of marriage, she never knew that Hart kept a manila envelope on the top shelf of his side of the closet. She tossed the shirt and took down the envelope to look inside.

It contained three photographs. The first was a black-and-white snapshot of a woman posed in the doorway of a hotel or an apartment house. She was wearing white ankle-boots and an oversized mod-style cap and a very short skirt—an Audrey Hepburn kind of outfit. She seemed beautiful, with generous but chiseled features and, under the hat, masses of dark hair. She had small, girlish breasts. One hand was on her hip, the other hung straight down. She was not smiling. Emily turned the photo over: *Marge '64.*

Well. In 1964, Hart would have been ten years old. He was the middle child, he said, so at least his three older siblings were already in existence, plus, probably, a younger one or two. Emily looked again at the photograph. *This* was the famous Marge Hartwell, the brutal, unstable, and ignorant woman who had given birth to seven children somewhere out in Wisconsin and mothered them so inadequately that Hart in desperation had to leave home at sixteen? *This* the woman who sent her children to school without books and gloves and warm hats? Who locked little Tab in the cellar for an entire twenty-four hours because he wouldn't finish his dinner? Who so henpecked and browbeat her husband that Hart could barely remember the old man uttering a dozen sober words the whole time he was growing up? Emily had pictured a schlumpy, drab woman in a house dress. Who was this glamorous mom with the funny hat and the sad eyes?

She picked up the next photo, another snapshot, in color this time, and unidentified, of a child who was undeniably Hart at the age of seven or eight—a handsome, robust little boy dressed in shorts and a T-shirt. He was standing with a red bicycle on what looked like a suburban street—sidewalks, lawns, neat houses set back. Hart was smiling widely—a smug, happy sort of *I've got a brand-new bike* smile—and the bike did indeed look shiny and new, and it was summer, and Hart's birthday was in August. But Marge Hartwell never sounded like a bicycle-giving sort of mother. And his father, Hart said, old Jim Hartwell, had never come out of his alcoholic funk long enough to give his kids anything but a slap. And hadn't Hart specifically told her that he'd always longed for a bicycle but never got one?

Who could have known this cute little boy with the appealing grin would grow up to be a liar and a sleazebag, a man who would order Thai food and then not pick it up?

The third picture, also in color, appeared to be of one of Hart's brothers. He had either three or four, Emily couldn't keep them straight, and Hart never said much about them. She couldn't even remember their names. Pete? Paul? Phil? Anyway, this one was small, thin, altogether inconspicuous. He was sitting on the front steps of an old house, squinting a little into the camera, not exactly smiling but looking hopeful and expectant. He was holding a thick book, like a telephone directory, on his knees. He wore jeans and a sweatshirt with a large 7 on it. The front end of a dog was visible lying at his feet, head on paws, tail outside the photograph. Emily turned it over and was surprised to see *July 1991*. Not a brother, then—too recent. *It must be Hart's son,* she had thought with a shock. "Yeah, I've got a kid somewhere," he had told her casually one day, and when Emily pressed him for more, he said, "He lives with his mother, and his mother's none too fond of me, and that's all I want to say about that. Okay? It was a long time ago." He would never say any more about the boy. *Total estrangement,* he'd said. *A couple of wackos. Get off my back with the family stuff.*

Hart's son. He looked like Hart, but Hart reduced, thinned down, made wispy somehow. A shadow Hart. But the resemblance was there.

Emily still has the photograph. And she remembers when she first met Marcus, and how, slowly, she began to think that he was who he was. It was the phone book that made her suspect, and things he has said over the last year have almost confirmed it. And every once in a while, when he raises his head and the light catches his greenish eyes . . .

"It's funny," Anstice is saying, "because your father died when you were fifteen." Her mouth is full of cookie, and she chews and swallows before she goes on. "Women who lose their fathers so young usually seek out father figures. And here you are in love with a son figure."

"Go figure," Emily says.

"Of course, you probably did the father figure thing already, with Hart."

"Was that what it was?" Emily chews pensively, then pours herself another cup of tea. She often tries to reconstruct her marriage to Hart—not its details, but its rationale. *Why did I marry him?* She has asked herself the question over and over again, and has come up with a number of answers. *He was there, he said he adored me, he was cute, it was what people did, Mom was thrilled, I was lonely.* Sometimes she thinks it was just that she felt sorry for him because no one seemed to like him much except for his friend Joe Whack—that maybe if someone cared about him he could change and become nicer. None of these answers were enough, but there it was: four years of marriage like four years of a strange dream. "I don't know, Anstice," she said. "I'm not crazy about the marrying-your-father theory. Hart had nothing in common with my father except that he was older than me."

"He was one weird guy," Anstice says.

"Still is, probably," she says cheerfully. "Weirder."

"He always kind of reminded me of Bugsy at the Pet Pound, yelling his own name but with no one really paying much attention."

"Yeah. Hart's life was pretty much all about Hart."

"And what about Marcus?"

"Marcus?"

"I mean, is he like your father?"

"Oh. No, not a bit. Marcus is strange and intense and brooding and obsessive, and my father was one of those fun guys who fit in anywhere. He was always joking. He and my mother both. They were always in a good mood."

"Parent-wise, they sound great. It's so crazy you had a happy childhood."

"As H. L. Mencken said, 'My early life was placid, secure, uneventful, and happy.' I guess that is a little odd." Emily ponders the adjectives for a moment: *uneventful?* Yes, *uneventful* is exactly what children want. Let nothing happen except what always happens: Mom and Dad there when you get up in the morning, pizza after the movies, school letting out in June, "Silent Night" and "Jingle Bells" at Christmas, your old green blanket. She sighs. "Until my father died. Then things weren't so great."

They eat in silence, thinking of how Emily's father dropped dead of a heart attack while ordering a hot dog at a county fair. Emily remembers her mother's grief, how she sobbed in the night, and how she said that she used to think time went by so fast and now without Theo it was so slow, so slow. . . .

Two of Anstice's cats join them; the gray tabby sits on the arm of Emily's chair, looking intently at her cookie. Emily holds out a crumb and the cat eats it. Emily is remembering the game called Worm Words that she used to play with Milo and Laurie, how they used to turn *Mom* into *law* in five steps *(Mom-mop-lop-lap-law)* and how she once sent her brother to hell *(Milo-mill-hill-hell)* in four. *Marcus Mead. Lime to Mead.* She thinks hard: *Lime-line-lane-land-lend-lead-Mead,* she comes up with, and smiles.

"But what about you?" she asks Anstice. "Didn't you have a happy childhood? Only child? Wealthy parents who adored you?"

Anstice shrugs. "It was okay. Yours sounds better."

"You had a pony!"

"You had fun!"

"Your pony wasn't fun? Anstice, don't you know that all kids think that if they had a pony they would have nothing but pure and total fun every single minute for the rest of their lives?"

"My pony was okay, but I had to muck out her stall, and once she kicked me in the shin, and then I got unpleasantly plump and didn't like to ride her any more. We gave her to my cousin Martha."

"I wish I'd been your cousin Martha."

"No, you don't. She married the golf pro at her parents' country club and had five kids, none of whom turned out well, and her husband left her, and her second husband is almost seventy, and they live in a high-rise condo in Florida."

"Oh."

"See?"

The gray cat settles down on Emily's lap, purring. "Well, at least she wasn't poor."

"Nope. She was loaded. Still is."

"I don't care what you say, loaded would definitely be more fun." Emily remembers Trollope's Miss Dunstable, heiress to a patent medicine fortune, who, when someone told her that her ringlets were out of style, replied, "They always pass muster when they are done up in banknotes." Everything does, she thinks, and starts feeling sorry for herself again. "Poor isn't fun," she says, knowing she is whining. "We were already poor when my father died—he was a high school math teacher, for heaven's sake. And then my mother started law school. My mother was a student! We had nothing! We struggled!"

"Really? You had nothing?"

"Well, Mom had to keep calling her parents to ask for money for groceries."

"Oh, horror," Anstice says with her mouth full.

"They were really stingy." Emily offers the cat another crumb; this time the cat turns her head away in disgust. Emily and Anstice look at each other and shrug: *Who can fathom the mind of a cat?* "They hated it when she asked for money. Once she made me call. Believe me, we were a severely stressed family. I had a part-time job from the time I was fourteen. My brother had two."

"You sound like the Five Little Peppers. Everybody pulling together to help Mamsie. Remember when Ben had to plug up the hole in the stove with an old boot so they could bake a cake for her birthday?"

"At our house, it was everybody helping Mamsie write her brief for Moot Court."

"That sounds like fun."

"Oh, Anstice. The fact remains that, happy childhood or not, I'm in love with a man half my age who doesn't even love me back."

"He's not half your age. He's more like five-eighths your age."

"I don't trust your math. Or mine, either. He's just very young. His skin is so pure and unwrinkled. His eyes are so clear, and the whites are so white." She pets the gray cat, who digs her claws gently, blissfully into Emily's thigh. "Marcus is a lot like a cat," she says. *Who can fathom the mind of a Marcus?* "Or a bird. Like Izzy. Or like—hey, remember the crow who could make a tool out of a piece of wire and use it to get food? In the news last summer?"

"I do remember. It was the same week those rabbits in England found the rare medieval glass window. A great week for animals." Anstice frowns. "Wait—how is Marcus like the rabbits?"

"I didn't say he's like the *rabbits*. I said he's like the crow. I mean, he's intelligent and lovable and funny and yet there's something in the way, some barrier—like the barrier between birds and humans. He's—somehow—distant. Removed." A thought strikes her. "That's how Gene Rae once told me I am."

"Distant?"

"Yeah. Oblivious to things."

Anstice considers this. "Well, yeah, you are, a little. But maybe that means you and Marcus could actually live together in perfect felicity. You know, making tools out of wire and stuff."

"Perfect felicity. I like the way that sounds. But we won't live together at all because Marcus isn't interested in me."

"He loves you."

"Yes, he probably does. But he loves me like a—" She pauses, shrugs.

"Like a brother?"

"Like a cat, I think. More like a cat. That's what I'm getting at. He doesn't seem to need people. Anstice?"

"Hmm."

"Is it okay that I'm distant? Removed? Oblivious? I mean, I like being the way I am, but I just wonder if it means there's something wrong with me."

"What nonsense. If Marcus is like a cat, or a bird, then you're like a dog, Em. You're like Otto: a human comes into the room and you go crazy."

"But—" She thinks of her idiotic marriage, of her lost boyfriend Peter, of a man named Kevin whom she slept with happily for a month and who suddenly stopped returning her calls, of other men who have come and gone. She thinks of the Dirty Gertie guy Pat and Oliver want her to meet, and of a nice-looking man she saw on the subway the other day, and of how she never expected to be thirty-six and alone, and of how at Thanksgiving her brother Milo and his wife took long walks together every afternoon, and how her sister Laurie spent two hours on the phone every day with her doctor husband, who had to stay home because he was on call at the hospital. She thinks of the E-mail she had from her mother a few days ago in which she said she's dating a colleague in the law firm where she's a partner. She remembers the wedding of Gene Rae and Kurt, where she was a bridesmaid and wept unashamedly into her champagne. She thinks of Marcus, who has no pets. She remembers something she read once—how, in a country she can't remember the name of, when a woman saw the reflection of the moon in the river, she would spoon up some water with the moon in it and drink and then, if she gazed into the water again, she would see the face of her future husband. Maybe she should go down to the East River on a moonlit night. . . .

"Em?"

Everything seems so hopeless. If she drank a spoonful of the East River she would probably not survive it.

"You okay?"

"Oh, Anstice—"

"What, sweetie?"

"I guess what I'm asking you is—do you think I'll ever have a boyfriend again?"

"Every dog has his day," Anstice says firmly. She passes the cookies, but Emily says she has to get home and take Otto for his walk. She goes down the stairs to her place, and as she approaches she can hear Otto begin barking and Izzy screeching with joy: They know her step, or her smell, or her aura. Something. When she walks in the door, Izzy squawks "Pretty boy" and flies to her head, and Otto bounds over to sit at her feet, grinning.

Murder for a jar of red ruM

Murder for a jar of red ruM

"**Y**ou should get yourself a little iMac," Saul is saying over two bowls of vegetarian chili at the bar in Vera Cruz, the Saturday after Halloween. He and Marcus are drinking beer and discussing, as they often do, the pros and cons of the Mac and the Dell. "The name of the game is tech support," Saul says, nodding. "And frankly, in that area, the Dell sucks."

Marcus is feeling good. He has just finished his dog-walking duties for the day, and the dogs always make him happy. So does talking about gigabytes and ROM. Computers fascinate Marcus, though he has never owned one. "But it's cheaper."

Saul narrows his eyes and points his finger like a gun. "But is it, in the end?"

Zerlenka, the bartender, gets into the discussion, which

becomes heated, as computer discussions always do. A couple of other beer-drinkers join in, and the debate is still going when Marcus leaves, just as covetous but definitely more confused. He suspects he'll never spend the money to buy a computer. The problem is not only that he doesn't like to own too many things, that he wants to take off when he wants to, without having to pack up bags and boxes; it's also that he can't think of anything he would use a computer for, except to play games.

Still, as he walks he ponders the pleasure of coming home in the evening and finding a killer crossword on the Web, or playing some complicated number game. There's a program called Mathematica that he read about in the *Times* and wonders if it's anything like the game of Numerabilis he used to play as a kid with Donnie Ryan. The tiny, unhatched egg of desire for all this is nested in his mind, like his urge to change his name, or go to veterinary school. It's something he thinks about when he's caught on the subway with nothing to read, or on a mildly beery walk home like this one.

When he gets there, he finds four phone messages from his father. The first says, "Hi there, sonny boy. It's your pop— obviously, heh heh. Just thought I'd remind you that—well, what can I say? The weekend is here. Give me a call, laddie." The second says, "Hey, Marcus. It's Hart. What's up? It's the weekend. Call me—okay?" The third says, "Marcus, this is getting serious. It's—what? Almost five o'clock on Saturday afternoon—and I've been expecting you to call all day, and I've got better things to do than sit by the fucking phone waiting. Would you get up off your butt and call me back?" The fourth says, "Hey. Marcus. You said you'd get back to me by the weekend. Well, this is *the fucking weekend!* God damn it, if you don't call me back, I'll take the L train over there and *rip your fucking heart out.*"

There is one other message. It's from Emily:

"Marcus! How about that Scrabble game? If you're going to be around tonight, I'll be glad to humiliate you. Also, I have Halloween candy left over. So call me? Please?"

Marcus puts the kettle on and makes himself a cup of comfrey-mint tea. He sits down in the chair opposite SEAMUS IS MY NEW BUDDY, waiting for his stomach to stop churning. His father on top of a bowl of extra-spicy chili is too much. That and the juxtaposition of Hart's voice with Emily's, as if he has somehow brought the two together: beauty and the beast, obscenely entwined, on his voice mail.

He breathes deeply and removes his mind to other matters.

At their most extreme, he recalls as he sips his tea, the Victorians wouldn't put a book by a man on the shelf next to a book by a woman unless they were married to each other. This reminds him, for no good reason, of the Monty Python skit that claims Chuck Berry actually wrote most of Shakespeare's plays, and this reminds him of his mother's death. One morning in the bitter depths of an upstate winter—the winter he disappeared into the woods and stayed there—he had been reading the sonnets and had come across the line "Summer's lease hath all too short a date."

He'd been struck by how true it was in that part of the world; also by the fact that he hadn't had a letter from his mother in over a week.

I'll write her tonight, he said to himself. He didn't have a phone, or a car, or even a bicycle. He did have paper and envelopes, and he would buy a stamp at the post office on his way to work. Summer knew he didn't welcome visitors, but she wrote to him regularly, as she used to write to Hart: meticulously printed letters telling him what she was cooking and reminding him to dress warmly when he walked to work.

Later that day, Tamarind came to tell him Summer had been found frozen to death in the woods behind her little gray house. She was wearing her blue angora mittens and a red-and-white striped stocking cap, but no coat, and no boots, just her sneakers with jeans and a sweatshirt. There was no sign of foul play, and no suicide note. It seemed that she had just wandered out to the woods and didn't come back. She was curled up under a tree, as if she had gone to sleep. She had been there at least three days.

Tamarind stayed with him all that afternoon. She made him tea and put whiskey in it, and told him she would help him with the funeral details. She made him promise not to despair, not to blame himself. Before she left, he pulled the book out to show her the line about Summer's lease. Tamarind smiled a little and then, after a moment, she quoted, "But thy eternal summer shall not fade," and Marcus put his head down and began to cry.

He tries not to think of his mother, alone in the woods in her blue mittens. He knows he has to call Hart, and he's drinking the tea in small, comforting sips, trying to decide whether to call later or right this minute, today or tomorrow, when the phone rings, and he leaps out of his chair and snatches it up. "Okay, give me a break. I just got in, for Christ's sake!"

"Um, Marcus?"

"Oh—Emily! Sorry. Sorry, sorry, sorry."

"Are you okay?"

"No—yes. I don't know." He sinks into the chair again. "I got all these harassing phone calls—not yours. I mean, yours was the only bright spot."

"Is your refrigerator running? Do you have Prince Albert in a can? That sort of thing?"

"Something like that. Leftover Halloween stuff. I guess I'm a little rattled. Or something. I'm sorry. Jesus." He sips tea. "Okay, then. Scrabble. Candy. Otto and Iz. It sounds great. What time?"

"How about eight? I'm sorry, but it has to be after dinner. I'd feed you, but—"

"I know. You're having a bowl of cereal and six dried apricots for dinner."

Marcus leans back in the chair. He's feeling better. He can deal with this. He can tease Emily about her eating habits. He can call Hart and—well, whatever. His mind stops there.

"No, actually, I'm having an egg—a nice egg, my mother always calls it. I'm having a nice egg and a piece of toast and, of course, leftover Halloween candy, and maybe a Bloody Mary. You can join me if you like. It's just not the sort of thing people usually serve to guests for dinner."

"That's okay. I'll just eat my three raisins and a turnip and half a hot-dog roll right here."

"I don't know why I thought kids would ring my doorbell. Like I could really afford all this stuff."

"This just isn't a kid neighborhood. Plus I think people are afraid because of the rapes."

"Nobody came to my door but Oliver and Pat. They were wearing their ostrich costumes."

"Not again."

"Yeah. They were on their way to the school, to chaperone a

party for the kids. I gave them some of those miniature chocolate bars, but there's still a ton."

"You did this last year, Emily."

"I know. I do it every year. Maybe it's time to admit I do it so that I can eat the leftover candy."

"Don't eat it all before I get there."

"I won't. Will you want a Bloody Mary with yours? I can go out and get some more tomato juice."

Marcus says he'll bring some, and when they hang up, he dials Hart's number.

"It's me."

"All I want is a simple yes or no."

"Simple yes."

There is a silence, during which he hears his father's breathing get progressively quieter. Finally he says, "Okay, son. Okay. This is good. This is excellent. There's money there for you, Marcus. Lots of it."

"Can we sign a contract or something? I mean—I want to be sure you'll pay me."

He expects Hart to blow up at this, but his father just chuckles. "Marcus? What are you going to do? Sue me? Take me to court? I'll pay you, for Christ's sake. Trust me."

"When?"

"Well, when is the event going to take place?"

Marcus has thought about this. He puts his feet up and gazes into the eyes of Rudy Giuliani's dog on the cover of the *Daily News*. "Thanksgiving."

"Thanksgiving? That's a month away!"

"No, it isn't. It's three and a half weeks."

"What?" There's a break while Hart switches the phone to his good ear. "It's what?"

"It's three and a half weeks to Thanksgiving."

"No, it isn't. What's today? November second? It's—okay, okay, it's three and a half weeks. That's a long time."

All Souls' Day, Marcus is thinking. Today is All Souls' Day. *Summer's lease hath all too short a date.* He blames Hart for his mother's death. It's absurd. He might as well blame Tamarind, or the social worker he knew she was seeing before she died. And he does, actually: He has blamed them all from time to time. He even blamed Summer, for dying as oddly as she lived— for dying at all. But the person he *wants* to blame is Hart: Maybe only Hart could have saved her. He has a sudden, ludicrous memory of a picture he saw last summer on the cover of the *Times,* of a large, gray, heavy, patient hippo being evacuated in a red sling from the flooded zoo in Prague. Blindfolded so it wouldn't panic.

The problem, of course, is that when he wakes up in the middle of the night it's himself he blames.

"Do you wanna tell me why you need to wait three and a half weeks?"

"I'm going to push her down the elevator shaft."

"Down the elevator shaft," Hart says slowly. "Wow. You mean that fucking freight elevator is still there? Miss Moneybags Anstice Mullen still hasn't brought the place up to code, eh?"

"I think she's applied for legal status, but nothing seems to happen."

"Ha! Damned right. *Jesus.* Williamsburg, Brooklyn. What a place. Nothing changes. It warms my heart." He chuckles uneasily. "Well. That's good, son. That's creative. Damned easy for someone to just slip over the edge when they're pulling the fucking cable, eh?" His voice fades away. Then he clears his throat and says, "But that doesn't answer my question. Why Thanksgiving?"

"It's easier with hardly anyone in the building. At Thanksgiving, everybody goes out of town."

"How do you know that?"

Marcus heaves a sigh. "They've already got me signed up. It's a major dog-walking weekend for me."

"What about her? Won't she be going out of town?"

"No. I happen to know she isn't."

"What? You're sure?"

"I'm sure."

Hart is silent, and Marcus can hear him thinking. He wonders if Hart distrusts him as much as he distrusts Hart. Then Hart says, "You're the only one I can trust, Marcus. I'm depending on you," and Marcus realizes that his father is alone in the world. As he has always been. Well, why should things be any different? He's a bitter, cynical, mean, half-crazy, and thoroughly disagreeable weasel. No, not a weasel, despite Grandma Mead. Weasels have a bad rep, but not for any good reason. They're prized for their pelts, for one thing: Minks, after all, are weasels. And sure, they steal eggs and chickens, but they also feed on rats and vermin. Marcus can imagine his father as a sort of Ozzy Osbourne feeding on rats, though he can't imagine anyone prizing his pelt. Hart has become distinctly scruffy in his middle age. For a moment, Marcus almost pities him. "You there, Dad?"

"You're really going to do this?"

"Yes."

"I'll be damned."

"So when do I get the downpayment?"

"A week from Tuesday." They arrange to meet at the Brooklyn Botanic Garden, Hart's idea. "There's never anybody there on Tuesdays but those Hasidic families. Eleven badly dressed kids, plus Mom in her tailored coat and sensible shoes. Let's say late afternoon. By then it's really dead."

"You go to the Botanic Garden?"

"From time to time. It's relaxing."

Marcus is strangely pleased by this, because the Botanic Garden is one of his favorite places, but he's also appalled: He hates to think of people like his father being there. He imagines him strolling the paths, thinking malevolent thoughts, ripping the blooms off the roses, sneering at the little Hasidic kids in their yarmulkes.

"Okay," he says. "A week from Tuesday. What? Four o'clock?"

"Four's good. You know the Japanese pavilion thing? With the pond?"

Marcus knows it well: the pond full of carp and turtles, the red torii gate, the little wooden bridge, the peace that is so un-Hartlike. "Yeah," he says without enthusiasm. "I'll see you there."

When they hang up, Marcus dials Emily's number. "Just quickly—I'm taking a sort of poll," he says. "Suppose you needed cash in a hurry. Where would you get it?"

"What? Marcus, I'm cooking my egg!"

"I know, but humor me. I'm compiling some statistics. You know. What people do. Where they put their—you know—money. Or whatever."

"Marcus? Is there a problem? Do you need cash?"

"No no no! Emily, this is all theoretical. Just tell me quick, before your egg overcooks. Let's say you need—oh, whatever— fifty thousand bucks."

"Fifty *thousand?* Why would I need that much money?"

"It doesn't matter. For the purposes of my inquiry, let's just say you need it. What would you do?"

"I wouldn't do anything! I have no way of getting that kind of money! I'd have to ask my mother. Or my brother Milo. He could take a second mortgage on his house or something. Or Anstice. I suppose I could go down on my knees and beg. But I just never would! This is a stupid question. I don't even like to think about it."

"But just—I mean, you don't have anything you could sell, you don't own anything valuable?"

"Marcus, no! I don't have anything! Just my Nikon. My Hasselblad. My dog. You know what I've got."

"But—"

"Listen, I want to do my egg now. I want my dinner. Can we talk about this later?"

"Sorry, Emily. Sorry. Okay. I'll see you around eight."

"You are getting so peculiar," Emily sighs, and hangs up.

Marcus finishes his tea. Hart is obviously insane. But meanwhile, he'll pick up ten thousand at the Japanese pavilion, money that his father owes him, fair and square. All those years of poverty, living with Summer while their small bank account dwindled away. Delivering papers. Working at a gas station. Hart owes him for all those cold afternoons pumping gas.

With that much money, he can go home.

His goal has been to save thirty thousand; Hart's ten will put him over the top.

Aside from Tamarind's occasional visits, Summer's house in Honesdale has been vacant for more than three years. He knows it needs work. And he has to have a vehicle. And some money to live on until he gets the house in shape and can start to earn a living. He has an idea that he'll work for the little old-fashioned railroad down there. Or learn to train dogs, or teach himself to cook. Marcus doesn't worry about earning a living: If he can make money in Williamsburg, he can make money in Honesdale. What he worries about, increasingly, is leaving Emily.

But he doesn't think about that now. He sits down with that morning's *Times* crossword—Saturday, the hardest—and, though he finishes it off in fourteen minutes, he enjoys doing it: Like the tea, it's soothing. Then he cuts an avocado in half, removes the pit, salts both halves and eats them from their shells with a spoon. When he's done, he puts on his coat and heads out to Emily's.

He stops at the Syrian deli on Berry Street. Elliot C. is at the counter, buying cigarettes, and Marcus is jolted by a visceral revulsion at the sight of his brown leather jacket, dyed blond hair, and arrogant little body. Cigarettes in New York City are now $7.50 a pack. He hopes Elliot C. will go broke buying them and also get emphysema. Then he's vaguely ashamed of himself. He has no reason to dislike this person. Elliot C. turns, looks Marcus in the eye, smirks, and goes out without speaking. Marcus picks up the tomato juice and pays for it, feeling as if a cruel, wintry wind has blown through the place.

Summer's lease hath all too short a date, he thinks.

And so does everyone else's.

11

Eve damned eden. mad evE

Eve damned eden. mad evE

(Mid-November 2002)

Emily comes in from a photography session and checks her E-mails. There are five. The headings are:

Emily, your dog can be smarter!

Eddie Bauer pre-Christmas Outerwear Sale!

Work at Home for BIG $$$$$!

Emily Limo! Your Mortgage Has Already Been Approved!!

Thanksgiving? London? Mom? California? Guilt? Help?

The last one, she knows immediately, is from her sister Laurie telling her that she's thinking of not going to Berkeley for

Thanksgiving. She and Jonathan want to go to London and see some plays, and what does Emily think about all of them meeting up at Mom's for Christmas instead?

She E-mails her sister that she has already decided to fly out only for Christmas this year, not Thanksgiving, and reassures her about the lack of necessity for guilt: Mom's new beau is helping her make the Christmas fruitcakes, so it's serious—she probably won't notice whether her kids are there for Thanksgiving, Christmas, or Groundhog Day. Emily cc's her brother on the E-mail, puts in a wash, and then curls up under her quilt with Otto and *Miss Mackenzie*. But she's distracted from the book by the need to contemplate her life.

Emily is tired of being poor.

Her sister Laurie, two years younger than she, is a senior curator at the Art Institute of Chicago, specializing in sixteenth and seventeenth century English needlework, and Laurie's husband Jonathan is a pediatrician with a large practice. Emily's brother Milo is a building contractor in Ann Arbor, married to a well-known novelist who teaches at the university there. Both her siblings will offer her money for a plane ticket to California at Christmas, and so will her mother. She will debate whether to accept it from one or the other of them (and make things easy on herself), or scrape together the money (as she usually does) by a creative combination of late rent, a maxed-out Visa, frugal eating, and hope. Hope is not entirely illusory; Dr. Demand has bought photographs from her on four of the eleven Christmases she has lived in Williamsburg. But hope is also, as Emily Dickinson and the posters in the Hallmark shop have it, the thing with feathers, and it can soar into the air faster than Izzy does when he hears a ringing phone.

In the end, she knows she will pay for her own ticket.

But what she will do about gifts for everyone is another question.

Last year, when she made fudge for her family and begged them not to give her presents, they all got together and presented her with a check so large she couldn't bring herself to cash it until Milo flew to Brooklyn in March and escorted her personally to the bank. The year before, she suggested they all draw names: She drew her mother and gave her three pairs of striped socks and a loaf of home-made bread; Jonathan drew Emily and gave her the rare antique "Hummingbird" pattern quilt that she is presently snuggled under with the dog.

Outside her windows, she can see an occasional aimless snowflake. The air was brisk when she was out with her camera, and now her life seems as bleak as the view. The woes of the world are so many, and they come to her at random: *the hole in the skyline, the hopeful unadopted cats at the Pet Pound, the memory of her father's sudden death and her mother's weeping in the night, the Greenpoint winos with their brown-bagged bottles, her sister's two miscarriages, the story in the morning paper saying the average teenager reads two books a year.* Her own life is aimless, precarious, stalled. The old Volvo was ailing today, so she took the subway to the Village. She didn't find much—an ugly TIME from a billboard, a possible DOG on a peeling wall on West Fourth Street, another nice TIME with a truck parked in front of it so she couldn't get a good shot. She just had time to walk Otto before it started getting dark, and now the river and the skyline are dimming against a smoky sky. The rhythmic chug of the washing machine performs its whiny three-note noise, the start of a Strauss waltz, against the Bach cello suite on the CD player. The CD player, she reflects, was also a gift—from her mother, for her thirty-third birthday. And so were the Bach cello suites.

She looks around her loft, suddenly appalled.

How many of her possessions has she actually bought and paid for?

There's her big maple bed, a castoff from Laurie. The pretty little rag rug on the floor next to it, which Lamont found in the trash and mended and cleaned for her. The wall of bookcases Anstice had made for certain selected tenants the year she gave them a marginal rent raise and then felt guilty about it. The coffee table and rocking chair Emily found on the street and painted yellow. The funny little pink lamp: She and Pat both spotted it at the Salvation Army, and fought over it, and Pat bought it for two bucks and ended up giving it to her anyway. The kitchen table she made herself out of a piece of plywood, some oil cloth, and a set of fancy legs from her mother's attic, and the four chairs one of Sophie's clients begged her to take away when she was remodeling her kitchen. Izzy, found on a rooftop, and Otto, given to her by Hattie and Gaby after Harry died and Hart left her. Even the washer, chugging away, is a relic of her marriage—her divorce settlement consisted of the washer, the dryer, the car, the Trollopes, and the junk upstairs in Anstice's storeroom.

The snowflakes are gathering in greater numbers, like crowds surging onto a subway platform at rush-hour. Winter is coming, which means not only cold and dark and the occasional snow or slush but also freedom from her gardening job and time to do more photography. Given the unprepossessing elements of her life (no money, few prospects, wealthy siblings, unrequited love), she realizes she has no right to be as happy as she actually, usually, is. Her failures nag at her, but they are unchangeable elements of her existence, and she tries to accept them, as she accepts the polluted air of Williamsburg and her size nine feet. With an effort that is partly physical, inhaling deeply through her nose and exhaling through her mouth the way she learned in a yoga class she took years ago at the Greenpoint YMCA, Emily banishes her bad mood to the furthest, dimmest cellars of her mind.

She's just finishing up Chapter Three of *Miss Mackenzie* ("This was the first occasion in her life in which she had gone to a party, the invitation to which had come to her on a card, and of course she felt herself to be a little nervous") when the phone rings. Izzy, as always, squawks and flies to her head. Otto, asleep beside her, wakes up and gives the bird his what-a-jerk look. (*What does he think? That it's for him?*) Emily considers ignoring the phone, but it could be Marcus, who has been elusive: *After he has walked the dogs, what does he do all day?* She hasn't seen him since they went to the polls together on Tuesday, when he entertained her with choice presidential quotes, like "A low voter turnout is an indication of fewer people going to the polls," cracking up all the English-speaking Williamsburgers in line. The Saturday before that was her triumphant Scrabble coup, when she clobbered him with *aquifer* on a triple word. Emily smiles, remembering his pathetic comeback with *squire*, using a blank and wasting an S for a measly fourteen points before going on to beat her in the next two games—but narrowly. Suddenly she misses Marcus desperately, and remembers that she wants to tell him, among other things, her discovery that "two plus eleven" and "one plus twelve" not only have the same answer but use exactly the same letters. On the fifth ring, she picks up the phone.

"Hello—is this Emily Lime?" a man's voice asks.

"Yes."

"Well, hi Emily, my name is Hugh Lang, I'm a friend of Pat and Oliver's." He begins talking too fast. "Well, not a *friend* exactly, I'm the father of a couple of their students at Taggart, but we have, actually, become friendly over the last year or two, you know, they teach my children, and so I have a certain amount of contact with them."

Emily says nothing, and there's suddenly a huge silence in her apartment. The cello suite is over. The washer has stopped its waltz and is waiting to have its clothes transferred to the dryer, which she should get up and do, but Otto has started his gentle snoring again, and she hates to disturb him. She looks out the window, thinking *Everything is dark except for the lights.* The lights in New York never go out, and the sky is never allowed to get black. Anytime, anywhere, in New York City there is someone awake, with a light on, a concept that is both comforting and worrisome. *The city never sleeps.* But maybe it should, maybe it should turn out the lights and get some shut-eye for a change. Somewhere out there, she thinks irrelevantly, is the Williamsburg rapist, the man in a mask and a hood who forces women at knife-point into alleys and to the roofs of abandoned buildings and down to the desolate wasteland by the river. His last victim was one of the Kent Avenue hookers, just two days ago—she also got her face slashed. The one before that was the young Polish girl who used to work at the Pink Pony Thrift Shop. After her rape, Emily heard, she went back to Krakow.

"Hello?"

Emily says, "Oh. Yes."

The man on the phone continues. "So they mentioned that you play poker, and I was wondering—well, you wouldn't believe how hard it is to find poker players in this city! You can find people who do every damn thing—you know, niche things—like my next door neighbor is a Greek acupuncturist who plays the bagpipes—but poker players are hard to find, for some reason. So I was wondering if you'd like to join our little game? Friday nights? Usually at my place—for obvious reasons. I mean, I'm single, so I have no—I mean, I'm not *single,* I'm *divorced,* actually, but my kids aren't here on weekends. What I mean is we do play poker here most Fridays, and we'll be play-ing this week, I'm on the Upper West Side, Amsterdam near Ninety-fifth, and if you'd like to come, that would be great. We play nickel-dime-quarter, a friendly game, none of us are sharks or anything like that, but we're pretty good, not amateurs, there are usually five of us, sometimes six, but we could use a new face, some fresh blood, and I think you might find it's quite a lot of fun. . . ."

Hugh Lang's voice trails off. Izzy, on her head, is murmuring softly, and Otto's snore rumbles against the inside of her left arm. She knows she has to speak, and though she knows what she will say, she is reluctant to say it. She doesn't like to lie, and yet she doesn't want to tell the truth, either, which is that she has no interest in Hugh Lang's poker game or in Hugh Lang, that she is mildly angry at Pat and Oliver for having given him her number, and that she hopes he will never bother her again.

She takes a breath and says, "It really does sound delightful, and I'd love to come, but I'm afraid I can't. Friday night is my—" she hesitates for only a moment "quilting night." She looks down at her black and red quilt and smooths a seam that was meticulously stitched by a woman named Melicent Harris in Pennsylvania in 1845. "My quilting *bee*," she corrects herself. "Every Friday. Seven o'clock sharp. We're a very dedicated little group."

"Really." His voice is deflated. "Well, I'm sorry."

"Yes, me too. It's a shame, but—well, there you are. Isn't it weird how everything is always on the same night, so that you never really get to do anything?" She doesn't wait for him to answer. "I do appreciate your thinking of me, though."

This is a sentence that, she hopes, indicates she wants to hang up now. He gets the hint, and after a few more stilted exchanges they say good-bye. She immediately feels awful. What crazy Yogi Berra thing did she just say? *Everything happens at once so you can't do anything?* Her only consolation is that Hugh Lang probably found her such a dingbat, not to mention a transparent liar, that he is relieved she didn't agree to join the game.

Remorse makes her energetic, and she eases herself out from under Otto and puts the clothes in the dryer. The washer and dryer, combined with the poker game, remind her of her married days, when she and Hart used to play poker with Joe Whack and Jeanette Jerome, the Jeanette whose loft Elliot C. is subletting while Jeanette is in London for a year, on sabbatical from her job teaching American literature at Brooklyn College. It was a pathetic poker game. Joe was really sick then, and Hart was a mediocre player who became sullen and offensive when he lost a hand. Emily was so busy trying to keep everyone happy that she couldn't concentrate, and so Jeanette always took all their money, gleefully quoting Hemingway's strategy—"Never call, always raise or fold"—as she raked in the chips. But Emily loved those poker nights anyway, and it occurs to her that she would, actually, enjoy very much playing in a poker game exactly like the one Hugh Lang just described.

She stops, suddenly, with her hand on the dryer knob.

What is wrong with me?

It's such a familiar question she doesn't even bother to grope for an answer. She stands holding the knob, contemplating the zipper around her wrist. She does her deep breathing. *Think of something nice,* she instructs herself, and she shuts her eyes and lets her mind travel back to 1977, the day Elvis died. Her mother wept on her father's shoulder, her brother Milo put on an old Elvis album, and her parents slow-danced together to "I Want You, I Need You, I Love You," while their children watched, entranced, swaying in time to the music. Emily was eleven.

Feeling better, she starts the dryer.

Then she pours herself some tomato juice (left over from the Scrabble session), puts on the second CD of the cello suites, and returns to Miss Mackenzie, who in the course of Emily's evening goes to Mrs. Stumfold's tea party, is called on by the handsome Mr. Rubb, spends Christmas at the Cedars with Lady Ball and her eligible son, and attends a dinner party in London. Miss Mackenzie makes Emily ashamed of herself. But, as Marcus reminded her at the polls, President Bush once memorably declared, "The future will be better tomorrow."

Emily snuggles up with Otto, feeling sure that this sentiment, while stupid, is probably true.

12

No! it is opposition

No! it is oppositioN

Marcus gets to the Botanic Garden early, so he can take a walk before his father arrives and transforms it from a green and beautiful refuge into a place of bad memories. So far, Marcus has only good memories of the garden, which he discovered soon after his move to Williamsburg in the fall of 2000, when he was nineteen, and had only a hundred dollars in his pocket. He was drawn to Brooklyn by the presence of his father. Broken and motherless, Marcus was too realistic to expect to find family, connection, or roots, but he was also vulnerable enough to want something that at least resembled those things. And he needed money. Hart, he heard from Tamarind, was still some kind of art dealer, with a gallery of his own, and he was married and living in a loft on North Third Street.

Marcus figured he must have improved since the Honesdale days.

But when he arrived and called the number he was given, a

woman's voice told him, curtly, that Hart no longer lived there and no, she didn't have a new number for him. As it turned out, though, Hart wasn't hard to find—he had emigrated across the river, and was renting a place on Crosby Street. He was the proprietor of a small gallery, trendily located in Chelsea, that specialized in what Hart called "the aesthetic of blood," including the work of the soon-to-be-famous wound-painter Selma Rice.

A big surprise was that Hart wasn't sorry to see Marcus. His son's sudden appearance in his life seemed to amuse him—a son who, as he gleefully pointed out, had failed to take his advice, and now look at him. "Did I tell you to get out of that fucking backwater, or what?" he asked, more than once. He was still a smoker, and his voice was a rasp, like a saw that needed sharpening. "But did you listen to your old man? Huh?" He cuffed Marcus on the shoulder. "But hey, kid, I'm glad you turned up." Hart put Marcus up for a night on the couch in his shabby apartment, and gave him an old but warm tweed overcoat, a couple of shirts, and a pair of leather gloves that needed repairing. They were all too big on Marcus, a fact Hart enjoyed ("Jesus Christ! My son the twerp"). Marcus endured his merriment in exchange for enough money for a security deposit on an apartment and a month's rent. Hart had not, in fact, changed much, except that he looked older and was actually willing to part (condescendingly, chuckling, with a couple of remarks about losers) with some of his money.

They went out to dinner in a bar at the top of the World Trade Center—champagne in an ice bucket, and the city like an open jewel box far below. Marcus gazed down at the view, which was both sublime and frightening, while his father launched into a tirade reminiscent of the long-ago night at Mario's Olde Italian

Inn—people are jerks, illogic rules the universe, the art world is stupid and venal, etc. etc. Marcus let his father continue talking until Hart's steak arrived. Then, after a suitable interval as his father attacked the meat and Marcus worked on a vegetarian mushroom-and-pastry thing that reminded him pleasantly of his mother's cooking, he asked one of the questions he had come to New York to hear the answer to.

"So, Pop—why didn't you ever marry Summer?"

Hart looked up from his steak and surprised him by actually answering. "I'm not the marrying kind, son."

"But you married that other woman."

"You know what her name was?" His father smiled. "You'll like this. Emily Lime. Get it?"

But Marcus wasn't listening. "So if you aren't the marrying kind, why did you marry her?"

Hart's smile dissolved into a frown, as if the question truly puzzled him and he was actually searching for some kind of self-knowledge. He gazed off into space for a minute, sipping his champagne, and then he said, "I'll tell you the truth here, Marcus. I think I thought I could become the marrying kind by, well, by getting married. You know—walk like a duck, talk like a duck. . . ." He shrugged.

Hart's face was sneer-free, and his words seemed sincere. Not for the first time, Marcus wondered if his father was all that bright. He remembered Tamarind once saying to him, "You know I loved your mom, but sometimes I wonder how in hell those two managed to produce *you*." She added that it would be hard to believe Hart was actually his father if Marcus weren't a kind of elfin version of the old man, a description that made him cringe but that he knew was accurate.

The two of them chewed for a while in silence. Marcus ate his mushroom tart slowly, trying to make it last. He wondered why Summer had never aspired to be a chef, and imagined her rich and happy working in a place like this, messing with mushrooms and pastry, instead of poor and melancholy, schlepping around her house, killing the hours until she could start cooking dinner. The thought was painful. *If Summer hadn't died. If Summer were alive now.* He could bring her to New York, send her to cooking school, see that she got a job and was happy. All through his adolescence, mooning around the house and prowling through the woods and reading and watching TV, he had thought his mother was so difficult, so hopeless. Maybe she wasn't, maybe she was easy, like a chess prodigy or a musician. She could only do one thing, but it's a thing you can make a living doing. Why didn't he know that then? Why didn't anyone?

"My turn, then, laddie," Hart said suddenly. "Another question. What brought you to Williamsburg?" He pointed his fork at Marcus. "And don't tell me it was the zip code."

Marcus considered. There was no way he would tell his father he had moved there because of him. "It was, actually, the zip code."

"Let me get this straight." Hart wore little half-glasses on the end of his nose, presumably so he could see his steak when he sliced into it. The steak, which Hart had ordered rare, reminded Marcus of the paintings he'd seen in his father's gallery—raw, oozing, lurid, brutal. "You own your mother's house. Right?"

"Yeah, pretty much. Sort of." He hadn't been back to the gray farmhouse since Summer's funeral. He tried not to remember how he got high in the men's room at the funeral home on some reefer Tamarind, mercifully, slipped him. He really didn't remember much else about that day except that the weather that had killed his mother had thawed, and the cemetery was a mess of mud and slush, and his father didn't show up. "I owe some back taxes. But—yeah. Basically."

He wanted to keep it vague, didn't want Hart to suggest that he sell the place and pay him back the money he'd just given him. Marcus had his own plans for his life, his money, and his mother's house.

But Hart didn't pursue it. He asked, "So you couldn't live in the drab, boring, jerkoff zip code of Honesdale, Pennsylvania, whatever it is—"

"18431."

"OK. I see. 18431 isn't numerically interesting enough for you." Hart's face was amused and expectant, as if Marcus was about to provide the punch line to a great joke. Marcus could have told him some ways in which 18431 was, numerically, extremely interesting, but he knew Hart didn't want to hear them. And of course it was true that, interesting or not, 18431 was very far from the palindromic beauty of 11211. "So you've got to move to 11211. Is that what you're saying, son?"

"Well, I could move to 10001, over in the West Thirties, but I can't afford to live in Manhattan."

"Ha!" Hart's laugh burst out. "You couldn't afford to live in Brooklyn if I weren't staking you."

Marcus sighed. "Right, Dad, but I figured I could only squeeze so much out of you."

Hart looked at him with what seemed to be approval. "That's my boy," he said, and sloshed the rest of the champagne into Marcus's glass. "Drink up, son. This is a historic moment. Damn it, I haven't seen you since you were—what?"

"Ten."

"Ten. And now you're—what?"

"Nineteen and a half."

"Holy shit. You look about fourteen."

Marcus knew this was true.

Hart finished the steak, removed his glasses, pushed his plate back, and signaled for another bottle of champagne. "So did you ever go back to school, or what?"

"Nope. Never did." Marcus had almost reached the point where he thought it might have been a mistake to stay out of school all those years, to escape the horrors of Honesdale High, simply because no one noticed he wasn't there. Maybe people needed to endure things like that. Maybe it's a kind of refiner's fire, it normalizes them.

"They *never* made you go to school?"

"Apparently, once I got off the radar of the Wayne County Board of Ed., I never got back on."

"Holy shit. So you've never been past sixth grade?"

"Fifth. I'm probably one of the few people who doesn't have that dream where you're late for a final exam you haven't studied for."

"So what the hell were you doing all those years? After I left your mother?"

Marcus doesn't bother to correct his father's version of events. "Not much," he says. "Eating Summer's cooking. Reading. I read all the books in the Honesdale Library. The only problem was I had to go there after school hours and on Saturdays so the librarians wouldn't get suspicious." He doesn't tell Hart about his winter in the woods, when he abandoned Summer to live on his own way up near Damascus, working in a gas station, feeding a family of raccoons, sleeping long hours, reading Shakespeare's sonnets. He would never tell anyone—he could barely admit it to himself—that he'd left home because by the time he was a teenager her oddities were getting to him, and that he even felt a certain sympathy with Hart and his absences.

Hart, who had drunk two scotches before dinner and most of the champagne during it, was sloshed. He lit a cigarette, having some trouble with the match, and then his sneer reasserted itself. "So what are you going to do now? Write your memoirs? Memorize the phone book? Rob a bank?"

"Probably not, Dad," Marcus said evenly. He had already noticed that Williamsburg seemed dog-heavy, and contemplated a pet-sitting/dog-walking business. He ate the last bit of mushroom, considered picking up the plate and licking it, decided not to. "Probably something else."

Now, as he walks the fragrant paths of the Botanic Garden, Marcus counts up the times he's seen his father since he's lived in Williamsburg. He'd seen him one more time that first year. Then three times in 2001, not counting a maudlin phone call from Hart right after 9/11 that makes Marcus cringe when he thinks about it. Now this would be their fourth meeting in 2002. The encounters are increasing by one a year, a fact he finds dismaying.

Another reason to get out of town.

A little before four o'clock, he leaves the Shakespeare garden, where he has been contemplating a hefty stand of *Rosmarinus officinalis* with its inevitable rosemary-for-remembrance quotation from *Hamlet*. He walks across to the Japanese one, recently renovated, but which (in its autumnal guise) is still very much as he perceived it when he first took the Number 43 bus to see it nearly two years ago: elegant, spare, and—in spite of its mannered precision and air of absorbed cultivation—a magnet for the wild creatures Marcus continues to miss in the brickstone-asphalt world of Brooklyn. There are turtles on a rock, koi in the depths, brown ducks riding on the khaki water, rabbits on the grass, an occasional snowy egret perched on the faded red torii gate. Just the sight of them eases his mind, the way a romp in the park with Rumpy and Elvis can do. Or a Scrabble game with Emily. He smiles, thinking of her and her damned *aquifer*, and he's still smiling when he hears the crunch of leaves and looks up to see his father coming down the path. If Hart only knew he was thinking with such affection of Emily Lime, whom he is about to be paid ten thousand dollars to murder. . . .

As it turns out, however, Hart has only nine thousand four hundred on him.

An emergency came up this morning, he says, and he needed some cash.

Marcus had expected his father to either not show up, or show up with no money at all and an excuse. Instead, there are ninety hundred-dollar bills, plus a short stack of twenties—all of it stuffed into an envelope that once held Hart's Con Edison bill. Marcus is stunned. He sits on a bench in the pavilion, which is deserted except for a spider in one corner poised in an enormous web. His father looms over him, leaning against the frame, looking as if he wishes he had a cigarette, while Marcus counts the cash. The bills aren't fresh, the way a bank would hand them out, but wrinkled and tattered, as if Hart has been saving up for his ex-wife's murder for years, a hundred at a time. As he counts, Marcus feels a creeping chill of fear: Hart is not a man who fools around with money. The idea is suddenly real that, to his father, this cash is not a used pick-up truck, as it is to him; it is the broken body of Emily Lime at the bottom of an elevator shaft. Marcus finishes counting and looks up at his father. Hart needs a haircut, his leather jacket has seen better days, and he's compulsively biting his bottom lip.

"No other way, eh, Dad?" he asks quietly.

"Of getting what I need?" His father jerks his head. "Sorry. No."

"Can you tell me—?"

"Nope. It's complicated. All part of a little agreement I made with my ex-wife." He smiles down at Marcus. "Grown-up stuff, kid. Don't ask."

"You couldn't just—"

"Nope. Everything's locked up tight."

"But—"

"Hey!" Hart bends toward Marcus and holds his hands in the air, stiffly, as if he is held back from grabbing his son by the throat only by the presence of a Botanic Garden employee chugging by in a cart on the path behind them. "Listen to me, you little twerp. Are you going to do this or not? I can take the money back, you know. I'm trying to be a good father to you for once, but I can find other things to do with my hard-earned cash."

Marcus sits there with the envelope in his lap. He has just taken money from his father in exchange for the promise to commit a murder. Is he now going to meet the same fate Phoebe did? A quick death, followed by burial in an unmarked grave? Then his mind shies away—*there's no proof his father killed his dog.* Marcus looks out over the water toward the red gate, which is a copy of one in Japan that stands in the sea at Miyajima. He knows that the inscription on it means "spirit of light."

He usually admires the gate, but today it looks to him like a gallows. "No problem, Dad," he says. "I'll do it."

"You're not fucking with me, are you?"

"No."

"Okay then." Hart straightens up and his frown smoothes out, leaving only a yellow-toothed smile. "That's my boy."

Marcus sits there for a while after Hart leaves, watching the spider. For a long time, it doesn't move, and he wonders if it's dead. Then, with sudden and surprising speed, it starts scuttling toward Marcus, and Marcus pockets the wad of money and heads home.

13

Oh! cameras are macho!

Oh! cameras are machO!

"We should mobilize," Gene Rae says. "Take back our neighborhood. Five rapes in this neighborhood in two months? I say we should fight."

"With what?" Emily asks her. "Guns?"

Gene Rae—eyes narrowed, gazing into space—considers this. She is sitting, with Izzy on her knee, on the sofa Emily found on the street years ago and covered with a chenille bedspread from the Salvation Army. Against the white bedspread, Gene Rae is vivid, with her frizzy red hair and startling blue eyes. She wears turquoise sneakers, and her earrings are long silver chains with silver cats spinning on the ends. Her yellow sweater stretches over Roland the fetus, now past his seventh month. "No," she says finally. "Guns are dangerous. I mean, I personally would

welcome the chance to pick this guy off with a little .38, but—
no."

"No," Emily echoes, feeling enormous relief. She is willing
to cope with the Williamsburg rapist simply by not going out
alone at night, though she knows that if Gene Rae comes up
with some other way, she will go along with it. Gene Rae once
said, "Every woman should know how to use an electric drill,"
and Emily got herself one, learned how to use it, and has never
been sorry. But a gun is different.

"But *something*," Gene Rae says. "Something besides cow-
ering behind our men, Emily! I can only go out after dark now if
Kurt is with me. How degrading!"

"I feel okay with Otto."

"Right. Men and dogs. Has it come to this? That women
have to come in third, behind men and dogs?" She takes a sip of
cocoa. "Not that I have anything against men or dogs. I mean, I
have one of each with another one on the way. But."

Gene Rae often ends a sentence with the word "but," especially when she's with Emily. They have known each other for so
long—since high school, and then they went to college together—
that they can read each other's minds. Sometimes they just sit
together for long minutes, thinking, occasionally nodding at each
other. They do this now, while Izzy circles around Gene Rae's
knee and walks down her leggings to her sneakers, where he pulls
happily at the laces with his beak.

Finally Emily says, "Well," and Gene Rae says, "Yeah."

They sip their cocoa.

"So are you on vacation yet?" Gene Rae asks.

"After this week. Sophie and I have to finish the fall cleanup
at the Ramseys."

"They're the ones with the turtle sculptures?"

"Yeah. She can't seem to stop buying them." Victor and Tilda Ramsey have divorced, and Victor's new wife, Siena, who is an astrologer to the rich, has an idea that in a previous life she was a turtle. "I'm sure she's spent a fortune."

"They sound kind of cute."

"One was cute. Two were cute. Even three were still almost cute. Fourteen is a little scary."

"That's a lot of turtle."

"We're always tripping over them. And they're a magnet for pigeons. At least we don't have to clean off the poop, the maid does it." Emily sighs. "I hate to see fall come, in a way. I love having all the free time, but I'll miss those posh rooftops."

"'Margaret, are you grieving,'" Gene Rae quotes, "'Over goldengrove unleaving?'" They were literature majors together.

"I am, Genie. I'm getting old."

"If you are, then I am, and I'm not, so neither are you."

"That seems reasonable, I admit, but still—I've been feeling sort of over the hill lately." Emily reaches for a Mallomar. Gene Rae brought the cocoa, milk, and cookies with her, knowing Emily's slender larder can't support the nutritional demands of pregnancy. Mallomars sit proudly at the tip of the Personal Food Pyramid Emily and Gene Rae concocted long ago, just above apples, poached eggs, chicken peanut curry, tomato sandwiches on toasted Wonder bread, Cherry Garcia ice cream, and celery stuffed with cream cheese. "These are *so* fabulous."

"They're great when you're pregnant, because they like being washed down with lots of milk."

"My mother has a new boyfriend," Emily says.

"Your mother is so completely cool for her age." They are

silent again, reading each other's minds, and then Gene Rae adds, "I often think you and St. Francis of Assisi would be perfect for each other."

Emily's heart lurches. St. Francis of Assisi is what Gene Rae calls Marcus.

"If only he weren't young enough to be your son."

"He could only be my son if I'd been a teenage slut."

"You were a teenage slut," Gene Rae reminds her.

"Okay, if I'd been an unlucky teenage slut." Emily sees herself with a little mound under her sweater, and inside it is Marcus. "I wasn't really a slut anyway. It was just Jeffrey Norris and Neil Saltzman. Mostly."

"Mostly."

"Those were the days," Emily says, but the remark is ironic, non-nostalgic. High school was the low point of their existence. Emily is happy to be a grown-up.

But she's still thinking about Marcus.

He told her a few days ago about the paper route he had as a kid, how he used to go out on his bicycle in the misty early mornings, when it was still nearly dark, with his canvas bag of papers slung over his shoulder. No one would be out but him and the deer, who'd stand on the roadside in clumps, staring at him, and then, quick as a blink, vanish into the trees. Marcus is not very communicative about his life, and Emily hoards stories like this one, typing them into a secret file on her computer titled SCARUM. The image haunts her: young Marcus bicycling down a country road in his corduroy jacket and little cap—though she's had to invent the jacket and cap, Marcus couldn't remember what he used to wear when he delivered papers. The image seems emblematic of Marcus: his work ethic, his aloneness, his feeling for animals, and his ineffable cuteness.

"So who's your mom's new squeeze?"

"One of the attorneys at Foley, Levine, & Kirk. His name is Enrico. His wife died a couple of years ago. Mom says he's got the most beautiful curly gray hair she's ever seen."

"Sounds adorable."

"And he has two cats and a new puppy."

"I hope she snaps him up!"

"It would be hard," Emily confesses, "to go to my mother's wedding before she comes to mine."

Gene Rae looks at her sympathetically, one hand spread across Roland. Emily's inability to find Mr. Right is an old story. "Realistically speaking, Em, it is sort of hard to imagine you and Marcus walking down an aisle somewhere. Everybody would think he was the ring-bearer." Gene Rae makes her voice high and squeaky, the voice of an imaginary crowd. "Where's the groom? Where's the groom?" She finishes her cookie, takes another. "Still, it's a shame. In a weird kind of way, you guys seem like soulmates."

After Gene Rae leaves, Emily gives in to the urge to get out of her apartment and into the streets with her camera, while the light lasts. She walks up Berry Street, past the tavern Mae West used to live upstairs from, past the brewery, to Greenpoint, the Polish neighborhood that, if you walk far enough down Manhattan Avenue, evolves into a Hispanic one, places where it's rare to hear English. This is one of Emily's favorite walks, and she has already scoured these streets for BREAD, DOG, and TIME. She knows she won't turn up any new ones, but she's hoping to find something else. She has decided recently to expand what she is embarrassed to call her *artistic vision* by taking photographs of the neighborhood itself—fast, unstudied photos of Brooklyn's joyful jumble. She hasn't told anyone about it because it sounds so supremely uninteresting, but she finds herself getting excited as she walks along—not quite ready to shoot yet, just window-shopping.

She knows every store by heart on Manhattan Avenue: the notions shop with its window of scissors and thread, the God Bless Deli, the Polish Wicca shop, the fishing tackle store, the store selling Eastern European housedresses. The tiny place called White Dream that features only white clothing. The beauty shops named by people with an imperfect command of English—Hair Crazy, Hair Fever, and her favorite, Beautiful Again, with its implication that everyone was once beautiful and will return to that state as soon as those split ends are taken care of. She walks by the market; canned salmon is on sale, and she makes a note to stop in on her way home. Canned salmon isn't anywhere near the top of her food pyramid, but it's cheap and good for you and tastes okay tossed in mayo with pickles à la Mrs. Buzik. Old Mr. Suarez waves to her from where he waits in line at the outdoor can redeemer with Eddie the Chihuahua. She passes the bad drugstore (large, chain, rude) and the good drugstore (small, Polish, polite), Mrs. Ronnie the Psychic, the gift shop with the handmade straw hens from Czechoslovakia in the window, and the produce markets with their outdoor bins overflowing with peppers and apples and cukes. Through the window of Dee & Dee she spots Hattie of the Pet Pound browsing through a rack of flannel shirts. Then, glancing down a side street, she sees the brown leather jacket and greased buzz-cut of Elliot C. going into the gym, and she turns away.

Even a quick glimpse of Elliot casts a strange pall over the neighborhood.

But then, when she crosses Greenpoint Avenue, she looks through her camera and is mesmerized by the beauty of it: Manhattan Avenue, stretching north to Queens, its colorful, improbable, crazy quilt of shops just touched with gold by the fading light. She snaps pictures from several vantage points until the light falls and fades, and tells herself that if she takes no other pictures today, this will have been worth it.

Luther comes out of the liquor store, which is famous for its handsome Polish clerks and its dozens of brands of vodka. "Russian Vodka," Luther says, opening the bag. "Something called Youri Dolgaruki. They were out of Krolewska. I'm going to make Cajun Kamikazes tonight. Why don't you drop over? Around nine? But bring Otto. Or get Marcus to walk you over. No going out alone, missy."

"I can't bring Otto." She has brought Otto over to Luther and Lamont's place in the past, and his attempts to play with the affronted Daphnes always break her heart. Last time, orange Daphne swiped his nose, drawing blood. She can still see Otto's hurt, baffled face.

"Then bring Marcus. The cats love him." Luther chuckles. "Maybe because he's not always trying to sniff their butts."

It's too dark for more pictures. The magic light is gone. How fast it fades! Emily and Luther walk back along the avenue, toward home. "How's everything?" Emily asks him. "How's Lamont?"

"Lamont. Lamont? Oh—La-*mont*. He's fine, I hear. I don't see that much of him nowadays. He has a new friend."

"Oh, Luther." Emily knows he means Elliot C. "I'm sorry. I'm sure it's nothing. I'm sure he'll get over it."

"I'm not sure of any of those things, Emily." Luther takes her arm. "But I'll tell you what. Let's not fuck up a beautiful evening by talking about it."

They're turning onto Lorimer Street when Luther says, "So what's this about Marcus moving out of town?"

Emily stops dead. "Moving out of town? Where did you hear this?"

"I ran into him at the bank this morning. We're just chatting, you know, and I say to him, 'Hey Marcus, you ever thought of buying yourself a little house here in the hood? Because I heard Mrs. Buzik's place over by the park might be available soon, she's thinking of moving in with her daughter out in Mineola.'"

"She is?"

"Yeah, she's not doing so well. Going in the hospital next week to have a toe amputated. And she's talking about unloading the place."

"What about Trix?"

"Going with her, of course. Can't you just see Mrs. Buzik and Trix out in the burbs? Sitting by the pool, soaking up the sun? Trix can do her business on a lawn that has one of those FED BY CHEMICALS AND PROUD signs on it."

"So she's selling her place," Emily says. She can't let Luther get off on one of his suburban-living riffs. "And so you said to Marcus—"

"Well, of course, the trouble is, the building is such a wreck she's not going to get much for it. But that's where I figure somebody like Marcus comes in. He's got his little nest egg going—he was depositing a fistful of cash this morning. Let me tell you, the kid is no slouch. He's smart, he's handy, he's personable, he'd be a cool landlord, even at his age. But then he tells me he already owns a place, in the boonies somewhere—I think he said Pennsylvania—his mother's place."

"Honesdale, Pennsylvania," Emily says, her heart sinking.

"That's it. Honesdale. Just south of Doohickey Falls and west of Bumfuck Center."

"I didn't know." Emily starts walking again, but her legs are rubbery. Marcus has told her about the little gray farmhouse, the pretty Victorian town. "I didn't know he owned the house."

"Sounds like there was nobody else to inherit it."

Why hasn't she realized that? Why hasn't she ever asked him what became of the house? Why hasn't she ever asked him the million questions she doesn't know the answers to? She has no idea what he wants, why he wants it, who he is. Marcus Mead. His mother's name was Summer, and she is dead, though Marcus doesn't talk about what she died of. His father left when he was ten. Marcus had a paper route and a long period of no formal schooling. He had a dog named Phoebe. There's a picture of him from 1991, with phone book and number 7 sweatshirt, squinting into the camera. He used to live alone in an unheated cabin. He's the son of her ex-husband, he's her dog-walker, he's somebody Luther ran into in the bank, he has strange green eyes, he is fond of avocados and Trollope and numbers and words, and he doesn't share her taste for Mallomars.

He's a cat, he's a bird, he's the crow who has learned to use a tool to get food. . . .

"So I asked him why he never goes down there, and he said,

well, one of these days he might, he'd like to set himself up with a truck and get down there from time to time and maybe even move there for good one of these days."

Emily stops again. "Marcus said that?"

Luther gives her a strange look. "Well, yeah," he says. "But just in a general kind of way. I mean, I don't think he has any plans to do it any time soon."

"Oh."

"It's like—hey, who doesn't get the urge to move to the country every once in a while?"

"Yeah."

"He's not going to find too many dogs to walk in a place like that. Sounds like the kind of place where they keep the dog in the yard and name it Bubba and only let it off the chain during deer-hunting season."

They turn onto Berry Street. Luther chats on about city life versus country life. Emily is silent. Why is she just realizing now that Marcus is an immense, panoramic, teeming, epic novel, stuffed with events and thoughts and feelings, and all she has of him is her pathetic, lovesick little SCARUM file: everything he's let her know about himself packed into—what?—fifty lousy kilobytes on her hard drive. Readers Digest Condensed Marcus.

She gives a little moan, and stumbles. Luther catches her arm. "Hey—you okay, Emily?"

She leans against him, and he puts his arms around her—the vodka bottle bangs against her back—and the two of them stand on the corner behind the automotive high school, while Emily lets herself weep over Marcus Mead, who is someone she has absolutely no claim on. She is nothing to him but a temporary friend. He would leave her in a minute for a house in

Honesdale, Pennsylvania. This is the hard truth. Marcus was all she had, and soon she won't have Marcus.

She searches in her pocket, finds an old tissue, and blows her nose while Luther stands there patting her back. Then she heaves a huge sigh. "Oh, Luther."

He tucks a lock of her hair behind her ear. "It's a bitch, ain't it, babe?"

They walk on. Berry Street is just Berry Street, and the river when she glimpses it is aluminum gray, flat and dull. In the brewery yard, she sees half a dozen of the scrawny stray cats who live there, foraging in Dumpsters and sleeping in the open and producing endless litters, and Emily thinks she has never seen anything sadder or more hopeless. *Brooklyn,* she misquotes slightly,

> *which seems to lie before us like a land of dreams,*
> *So various, so beautiful, so new,*
> *Hath really neither joy, nor love, nor light,*
> *Nor certitude, nor peace, nor help for pain . . .*

When they get to her door, Luther looks into her eyes and says, "We don't ever need to say another word about this if you don't want."

"Thank you, Luther."

"But on the other hand, if you ever want to talk about it, you can talk to me."

Emily nods, a lump in her throat.

Luther holds up the bag from the liquor store. "Come on over later."

"Thanks, but no, I don't think I will," she says. "I have to work tomorrow."

She watches him walk away, handsome, heartbroken, but maybe distracted for a minute from his own troubles by the troubles of pathetic Emily Lime. Soon he will start wishing he could talk it over with Lamont, and all his own sorrows will come rushing back.

Still, Emily remembers, she got some good pictures. Brooklyn is a dismal place, full of loss and betrayal, but it's also beautiful.

She goes upstairs to Otto and Izzy, and considers calling Marcus to ask him if he's really planning to move away. But she's afraid she will cry again if he says yes, and the horror of that is too much for her. Unrequited love. Is the word *unrequited* ever used except in that Victorian phrase? Or *requited,* for that matter? What kind of word is that? She remembers Johnny Eames in *The Small House at Allington*—the April selection of the Trollope group—whose passionate love for Lily Dale is one of the most famous unrequited loves in literature. The last sight Trollope provides of poor Johnny is when he is sitting alone in the dining room of the Great Western Hotel in London, moping over a mutton chop. The image has always seemed sad to Emily—all of them in the group felt bad for Johnny, who is a serious, decent young man. But now, in spite of herself, it makes her laugh—a mutton chop, after all!

But she sobers immediately: Will Marcus even be at the next Trollope meeting? *Marcus,* she thinks. *Marcus Mead. Dr. Maus came. Mama's cured.*

She is sitting by the window watching the lights come on across the river and munching the last Mallomar—*dinner of Mallomars and tomato juice is pretty good,* she is telling herself—when the phone rings. It's Gene Rae to say there has been another rape, a middle-aged waitress at Kasia's was attacked in the doorway of an abandoned building on Franklin Street. Same guy, same hood, same mask, same knife, and she's going out to buy a gun.

14

Deified

DeifieD

Marcus waits until nearly noon before he lets himself into Emily's loft with his dog-walker's key. Otto comes running to greet him, and Marcus tussles with him for a few minutes, throwing the old red ball until he wonders, as he often does, if Otto really likes chasing it or if he keeps fetching it because he thinks Marcus likes to throw it. When they both get tired, Marcus perches gingerly in Emily's yellow rocker and contemplates what he is about to do. So far he has only committed one crime—entering her apartment illegally—and it's a crime he could probably justify with some lame excuse if she walked in on him. *I had an uncontrollable urge to visit Otto.* Emily would probably fall for that one, though no one else on earth would.

But he is about to commit a much greater, utterly unjustifiable crime, and his only excuse is that it could save her life. And telling Emily Lime that her ex-husband, who happens to be his father, wants her dead is not something Marcus ever hopes to face. Half an hour of blatant snooping is infinitely preferable. Somewhere in her apartment there must be something that will shed light on what his father wants. Two things that Hart said on Tuesday have stuck with him: "My wife and I had a little agreement," and "Everything is locked up tight."

These two sentences, of course, could mean nothing.

The first could refer to a casual conversation, the second could be a metaphor.

But Marcus can't be sure until he looks, and that is what he is there to do. He wishes he didn't have to, but what if Hart had asked someone else to do the deed? Emily could be dead by now, and the whatever-it-is could be in Hart's pocket. *My wife and I had a little agreement. . . .* How, how, how could Emily ever have been Hart's wife? It's beyond him, and he doesn't like to think about it. He would rather think of Emily up on a roof somewhere in Brooklyn Heights right now, tying back vines and potting up tender plants and bundling rosebushes in burlap against the coming winter. It's a cool, sunny Thursday morning— a perfect gardening day.

The light is pouring in through the tall windows, and Emily's loft is a pleasant place to be. Except for its size, it always reminds him of van Gogh's painting of his bedroom in Arles: colorful, plain, a bit eccentric—and poor. He hates it that Emily is so poor. He knows she isn't eating much: She lives on eggs, apples, and canned salmon. She is appealingly slender, but one of these days she will be precariously gaunt, like a teenage supermodel. He had considered bringing over some groceries, leaving them on her kitchen counter with a note: *I went shopping while you were at work. Hope that's okay. Love, Izzy.*

But she would know it was him, even if he misspelled some of the words.

Marcus wants the whatever-it-is to transform Emily into a rich woman, and tells himself he won't leave New York until he figures out how to make that happen. Eventually, he gets up and goes over to Emily's desk, which is a piece of plywood balanced on two file cabinets. Emily has devised a keyboard holder under the desktop: a scarred maple cutting board resting on two pieces of half-round molding that stick out below the plywood like arms. Marcus always smiles when he sees it: It's primitive, sad, ingenious, and ludicrous, because the keyboard it supports is attached to a sleek and powerful top-of-the-line computer Emily bought during the Y2K panic with the proceeds from the sale of two BREADS and a DOG.

The computer is seductive: He's tempted to get on the Web and try to find the fiendish crossword puzzle site he heard about from Saul. But it's too risky, and Izzy chooses that moment to screech "Pretty boy!" as if warning him away. Who knows what time Emily and Sophie will finish for the day, or how long it will take him to snoop through Emily's possessions?

Hating himself, he opens one of the file cabinets. He is surprised by its finicky order, which is worthy of himself. It seems to contain only information relating to her photographs: correspondence with galleries, receipts from photo labs, lists of what she sold and to whom and when. It's in the second cabinet that he finds, instantly, what he knows instinctively he has been looking for.

In between folders marked GAS BILLS and MEDICAL STUFF is a thin one marked LEGAL, and inside it is a multi-page document headed STATE OF NEW YORK: DISSOLUTION OF

MARRIAGE. He has an unsavory desire to read it straight through—Docket No. FA-96 04587553F, Statement of Income, Marital History, Judgment File—but in his first quick perusal he sees a page headed "Schedule C: Personal Property to be Retained by Wife pursuant to Paragraph VIII of Agreement dated July 16, 1997." The list reads:

washing machine and dryer

1985 Volvo

54 novels by Anthony Trollope, "Everyman" edition

74 oil paintings, three notebooks of drawings, two pastels: work of artist Joe Whack

Marcus sits down on the floor, dazed, and stares at it. His first thought is the Joe Whack painting of the toaster and safety pins Hart gave to Summer, which is still hanging on the wall in the gray farmhouse. He'd forgotten all about it.

His second thought is: *What a shit.* At a time when Hart was making plenty of money, this is all she got. She probably couldn't afford a lawyer, probably in her Emily-ish way didn't even quibble: Sure, whatever, let's just get it over with.

He gathers his wits together, finally, and produces his third thought: *Whack.* It must be Joe Whack. His work must have become valuable. Posthumously, he has been discovered. Somewhere, somehow, somebody wants Whack. Hart knows this, Emily doesn't.

Emily has seventy-four Whacks.

He looks vaguely around the loft. Where the hell are they?

He is putting the document back when another one catches his eye. It is badly typed on flimsy paper, and it is headed JOINT

TENANCY AGREEMENT, dated March 14, 1995. Feeling slimy, Marcus peeks at it. It is written in legal gobbledygook that sounds to him like a parody:

"Notice to whomever it may concern, now and hereafter and in perpetuity," it begins, and goes on to say:

> the artist herein named and whose signature is below, I, Josef Whack, do hereby transfer the property that comprises my life work, namely 74 paintings, 2 pastels, and 3 notebooks, to Tab Hartwell and Emily Lime, which they will own jointly now and forever, to do with what they wish, and in the event of the death of one of them, the works of art in question, namely said paintings, pastels, and notebooks, become the sole and exclusive property of the other.

The document is signed by Josef Whack, Emily Lime, and Tab Hartwell and notarized with a signature that is barely readable but looks female, Polish, and in a hurry.

In the event of the death of one of them. If Emily Lime's dead body is found at the bottom of an elevator shaft, Hart will get back the Whacks he gave up, plus pastels and notebooks. But if Emily Lime's death is averted, Hart will own nothing but his own twisted soul, and Emily could be a wealthy woman. Or at least a wealthier woman. Or is a Joint Tenancy Agreement some kind of binding lifelong covenant that Marcus doesn't understand? Do Emily and Hart, bizarrely, still own the paintings together, as if they were a child in joint custody?

But—again, the vital question—where are the paintings?

Marcus returns the document to its folder and closes the file drawer, ignoring the urge to wipe off his fingerprints. Then he exchanges a few "pretty boys" with Izzy, pets Otto until the dog starts to get wild, and lets himself out. He has to wait for the elevator, which is above him on the sixth floor. The elevator makes Marcus nervous. Whenever he takes Otto out, he's always terrified that, in his zeal to get to the park, the crazy little guy will fling himself over the edge.

Marcus leans out into nothingness to pull on the cable and he looks up the open shaft, where he can see the dark steel cube that, Emily has told him, Anstice is planning to replace with a regular elevator, one with numbered buttons and automatic doors. Anstice can't bring herself to do it yet, because during the time it's being worked on (conservative estimate: a month) she will have to walk up to her sixth-floor loft. And until the building achieves legal status, nobody says she has to do it.

Marcus moves back, well away from the shaft, knowing that if he looks down he will see the bottom of the long vertical tunnel where he has told Hart that Emily's body will lie in a broken heap. He leans against the wall and squeezes his eyes shut, and into his mind comes the image of a body at the bottom of the shaft, and it's not Emily's, it's Hart's.

Finally, the elevator grinds into action, descends noisily, and stops in front of him. He wrenches open the door and sees Anstice and Dr. Demand, each of them wearing the pleasant and elaborately neutral look worn only by people who have just sprung guiltily apart.

"Oh! Well! Hi, Marcus," Anstice says. She is wearing what appears to be a nightgown under a quilted Chinese jacket. "Nice to see you. I'm just going down to get my mail."

"Hi," Marcus says, nodding at them both. "I stopped in to

see Emily, but I guess she's not home. Her buzzer doesn't seem to be working."

"Oh, right," Anstice says vaguely. A smile hovers around her lips. "Those damned buzzers, always wimping out when you need them."

Dr. Demand hauls on the rope, and the elevator starts to descend. "I had to deliver something to Anstice," he says. "A small dental complication." He glances at Anstice and shrugs, looking suddenly helpless. "Something minor, but, you know, major."

"It was so nice of you, Doctor," Anstice says, and the smile breaks out.

Dr. Demand gazes at her, then turns with an effort to Marcus. His face is bright crimson above his nattily knotted blue tie. "Great weather we're having, eh?"

"Pretty good, Doc." The elevator is agonizingly slow. Even on a cool autumn day, the smells of cinnamon and cloves linger in the building, permeating the elevator. There is an awkward pause, which Marcus figures it's his turn to break. He says, "Running into you like this reminds me I should probably do something about that broken tooth."

"Ah—yes." Dr. Demand visibly struggles to remember the tooth. When Marcus chipped a piece off a year ago on a frozen candy bar, the dentist said it wasn't serious, not to worry unless he lost some more of the tooth, which is one reason everyone goes to Dr. Demand.

"Snickers bar," Marcus prompts him.

The dentist's face lights up. "Second bicuspid in the upper right quadrant? I still think you can wait on that, Marcus, but if it's bothering you, give Renata a call and make an appointment. I'll be glad to take another look."

"Will do," Marcus says, and the elevator lands, with a little bump, at the first floor, and they all file into the lobby.

Anstice says, "Well—guess I'll get that mail," and Dr. Demand says, "Guess I'll be off to pull some teeth." But neither of them moves.

Nor does Marcus. He stands there, suddenly struck by an idea. "Anstice," he says.

She wrenches her gaze away from Dr. Demand. "Hmmm?"

"I wonder if I could talk to you about something."

Anstice gives him her full attention, genuinely surprised. "Sure." She looks at Dr. Demand, back at Marcus. "You mean—now?"

"Well, yeah. I mean, if you're not too busy."

"No, no, of course not. I'm just . . ." She looks down at her feet for a moment—she is wearing what Marcus believes are called mules—pink ones—and then seems to pull herself together. "Sure. That's fine." She holds out her hand to the dentist. "Thanks, Dr. D. For stopping over and everything."

Dr. Demand takes her hand, and Marcus turns away for a moment, hands in pockets, whistling a little, so that they can exchange the kind of look they seem to want to exchange. *Anstice and Dr. D. Well, well.* He doesn't know what to think. He is aware of the usual combination of boredom, bafflement, and envy, but it's like distant hoofbeats, going someplace without him. *When wolves howl,* he thinks, *they sing in harmony, like a barbershop quartet, each wolf on a different note. The songs of whales, on the other hand, are intricately structured,*

*and they come and go like pop tunes. For a couple of months,
they sing the same song, then it changes. . . .*

"I'll be seeing you, then, Marcus," Dr. Demand calls. "You
and your bicuspid."

When Marcus turns, the dentist is going out the front door,
with a jaunty wave, and Anstice is looking blissed-out with an
overlay of puzzlement. "So—Marcus? You want to talk to me
about something?"

"Well, yes—I do."

Marcus looks around the big, bare, industrial lobby, as if a
conference room might present itself—maybe a room hung with
rugs, a hookah in the corner, where spice merchants in turbans
once gathered. Anstice smiles apologetically as if suddenly
remembering that she is well brought-up and that she is wearing
a nightgown and mules and a quilted red Chinese jacket. "Can I
offer you a cup of tea?"

"Yes," Marcus says, with relief. "Tea would be great."

They go back up in the elevator in silence until, at about the
fourth floor, Anstice blurts out, "Oh, all right, then, *yes*. Yes, we
are seeing each other. I know it's—well, I mean I know he—
okay." She takes a deep breath, her bosom heaving, tears in her
eyes. Marcus stares at her, stunned. *No, Anstice! There's no
need to do this!* "He has a wife on Long Island. Betty. We all
know that. And three little kids. Okay. But this is real, Marcus.
This is it. This isn't a fling, or—"

They arrive at her floor. Marcus opens the door.

He has no idea what to say.

He stands aside and lets Anstice precede him out of the elevator and follows her down the hall to her loft. They go in—his

first impression is *cats*. She turns to him. Her eyes are wet, pleading. "I am not a home-wrecker!"

"Anstice," he says, putting out a hand and touching her red Chinese sleeve. "I have a lot on my mind. You don't have to worry about what I think. I don't think anything. Really."

They look earnestly at each other for a moment. Slowly, Anstice reaches into her pocket, removes a lace-bordered handkerchief, dabs at her eyes. Then she sighs, and her little smile returns. "Okay," she says. "Thanks, Marcus. You're a very nice person."

She goes off to put on the kettle, and Marcus sits down in the striped wing chair. Sun pours through the window; the river in the distance is pure blue. The cats come over to sniff at his pant legs. He counts five, and then a sixth emerges from under the desk—a tiger cat who jumps to his lap, kneads briefly, and curls up there, purring. Marcus is aware that Anstice's loft is beautiful and perfect, but he takes it in no more thoroughly than he took in her romance with Dr. Demand. *The Whacks*, he is thinking as he pets the tiger cat absently. *Where are the Whacks?* He has no idea how he will ask this question, and he has no way of being sure Anstice will know the answer, but she is where he has to start because, at the moment, she is all he has.

Anstice returns, with a silver tray bearing a teapot, two mugs, and a plate of molasses cookies. She has changed into large white pants, a matching sweater, and fluffy red slippers, which Marcus finds himself staring at. "Well," Anstice says brightly. "What's up, then, Marcus?"

Without thinking twice he blurts out the whole story before the tea finishes steeping: Hart, murder, money, snooping, Whack—it all tumbles out in a rush while Anstice sits opposite him nibbling on a cookie. All he wants is to get rid of it, to lay the story down for someone else to deal with, and as he talks he wonders if he has ever done this before, and he can't think of a single time. It's probably a huge mistake, Anstice will either think he's nuts or she'll call the police. But he can't stop himself, doesn't want to stop, wouldn't stop if he could. He finishes with the Joint Tenancy Agreement, quoting its flowery language, and then he pauses for breath and says, "So I wondered if maybe you know where those paintings are. Since you were Whack's landlady. And you're Emily's friend. And I don't know who else to ask."

Anstice is chewing, and when she finishes she pours tea for them both, takes a sip, and sets the mug back down on the coffee table. "You actually saw these documents? This joint tenancy thing and also the divorce decree? There's no doubt that she owns the paintings outright? I mean, the divorce agreement gives her the paintings? For sure?"

"It seemed to. It looked pretty official. Unless a joint tenancy agreement is—you know—perpetual or something."

"And am I losing my mind, or did I just hear you say that Tab Hartwell is your father?"

"He's my father."

"And he asked you to kill Emily for these paintings?"

"Yep."

"Holy shit." She puts her hand to her chest and takes a deep breath, like an actress in a melodrama. But it seems perfectly appropriate. Marcus feels like doing the same thing. "Okay," Anstice says. "Give me a second here. I need to think."

Marcus picks up his mug and sips some tea. He's a little shaky. He was so nervous about snooping at Emily's that he couldn't eat breakfast. He touches the cat on his lap, feeling the powerful purr under the fur. *If you could harness purring*, he thinks, *you would solve the energy crisis. An endlessly renewable source. All you have to do is pet them or give them some chicken. Sometimes you just have to talk to them in that funny voice they like. Or catnip—with enough catnip the average cat-loving community could take care of all its energy needs.* Marcus looks out at the river, which is still the intense marine blue of an autumn afternoon. A red tugboat is chugging by. *Life*, he is thinking. *Life is—*

He puts his head back against the chair, afraid suddenly that he might, mysteriously, start to cry.

"Okay, then," Anstice says. "Two things." She is holding up two fingers, and she ticks them off as she speaks. "One: the storage closet down the hall. Two: Wrzeszczynski."

Marcus sits up straight. "Wrzeszczynski?"

She nods, smiling, ticks off the two fingers again. "Storage cupboard. Wrzeszczynski," she says, and smiles so hard it turns into a laugh. "I believe this whole thing is going to be very beautiful." She stands up. "Let's go."

Marcus lowers the cat to the floor. Anstice grabs a set of keys from a hook by the door, and they go out into the hallway, to a door at the end. On it is a brass plaque, a match to the one on the door of her loft: STORAGE, it says in precisely incised letters. There is also a discreet little burglar alarm box. Anstice punches in a code, there is a double beep, and she opens the door with a key. "My junk room," she says, and they walk into a room that's about the size of Marcus's apartment. It's lined with built-in cupboards and shelves, some of them padlocked.

"Down here." They walk through to the far end, where a tall window lets in hazy light. They pass a rack of garment bags

("Clothes from my thinner days," Anstice says. "Can't bear to get rid of them.") and a tower of cardboard cartons labeled AGNES'S KITCHEN STUFF ("Grandma Mullen's cook's *batterie de cuisine*. Ditto.") and a collection of engraved silver urns ("Various family cats, R.I.P."), until they get to a row of six cardboard cartons. Each one contains a dozen or so canvases, showing only their backs where the canvas is stapled to the stretchers.

"Ready?"

He is not, actually. "These are all Whacks?"

"To my knowledge, yes. Whacks are pretty unmistakable. Ever seen one?"

"Just one. Once. Long ago. It was some toast, as I recall, with safety pins and a broken cup."

Anstice chuckles. "Bingo! That's a Whack, all right. I've been thinking that it's hard to believe anyone would want these, much less pay big bucks for them, but given what's passing for art over in Manhattan, I guess it's not so crazy. Do you ever go to the galleries? Hilarious!"

"Could we—"

"Oh. Sure." She gestures. "Be my guest. Take a look."

The canvases are all the same size, and they are not very big. It takes him a few minutes, but Marcus pulls each one out of its box and looks at it. There are indeed seventy-four of them. In the light from the window, their drab grays and off-whites take on an eerie glow, and the occasional jolt of color is startling. Each of them is a semi-abstract still life similar to Summer's toast and pins. There's an empty jar with a spoon in it on a table with what appears to be a postcard. There's a crumpled tissue, a paper clip, and a wine bottle. A wristwatch, a golf ball, and part of a birdcage. Candy wrapper, milk bottle, bit of carpet. Book, transistor radio, oil can.

"It's always three things."

"Oh, yeah," Anstice says, with an emphasis on the *Oh*. "Part of the general weirdness."

"There should be some pastels, too. And notebooks?"

Anstice goes to a shelf and pulls down another box. Inside are three notebooks. Leafing through them, Marcus sees endless pencil drawings of the sorts of things Whack painted—he pauses at a particularly beautiful and detailed broken cup that must be the one in Summer's painting. The two pastels are pressed flat in a folder: both portraits, both recognizably the same man, though in one he is young and, while not handsome, at least full of vitality, his cocky gaze aimed straight at the viewer. In the other he is wasted, sick, his eyes cast down as if he's just heard his death sentence.

"Christ."

"That's Joe."

"What did he die of?"

"I don't really know. If it wasn't AIDS, it sure looked like AIDS. It could have been cancer. Could have been a combination. He was from the Midwest, somewhere. Michigan? Arkansas? Someplace like that. I don't think he had any close relatives, and as far as I know his only friends were Hart and Emily. There was some kind of memorial service for him here, but I didn't go. To be honest, I didn't much like him. Nobody did, really. He was a surly bastard, and he refused to have any animals." She picks up a painting—candy wrapper, milk bottle, carpet—and carries it closer to the window.

"It's funny. I haven't looked at these in years. They aren't as bad as I remembered. Not that I know much about it. But they have a point of view, at least, don't they? I mean, they're not *bland*. And the guy could paint, I'll give him that." She puts the painting down, picks up another. "Jeez. I'll buy one if Emily gives me a decent enough price," she says, and laughs. "Who woulda thought it? I've been living down the hall from a gold mine."

Marcus reminds her that he could be wrong, maybe it's not the paintings his father wants. Or that Hart could be wrong, and they're not really worth much of anything. Anstice says, "That's where Wrzeszczynski comes in."

"I don't really know Wrzeszczynski." Wrzeszczynski is the periodontist who shares an office with Dr. Demand.

"Never had your gums done, eh? Lucky you."

They stack up the paintings again, lock up, and go back down the hall to Anstice's place. "Unfortunately, I know Wrzeszczynski only too well." She bares her teeth, revealing pricey pink gums. "Well, maybe not *unfortunately*. If I hadn't spent so much time in that office, I doubt that—well, you know." She shows her teeth again, this time in the shy smile of the elevator. "So. Okay. Wrzeszczynski owns a Whack. Maybe more than one. But I remember that he bought one, because Joe told me one time when he paid his rent. This was back in—oy, let me think— probably ten years ago, maybe longer. I doubt he paid much for it. Anyway, I'll give him a call. Maybe he knows something about their value nowadays. Or maybe he'd like to buy another one—who knows?" When they go in the door, the six cats come running, weaving around their legs. "Sit," Anstice says, and Marcus realizes she's talking to him. "Have some more tea. And a cookie—please. You didn't touch a one. Grandma Mullen's feelings would be hurt. Agnes is probably having a heart attack in her grave."

Marcus sits down again in the wing chair, and the tiger cat repositions itself on his lap as if they're old friends. Marcus realizes that his heart is pounding, and he is suddenly very hungry. He bites into a cookie. Anstice settles opposite him with a cordless phone. She hits a "memory" button and says into the receiver, "Renata, sweetie? It's Anstice Mullen. I need Dr. Wrzeszczynski, if he's there. I think it might be an emergency." She winks at Marcus. "Thanks, doll." While she's waiting, she puts her hand over the receiver. "Hey Marcus? Why didn't you just carry this story to Emily?"

Marcus finishes his cookie. It is the best cookie he has ever eaten. "I didn't want her to know Hart is my father."

"Well, I guess I can't blame you for that. But shouldn't she at least know that someone is gunning for her?"

"How could I tell Emily someone wants to kill her?"

Anstice looks at him reprovingly. "Jeez, Marcus, she's not a child."

"No, but—" He has to struggle to explain, and he feels ridiculous, since Anstice and Emily are both so much older than he is. He hates feeling like a kid. "She's—I don't know, she's sort of like an animal. I mean, innocent like that. Like this." He scratches the head of the cat on his lap, and the cat rubs vigorously against Marcus's fingers. "She lives in a world that just doesn't have people wanting to murder her in it."

"Well, Marcus, most of us live in a world that doesn't—Hey! Dr. Wrzeszczynski! It's Anstice. How are you?" There is a pause. "Well, yes, but it's not a dental emergency, it's an art emergency. I hate to take you away from those lovely bleeding gums, but I just need you to answer one quick question. What's with Joe Whack? I mean, what do you know about his paintings? My friend Marcus has just discovered a bunch of them." Another pause, and Anstice listens, looking at Marcus the way people do when they're on the phone. Her eyebrows go up, then down. From time to time she says, "Oh, *really*?" or "Wow," or "Hmmm." Marcus wants a second cookie, but hesitates. Anstice leans over, holds out the plate, and Marcus takes another. "Hmmm, wow," Anstice says, and raises her eyebrows again at Marcus. "Well, *that's* interesting. Sure, I think so. Just a second." She covers the receiver and says, "Wrzeszczynski wants to meet you in an hour. Can you be there?"

"What? Yes. Where?"

"He'll be there," she says into the receiver. "What's the— okay. Fabulous. Bye, Dr. W. Give my regards." She hangs up and says, "He's freaking out. He wants more Whacks. He says he's waited for this moment for years—somebody to call him up and tell him there might be more Whacks in this world. He's calling his friend Sztmkiewcz right now. Crazed Polish Whack collectors. God only knows what's going to happen to the poor slob in his chair, probably lying there with his gums gaping open."

Anstice stands up and begins walking around the room, stepping around cats, her hands clasped at her bosom.

"God, this is so exciting. Isn't it? Marcus—are you sure we shouldn't call Emily right this minute? I can get her on Sophie's cell. She could go talk to Wrzeszczynski. I mean, do we have a right to leave her out of it, at this point?"

"It's not that I want to leave her out." Marcus looks down, thinking, and sees that the legs of Anstice's desk end in dainty paws. "I just don't want to give her false hope," he says. "I'll do the legwork, find out what Wrzeszczynski knows, and pass it on to her. But I'm not telling her about Hart."

"God damn that guy, he should be in jail."

"Anstice, we can't tell her. And that means we can't tell anybody."

"No, no, no—you're right. She doesn't need to know that. I see what you mean about the animal thing, too."

"I always—" Marcus hesitates: He is often afraid, not without reason, that the things he thinks sound weird to other people. "I always think Emily is kind of like the last pigeon. You know, all the pigeons on the sidewalk fly away in a panic when a human comes along, but there's always one that just stays where it was, pecking at the stale bread crust, refusing to be moved, refusing to give up. Trusting that nothing bad will happen. She's like that, I think. So smart and plucky, and—well— sort of in her own world, but—you know—lovable."

"How very interesting." Anstice sits back down. "You have no idea." She stares intently at him. "And it's true, you do have the most amazing eyes."

Marcus looks down in embarrassment at the cat in his lap, who is managing to sleep and purr at the same time. Anstice, seeing she has made him uncomfortable, says, "Would you like another cookie? I have tons. Lately, I can't seem to stop baking things."

"No, thanks, really."

"Don't be polite. Take one home if you want to. Take two."

Marcus takes two cookies and slips them into his pocket. Anstice looks pleased.

"Okay, then, Marcus," she says. "This is the thing. Don't tell Wrzeszczynski exactly what she's got. Just say there may be some

Whacks out there somewhere—okay? And you want to know on behalf of a friend how they might be sold, what kind of prices they're bringing. Is there a gallery that carries his stuff? Or could your friend deal with private collectors? Don't say too much."

Marcus nods. "Where do I meet him?"

"His house in Greenpoint, 120 Java."

He imagines the scene in which he breaks it to Emily that she owns something of immense value and is no longer poor. He imagines Emily wearing expensive clothes like Anstice's and filling her loft with antiques and having caviar and champagne for dinner instead of poached eggs and leftover Halloween candy. This is an unexpectedly elusive vision.

At the door, Anstice says, as if reading his mind, "It seems crazy, doesn't it? And yet these things happen sometimes. Look at that guy—what's his name? That friend of Lamont's who had a piece of junk pottery that he wanted to get rid of, and he sold it on eBay, and it turned out to be rare Majolica and it was worth like fifty thousand dollars."

"I've heard about him. Fred something?"

"Right. Total loser. But fifty thou! And that's chicken feed compared to the Whacks."

"I hope so."

"Believe it."

They stand there looking at each other and then, spontaneously, a little shyly, they giggle and hug each other. Hugging Anstice is like curling up with a big down comforter, and it is also—he tells himself, with a shock—like hugging Summer.

"Marcus," she says into his shoulder. "You won't—I mean, one of these days we'll go public, but we're not quite—you know."

"As far as I'm concerned, the elevator ride has already ceased to exist," Marcus says, and as soon as he has left the building, this lie becomes true.

Marcus walks to Greenpoint by way of the Three Flags Deli on Franklin ("MOWIMY PO POLSKU/SE HABLA ESPANOL/WE SPEEK ENGLISH"), where he kills a few minutes with an egg-and-pepper sandwich. Then he walks up Java Street, munching a cookie. Like most Greenpoint streets, Java is lined with remodeled brownstones. Wrzeszczynski's place is squeezed between a faux-shingled Cape Codder and a pink stuccoed Italian villa. The house has kept its dignity, and then some: It's a meticulously preserved triumph of mid-nineteenth-century rowhouse architecture, cornices and corbeled and bay-windowed, the pocket front yard surrounded by a curlicued wrought-iron fence, the door, at the top of a row of fancily molded concrete steps, a heavy oak beveled-glass wonder.

When he rings the bell, there is a melodious peal, and then the door is opened by Wrzeszczynski himself.

Wrzeszczynski doesn't have the look of someone who has just rushed away from a bloody set of novocained gums. He is wearing a pristine white shirt with a silky gray tie, his Cary Grantish chin is clean-shaven, little wire spectacles sit firmly on the bridge of his long nose. Marcus is acutely conscious of the fact that not only is he wearing his grungiest jacket and the sweater with the hole in the sleeve from the Salvation Army, but that he is probably strewn with crumbs and cat hair.

"You're Marcus." Wrzeszczynski's handshake is trembly with excitement. "Come in."

Inside, it's like a set for a PBS series about upper-crust New York society at the turn of the twentieth century: Oriental carpets, stately mantelpiece, graceful staircase winding up. Wrzeszczynski turns to Marcus and says, "I will show you my Whacks, and then we can talk."

Marcus follows him up the stairs. The wall is lined with small photographs in ornate gold frames. The subjects must be old-country ancestors: a stout woman and a black-bearded man in front of a farmhouse, a studio photo of a woman with a spit curl and a large hat, a fat baby in rompers clutching a stuffed horse, a bewhiskered man in uniform with a baton tucked under one arm like Field Marshal Montgomery.

The upstairs hall is hung with paintings. "I have a lot of art," Wrzeszczynski says, waving a hand. The gesture is almost dismissive, though the art seems impressive to Marcus; even the frames look expensive. "I collect many things. But come this way." Wrzeszczynski has a faint accent, like an American actor might have in a movie where he plays a spy from some Eastern European country. "This is the Whack Room."

He leads Marcus into a back room on the second floor, a stark contrast to the rest of the house. Here, the walls are white, the molding has been removed, the floor is the bland blond expanse of an art gallery. Each of the four walls holds a painting: all, quite obviously, Whacks.

There is nothing else in the room.

Wrzeszczynski and Marcus make their way from painting to painting. A piece of cheese, a pack of matches, an empty green vase. ("This I bought in 1990, when Joe was just beginning this amazing series, when he was finding his true vision.") A pencil, a large mottled stone, a set of keys. ("Slightly later, from the early nineties.") A flashlight, a folded wallet, a bottle cap. ("Another from around the same time, perhaps my favorite.") The last is somewhat different: a roll of film, a small opened book, and the edge of a mirror in which can be glimpsed, very faintly, part of a face.

"And this one," Wrzeszczynski says. "This one—the only known self-portrait."

He and Marcus stare at it together, and Marcus can tell that the dentist is choked with emotion. He's almost afraid of what Wrzeszczynski will do when he learns about the two pastels. "Such a tantalizing piece," Wrzeszczynski says, and then breaks down and has to wipe his eyes. "The poor man," he says, shaking his head. "The poor, poor man. What a loss."

They stand there a few moments longer, and then Wrzeszczynski takes Marcus by the arm. "Come. We'll talk."

Wrzeszczynski closes the Whack Room door softly behind them as if they are leaving a chapel containing the Holy Presence, and they go back downstairs to the front room, which Marcus has trouble calling anything but a *parlor*: velvet upholstery, marble tabletops, tufted chairs. From a decanter on a small oval table, Wrzeszczynski pours amber liquid into delicately etched glasses. He passes one to Marcus; his hands are beautifully manicured, with elegant, dentisty fingers. He wears a signet ring and a Rolex.

"To Josef Wakowski," he says. They touch glasses, and Marcus drinks, and everything is suddenly clear.

"Wakowski," Marcus says. "Joe Whack was Polish."

"A great, great Polish patriot and a magnificent artist. When he died, he took a piece of the heart of all Poles. I revere his memory more than I can say."

Wrzeszczynski downs the stuff in his glass and pours another, and tells Marcus the story of Josef Wakowski, who was born to wealthy Polish immigrant parents in the American Midwest. He traveled to Poland in 1970 as a fiery, idealistic teenager, inspired by the riots that led eventually to the fall of Gomulka. He went to art school in Warsaw, and later became a member of Solidarity, working with the movement until 1982, when he barely escaped arrest, made his way into France, and finally returned to America, settling in Brooklyn and devoting himself to his art. Every cent he could spare, however, he sent back to Poland, to his friends in the movement.

"And he died," Wrzeszczynski says, his voice breaking. "He died from the effects of the poison gas the Communists used in 1981. He was never well again. A long, slow, agonizing death. But he kept painting, right up to the end. Those," he says, pointing upward to the Whack room, "they are memorials to life. To what is around us. To the small nothings that are what our lives are made of. To the beauty of the insignificant. To Poland. To America."

They drain their glasses—Marcus has no idea what he is drinking, except that it is fiery and strong—and then they sit in silence for a moment. Marcus tries to remember the man who picked up his father that time in Honesdale, waiting in the car with the motor running while Summer wept. He remembers, a few years later, his father telling him how unappreciated Whack was, how poor, how struggling. That must have been just before Whack found his vision and Wrzeszczynski found Whack.

Wrzeszczynski takes a deep breath, smiles, and refills their glasses. "And now," he says. "Please, Marcus. Tell me about these Whacks."

15

No garden, one dragoN

No garden, one dragoN

Emily is obsessed with Trollope's mother's dog.

Was he or was he not a Newfoundland?

It's a bright morning, she is done with gardening for the year, and she has to go to the unemployment office. Instead she is surfing the Internet. She has discovered that Byron was a Newfie nut and actually wrote an ode to his beloved dog, and that the faithful Nana in the original *Peter Pan* was a Newfie, but she has not uncovered a single fact about the Trollope family dogs.

Nor did she find anything at the Brooklyn library, where she went to check out Trollope biographies. The library had one of Frances and three of Anthony, thick tomes full of interesting Trollopiana (Trollope at Harrow, a classmate said, was "without exception, the most slovenly and dirty boy I ever met"), but no dog specifics. She was so frustrated after that wasted morning that she had to walk down the block to the Botanic Garden for what Marcus calls an RBI: Restorative Biophilic Interlude, and where the egret and the yellowing gingko leaves and the big jolly Hasidic families cheered her up. She sat on a bench in the Japanese pavilion leafing through a book she took out of the library about Anthony's brother Tom Trollope, who lived in Florence, gave Anthony the plot for *Doctor Thorne,* and wrote his memoirs before he died peacefully at eighty-two.

The various Trollope brothers are all over the place, but their mother's dog is nowhere to be found, and Emily is ready to admit defeat, at least for the moment. She types one more desperately narrowed search into Google: "FRANCES + TROLLOPE + ANTHONY + MOTHER + DOG + NEPTUNE + NEWFOUNDLAND" and gets no hits at all.

She sighs and logs off. Before the noon light bleaches everything out, she should get out on the streets, to photograph them for her new project, "Disappearing Brooklyn," the memorialization of the neighborhood before it dies. Death is on the way, she knows. There will come a day when the Polish meat markets and the Hispanic delis will be replaced by fast food outlets. When bookshops won't be called *ksiegarnias,* when trilingual signs like DRUGSTORE/FARMACIA/APTEKA will be taken down, and garish plastic DRUGMARTCO signs raised in their places.

As she gets up from her desk, the phone rings.

"Emily!"

"Gene Rae!"

"Emily, something horrible. Susan Skolnick was raped yesterday, right on her own rooftop."

"Oh shit." Emily sits down hard, Izzy on her head. "How horrible. Is she okay?"

"I think she's okay. She was putting her key in the lock, and he comes along with a knife and forces her up the stairs to the roof. But listen to this. She *killed* the guy. She pushed him over the side. And it was that guy Elliot—Lamont's friend? Who's subletting from Jeanette? He pulled a knife on her, and there was a struggle, and he went over the side into the street. Did you hear the sirens? It was about six o'clock, just when it got dark."

"No. I got home late last night. Holy shit."

"The place was a zoo. Cops all over the place, ambulance, TV, newspapers. And the whole neighborhood, of course."

"And Elliot Cobb? *Elliot Cobb* is the Williamsburg rapist?"

"*Was.* Four flights down—he apparently died instantly. They took Susan in for questioning, but they let her go. He was ID'd by two of the other victims, and the fingerprints on his knife matched what they already had. Plus, it turns out the guy had a record a mile long, including serving time for assault. Can you believe it? But didn't he always seem like a creep to you?"

When they hang up, Emily's heart is knocking against her chest.

She saw Susan just two days before, when she and Marcus were at the park with the dogs. Susan was sitting like a rock on her bench, and Emily had passed right by, turning her head as usual to avoid having to speak. Otto, she remembered, had made a move to go over to Susan—in Otto's worldview, every human is worth a sniff—and Emily had pulled on his leash, roughly, so that he looked up at her in reproach. When she and Marcus walked home, Susan was still there, sitting alone in the gathering dark.

Emily puts Izzy in his cage and goes to the window. The cool white light of morning is over. She will wait until the golden light of late afternoon. The hours in between are useless for her purposes. She puts on her red sweater and hoists her bag on her shoulder and walks up to Bedford Avenue. Maybe it's her imagination, but the street seems more cheerful and alive, the mood not celebratory, exactly, but lighthearted, no longer haunted by the specter of a rapist. Emily stops at the florist for a bouquet of daisies, and then at the bakery for a pound of Polish butter cookies. Isa in the bakery is beaming. "Emily! You heerd?" Isa is a plump, middle-aged, white-aproned grandmother of seven, with an accent. "Somebody got dat fawking rapist," she says with satisfaction.

In front of Susan's building, the only reminders of what happened are a stray strip of yellow crime-scene tape and a damp patch on the sidewalk where it was hosed down. Except for the customers in the laundromat across the street, no one is around. The Skolnicks' front yard—dry birdbath, pachysandra border, bits of trash—is weedy and neglected, but the trellis still bears half a dozen late roses, brilliantly pink against the drab asphalt siding. Emily rings the bell and hears it rasp somewhere deep in the house.

The front door is opened by Susan Skolnick. "I looked out the window to see who it was," she says. "I'm expecting this woman from the *Post*, and I'm just not up for it. I saw you had flowers, so I couldn't not let you in."

Emily holds them out with the box of cookies. "I'm so sorry about what happened, Susan. I won't keep you. I just wanted to see how you're doing."

Susan looks at her for a moment, then opens the door wider. "I was about to make tea. You want a cup?"

"Sure, tea would be great, but—"

"I'm all right. Come on in."

The Skolnick apartment is on the first floor, and it's a mess. There are piles of dead newspapers, clothes thrown over chairs, take-out containers on the coffee table, a headless Barbie and her wardrobe scattered across the living room floor. They go to the kitchen in back—sink full of dirty dishes, wastebasket long unemptied—and Susan puts the kettle on. While it boils, she sits down at the table across from Emily. Susan looks terrible: The area around her left eye is blackened, with yellowish edges, and she has a bloody gash below it, across her cheek. Her black hair hangs around her face, uncombed. She is still in her nightgown, with a cardigan pulled around it, haphazardly buttoned.

"Susan," Emily says, hesitantly, "shouldn't somebody look at that cut? Can I take you to the emergency room?"

"I don't want stitches. I want the scar, to remind me." Susan speaks with surprising firmness, but in a flat, harsh voice. "It's an odd feeling, to know that you killed someone."

This is not what Emily expected her to say, and she has no answer. But she doesn't need one. Susan continues, "I'm not saying it's a bad feeling. Just an odd one. Everything is different afterward. Nothing can ever, ever possibly be the same."

Susan's face is closed, blank, uninviting, but Emily asks, "How? How do you mean, different?"

"I'm different." Susan says. "I was attacked. He didn't rape me. I killed him before he could do it. He had the knife at my neck. I didn't care what happened, he wasn't going to do that to me. We struggled. I pushed him and he started to go over. I pushed him again. The last thing I saw was his horrible red prick, sticking up. And his pants down around his ankles, going over the side. His shoes. Big black shoes."

"My God, Susan."

"So you want to know how I'm different? The big difference is I'm leaving here. I'm gone."

"What? Gone?" Emily tries to remember other conversations she has had with Susan, back before Glenda was put down. She can't remember much, a bit of chitchat at a meeting about the garbage dump, an exchange at the Greenmarket about the ripeness of peaches, a few doggy encounters in the park. She barely knows this woman. "Gone where?"

"I was lying awake all night after the police left, thinking about this. Murray and Vanna aren't here, you know. They're in Chicago for a long weekend. Visiting Murray's parents."

"So you're alone here?"

"I wanted to be alone. They kept me at headquarters for hours until they decided not to charge me, and the whole time they're saying I shouldn't be left alone. I got back from the station at midnight, and then they were here half the night. The policewoman wanted to stay, my upstairs neighbor wanted to stay. They made me see a police psychiatrist. They brought a rabbi—can you imagine? They wanted me to get stitches, get some medication, call Murray, go stay with somebody. I said no, I just wanted to be alone. I was fine. I took a Valium. As soon as I get rid of this headache I'm out of here."

"But Susan—where are you going to go? Shouldn't you—?"

"Wait until I can think more clearly?" Susan rakes her fingers through her hair, then holds her skull between her hands like a basketball. The gash on her cheek has opened up, producing a few beads of blood. "That's what my therapist said. I called her this morning at five-thirty. I figured she'd give me some support, and I ended up hanging up on her. I didn't want to hear it. I already knew I was going. I'm leaving Murray. I've wanted to leave Murray for so long. Why haven't I gone before this? I don't know. It's all I think about. I go to work, I think about leaving Murray. I walk around the neighborhood, I think about leaving Murray. I go to the grocery store, I cook dinner, I read the paper, and all I can think about is leaving Murray. And now I know I can do it. Why?" She lets go of her head, drops her hands to her lap. "Because I'm different. I want to be gone when he gets home. I want him to walk into this house and find the new Susan—the gone Susan."

Little Vanna seems a glaring omission, but Emily doesn't ask. It's none of her business. But, of course, none of this is her business. She has the odd feeling that she's listening outside a door to Susan talking to herself. She asks, "Where will you go? What will you do?"

The kettle boils. Susan sets down two mugs, a milk carton, a sugar bowl, a bottle of Tylenol. The whole time, she is talking. "The summer I was eight years old," she says, "my family and I went to Maine for two weeks. We stayed at a fishing camp on a lake, and my father fished all day while my sister and my mother and I swam in the lake and walked down a dirt road to pick berries. We played Monopoly on the screened porch and read Nancy Drew books and drove into town to the general store where they sold homemade ice cream and fresh tomatoes and corn." Susan takes two Tylenol, gulping them down with water from the sink. Then she sits across from Emily and continues.

"At night we'd eat the fish my father caught. Then he and my mother and the people in the cabin next door stayed up late and played cards and drank beer while Linda and I lay awake on our cots upstairs and listened to them and fell asleep with the smell of the pine trees coming in the window. One morning I woke up early and saw a fox crossing the lawn. And there were turtles in one part of the lake, a little hidden cove where we played pirates.

And every morning for breakfast we had blueberry pancakes. And sometimes at night we'd build a fire and toast marshmallows." She stirs sugar into her tea. "And I've never forgotten it."

"That's where you're going?"

Susan nods. "Lake Schoodic."

"Susan, shouldn't you—?"

Susan wears the stony face Emily recognizes. "Lake Schoodic."

"But—"

"Lake Schoodic, Emily. Lake fucking Schoodic. I'm out of here."

"Well," Emily says. "Maine. I've been there a few times, to visit a college friend in Bangor. She lives on the Penobscot River. We saw some eagles, and once we drove to Bar Harbor for the day. I remember those tall, straight trees. And the big, rugged rocks along the coast. The days were warm, the nights were cool. It was wonderful."

Susan doesn't smile or speak, just sits there with her gashed, naked, set face.

Emily waits a moment. Then she says, "Well. Lake Schoodic?"

"Lake Schoodic."

Emily shrugs, raises her mug and touches Susan's. "Okay, then. Lake fucking Schoodic."

Susan laughs, finally, then winces, as if laughter hurts her bruised face. "Cheers."

After they have sipped their tea, Emily says, "Susan, I want to apologize . . ."

Susan holds up a hand. "Don't bother. It doesn't matter. I'm leaving here. All the crap that's happened here is nothing to me.

I have been utterly, cosmically, crazily unhappy in Williamsburg. All I want is to get out, and I don't want to take anything with me. Not even your apologies. I want as few memories as possible. I'm starting over. My therapist says my anger should be directed at the guy who attacked me, not at Murray. She went on and on about it. I told her I don't even know this guy— Elliot Cobb? I killed some guy named *Elliot Cobb*. Some creep who pulled a knife on me, who called me a bitch and stuck his hand in my crotch, who slashed me across the face to give himself a hard-on, who made me push him off the side of the building. Who the hell *was* he? I don't know, and I don't care. It's Murray Skolnick that I know."

Susan winds down abruptly and lapses into silence again.

Murray Skolnick, as far as Emily can remember him, is a short, brisk, balding guy who works in Manhattan in . . . what? Insurance or something? *Surely Susan's therapist is right,* Emily thinks, *it can't be healthy to suffer a trauma like this and then walk out on your family. To just hop in the car with a black eye and a livid welt on your face, to drive to a lake in Maine and hope to recapture the impossible innocence of being eight years old?* And yet, for some reason, Emily trusts Susan's decision. She wonders why this is so. Maybe it's because Susan has fought Elliot Cobb and beaten him. Elliot C., whom Emily instinctively saw as bad. Or maybe because it's what she should have done herself, left Hart before he left her. Or maybe it's just that she has seen Susan, too many times, walking the streets of Williamsburg like a ghost.

Maybe anything is better than that.

Susan doesn't move; she stares in the general direction of the overflowing wastebasket. Emily watches her for a full minute, during which Susan doesn't blink once. There is dirt under her nails, and her naked wedding ring finger bears a white, ring-shaped indentation. On the floor in a corner is Barbie's decapitated head, her blonde hair splayed out as if she's been the victim of some terrible crime. Emily finishes her tea, sets down her cup, and pushes back in her chair.

Susan doesn't seem to notice. She sits with her elbows on the table, her chin on her clasped hands, staring, as if in the mess of cereal boxes and soda cans she is having a vision of Lake Schoodic, and a little house on its shore. Binoculars by the window for watching the birds, a glider out on the porch, strips of fly paper, a pick-up truck, and a job at the general store or the tackle shop. Maybe, eventually, a dog. Maybe, someday, a man who isn't Murray.

Finally, Emily stands up and says, "I should probably get going, Susan. If you don't need anything." She leans down and puts an arm around Susan's shoulders. "Good luck. Take the cookies with you to Maine. They're really good."

"Thanks," Susan says without acknowledging the embrace. "I will. Do you mind letting yourself out?"

In front of the house, a little white car with the *New York Post* logo pulls up to the curb. Two women get out, one with a notebook, one with a camera. "If you're looking for Susan Skolnick," Emily says, "she's gone."

She takes Otto for his noontime walk, thinking about Maine.

Maine is nice in the summer, when New York—as Lamont once put it—is like being panted on by a huge dog with bad breath. But she was there once in winter, and the snow was deep, pure, and shiny where the sun melted the top of it and it froze. It was aloof and frightening, and Emily, from Berkeley, California, had never lived with that kind of snow. She cannot imagine settling in such a place: nature so big, people so small. Maine is moose, she thinks, and blizzards, and lakes iced over so thick you can dig holes in them and fish; Brooklyn is tiny humans putting their umbrellas up as they hurry out of the subways.

Still, she has never been forced to a rooftop at knifepoint. She has never shoved a man off a four-story building. It would change you, as Susan said, forever.

Emily stops back at the bakery for a cherry Danish, and then she stands in front of the video store eating it, staring into the face of Julia Roberts, displayed on a poster in the window. Her talk with Susan, it occurs to her, has made her feel distinctly unsettled. She has not been happy since Luther told her about Marcus's house in Honesdale. But she knows it's not just the prospect of losing Marcus. *Honesdale isn't that far away,* she tells herself. She has looked at it on the map, measured out distances. She tries to spare her sickly car any trips farther than Long Island, but once she gets a tune-up, she thinks she could make it to Honesdale for a visit. And she can write letters. He might even write back. And there's always the phone; she and Marcus have always talked on the phone; and there's no reason that should stop, except for the problem of fitting long-distance calls into her budget. But it can be done, she is sure. If her life were a film starring Julia Roberts, Julia would slip gamely into her outsize grin, find a way to stay in touch, and probably end up marrying Marcus in the end—a scene that would be neither ridiculous nor improbable but truly, magically heartwarming.

Her life is very far from cinematic, however, unless some

eccentric filmmaker decided to do a documentary called *Broken Dreams;* even then, the audience would have walked out long ago.

And the problem is not just Marcus.

It's her ailing car, her phone bill, the coming holiday dilemma, and the fact that she just spent the ten dollars that was supposed to get her through the weekend on bakery stuff and flowers. It's the garden of gray hair growing near her left ear. It's her failure to do what she came to New York so many years ago to do: make a career for herself as a photographer. She replays in her mind the uncomfortable fact that she has made exactly four thousand dollars this year from her photographs. Last year she made five. Next year . . . next year she may very well not make anything. Dr. Demand, her best customer, seems to have enough BREADS and TIMES, and he's run out of friends and relatives to give them to. The gallery that was supposed to call her back hasn't. As for her new idea, it will probably be a dead end, too. "Disappearing Brooklyn" indeed. Who cares? Good riddance. And what if Sophie should move to Mexico, lay her off, get hit by a bus?

She is in a mood, she knows: By tomorrow this mopey Emily will have faded away, and her usual optimistic self will be back. *Which just proves what a sap I am,* Emily thinks, but she can feel herself cheering up already. She struggles to remember some lines from W. H. Auden that she used to know, something about *the baffle of being,* and about how, even when there's not much joy to be had, *a laugh is less heartless than tears.* And her father's old joke: Q. *Why are cats like radio announcers? A: Wee paws for station identification.* And gray whales like to have their bellies tickled. And gorillas, she read, run out and dance in the rain.

And then there is Otto, who is looking up at her with a look that is half adoration, half impatience, thinking, *What is she doing? I am so sick of waiting fuh huh*. She always imagines Otto, who was born in the neighborhood, with a thick Brooklyn accent.

She bids good-bye to Julia Roberts, and she and Otto turn up North Third to Havemeyer, then go back along North Sixth, a route Otto particularly likes because it takes him past Reba's house. Sometimes Reba is sitting in the window watching the world go by, her little long-nosed face darting back and forth between the curtains. Sometimes she is even in the front yard, tied to the fence, barking. Today she is nowhere in sight, but Otto sniffs around the fence anyway. "Come on, Otto. You'll see her at the park in the morning," Emily says, and, after she gives him the last bite of her Danish, Otto lets himself be dragged away.

Emily likes the route too, because they walk by Marcus's building. When Marcus moves away, she thinks, she'll walk by here with Otto every day. A pilgrimage. Like when the Mona Lisa was stolen and people lined up at the Louvre to look at the bare wall—or like tourists at Ground Zero gazing into empty space— she will walk by 222 North Sixth and think her thoughts.

She resolves to do what she's been avoiding: call Marcus and ask him if what Luther told her is true. If Susan Skolnick can pull herself up out of a violent assault ending in death and desert her family and relocate to the Maine wilderness, Emily Lime can make a simple phone call to ask Marcus about his plans.

As she is thinking these things, Otto begins straining at the leash, whining, and there is Marcus just coming out of his front door. She lets Otto go, and he bounds up to Marcus, who squats down and says, "Hey boy, hey boy, what's up, boy, hey Otto, how's my doggie, how's my boy? Hey hey hey hey hey," and lets

Otto lick his face. Emily stands beaming at them—her two great loves—until Marcus straightens up and says, "You're just the person I wanted to see, Emily. I tried to call you last night, but I kept getting your voice mail."

"Sophie and I finished up for the season, and she took me out to dinner to celebrate. We got slightly looped on Mojitos at a Caribbean place in Brooklyn Heights. I didn't get home until after midnight."

"So how's Sophie?"

Emily looks with happiness at Marcus's sleek hair, green eyes, and bright blue sweater, the one she especially likes, with the hole in the sleeve. How is it that Marcus always looks exactly right? So perfectly himself. Always so *Marcus*.

"Sophie's good. We were looking at a guidebook to Greece. She's going next week. The more I looked at pictures of that blue water and those little white villages, the more Mojitos I needed to drink."

"You should go with her."

"Right. And Otto should go with Reba to Las Vegas and play the slots."

"Come on in," he says. "There's something I want to talk to you about."

Her heart sinks: *It's true, then.* She follows him inside, wondering what he will be like when he's living in Honesdale in his old house, mowing the lawn, calling the plumber, cleaning out the gutters. It seems an odd life for a twenty-one-year-old person. Shouldn't he be in college? Or bumming around Europe? It's one more thing she has never asked him: Why he is a dog-walker in Williamsburg, why he is doing with his life what he is doing. Why he always seems like someone who is vacationing on earth but is a little bit sorry he ever left home. If he moves away, her questions will never be answered. Letters, phone calls, even an occasional awkward visit—it's never the same, and she knows it. The gloom threatens to re-descend.

"Take a seat," Marcus says. "Can Otto have a biscuit?"

Otto, who has flopped on the rug, leaps up. "Is the Pope's dog Catholic?" Emily asks. "You said the B-word, Marcus. There's no way you can't give him a biscuit."

Otto takes his biscuit and chomps noisily. Emily doesn't see Marcus's living room very often; their Scrabble games and weird little dinners are usually at her loft, because of the animals and the river view. His place fascinates her in the same way Marcus does: *It's true to itself,* is the only way she can put it. The room she is sitting in contains very little: Marcus's comfy chair with its batik pillow, a less comfy but still okay chair for guests, a coffee table made from a wooden crate, and—because Marcus is thrifty and also believes in patronizing the public libraries—one bookcase. Emily has looked at Marcus's books many times; when she and Gene Rae were in college, their motto was: *By their books ye shall know them.* But Marcus is as unknowable from his books as he is from anything else. Six dictionaries, several poetry anthologies, a volume of Shakespeare's sonnets, *In the Shadow of Man,* a couple of mysteries, a shelf of obscure novels by Eastern European writers, two Oulipo collections, a stack of phone books, and a whole shelf of Victorian novels, heavy on Gissing and Eliot, including the fourteen Trollopes he has read since he joined the group.

Today the place looks different. "Is your spare, minimalist decorating ethic a little sparer than usual, Marcus?" she calls out to the kitchen. "Something seems to be missing."

"I took a load of stuff to the Salvation Army this morning."

"Oh." *Now he will tell her.* "Just weeding things out, or what?"

"Live lightly on the earth." *No, he won't, not yet.* "Do you want tea?"

"No, thanks. I just had tea with Susan Skolnick."

"You did? How is she?"

"You heard?"

"Yeah, everyone is talking about it."

"She's okay. She didn't get charged with anything. She's got a black eye and a horrible-looking cut, but she seems all right. I guess. I hope." Away from Susan's kitchen table, Emily isn't so sure. Maybe Susan is in shock. Maybe her idyllic vision of Lake Schoodic is a crazed reaction to struggling with a rapist and pushing him to his death. Should Emily have talked her out of it? Called 911? Stayed to look after her, even though Susan quite blatantly wanted her to leave? "The whole thing is heart-damping," she says, a word she learned back in college from Coleridge, and that seems particularly expressive.

"Yeah, but—" Marcus sticks his head around the kitchen doorway. "I don't want to say what I want to say."

"I know." They look at each other. "It's wrong to be glad of anyone's death."

"Lamont will be upset. They were sort of pals. Or something."

"Lamont will be upset that he was pals with a rapist."

"Yeah."

"Gene Rae panicked. She said she was going to buy a gun. I wonder if she did."

Marcus brings his tea and sits down in his chair across from the *Daily News* front page. "I wish I had an update on that," he says.

"You could call her."

"No, I mean the dogs. Seamus and Goalie. How are they doing? There ought to be a hotline you can call."

"1-800-CELEBDOG."

"What a great idea. Isn't it? Somebody could make money with that idea."

She can't stand it another minute. "Marcus? What do you want to tell me?"

"Ah. Yes." He leans back in his chair, smiling. "Emily, Emily, Emily," he says. "Something very good could be happening. But first tell me what you know about Joe Whack."

"Joe Whack?"

"The same. You remember him?"

"Of course I remember him. He lived downstairs from me. He was a painter. He—Marcus, why do you care? What's with Joe Whack? He's been dead for something like six years. Seven years."

"Do you know what he died of?"

"Haven't a clue. He was wasting away for as long as I knew him. He was hospitalized for the last month or so. We—I went to visit him. He was a skeleton. He wasn't really responding. Then he died. It was horrible."

She hasn't thought of Joe Whack in a while, but now she remembers him in the hospital bed, she and Hart on either side. He was unconscious. His breathing was loud. That was all he was: the sound of breathing, the up and down of his wasted chest.

Once, he opened his eyes briefly and moaned, and Emily went running for the nurse, and when they got back he was gone. Hart was holding his hand.

"Emily?" Marcus's voice is gentle, wary, as if he's going to ask her a trick question. "You have his paintings, don't you?"

"What? Yes. There's a bunch of stuff up in Anstice's storage closet. Why? Do you want one? Take one! Take two! I have no use for them. They're up there gathering dust, and they can gather dust forever, as far as I'm concerned."

She is upset. She doesn't want to talk about Joe Whack, whose dying moan stays in her mind along with the thought of Elliot C.'s broken body on the sidewalk, the gash across Susan's face, Marcus mowing his lawn in Honesdale, the blank space in the air across the river. *Why does life, with all its beauty, have to be so cruel?*

"Would you mind if I showed them to someone?"

"Who on earth wants to see them?"

"You know Wrzeszczynski, right?"

"Wrzeszczynski the periodontist? Of course. Everybody knows Wrzeszczynski. He has a very nice TIME. Dr. Demand bought him one, years ago."

"He's a big Whack fan."

"Joe has fans? How can Joe have fans? He was a recluse. He didn't like to show his stuff to anyone. He hardly ever tried to sell a painting, just piled them up. This is ridiculous, Marcus! I don't know what Wrzeszczynski said to you, but it's all bullshit."

Emily has devoted even less thought to the paintings than she has to Joe Whack—those odd little still lifes, meticulously painted but drab and slightly absurd: collections of disparate objects on bare tabletops. Hart left them behind when they got divorced. And why not? She couldn't imagine anyone wanting them, much less Hart, who probably filled his new place with the sickening paintings of dead things that he favored. The garish watercolors by the severed-limb guy. And the work of the wound-art woman, who became famous and, no doubt, made Hart a fortune. "What? He wants a Whack? Great. He can have the whole lot for fifty bucks."

The thought of the Whack paintings is making her irritable. Everything is making her irritable. What she really wants to do is go home and climb into bed with Otto.

"Emily." Marcus comes over and crouches down beside her. He takes her two hands in his. "Listen to me. Those paintings are worth money. A *lot* of money. Wrzeszczynski is a collector. So is his friend Sztmkiewcz."

"Ziggy Sztmkiewcz, with the restaurant?"

"Yep. And he's not all. There are others, and not only here. There are collectors in Poland. There's a woman in Paris, Wrzeszczynski says, and a guy in Czechoslovakia. Some of these people are seriously rich, and they'll pay good money for a Whack. They had no idea there were more Whacks. And you've got *seventy-four* of them."

"How do you know how many I've got?"

Marcus flushes. "Anstice let me into the storeroom."

"What? When? *Why?*"

"She heard from Wrzeszczynski that he's interested and remembered that you've got a bunch of them. I just kind of . . . happened along. I was there. Somehow I got involved."

But Emily isn't listening. She has finally taken in what Marcus said, that the Whacks are worth a lot of money. *Well, maybe it's true. Who ever said the art world wasn't crazy?* But then she thinks of Hart. *Aren't they his?* She tries to remember what their agreement was. It was so long ago, and she didn't care, she just signed things. The paintings meant nothing to her: She didn't even keep one to hang on her wall. She remembers that she wouldn't have even agreed to hang on to them if Anstice hadn't offered her storage space. . . . She vaguely recalls carting them up there and leaving them, their faces turned to the wall, and being glad they were gone. "I don't know if they belong to me or not."

"What do you mean?"

Emily stares down at Marcus's hands, which are wrapped around hers. The backs of his hands are scattered with fine black hairs. There are black hairs on his knuckles. His wrist bones stick out. She observes the effect of Marcus's bright blue sweater sleeve against her bright red sweater sleeve. She remembers Anstice's words, that she and Marcus could live together in perfect felicity, and feels the familiar pang of sorrow: *Marcus is leaving.* When is he going to tell her that? Or isn't he leaving, after all? Or isn't he going to tell her? Like his father, will he just go out for Thai and never return?

Marcus is waiting. "Joe gave the paintings to me and my ex-husband jointly," she says. "Or something. One day when he was getting really sick but was still functioning we all went to this notary at the bank in Greenpoint and signed some sort of document. I don't know if it was legal or not, it was just a thing Joe typed up. Then when we got divorced I agreed to store the paintings upstairs in Anstice's closet. I don't remember any of this very well."

"You have copies of these documents?"

"I don't know. I think so."

"Let's go over to your place. Let's look at them and find out."

But Emily doesn't want to move. She'll go home and look at the documents in question, which have resided unexamined in her filing cabinet all these years, and they will show that the paintings belong to Hart. Hart will sell them and become rich. She'll be poor all her life. Thanksgiving is coming; she has nowhere to go. And then Christmas, that blasted holiday that is the scourge of the poor. *Yonder peasant, who is he?* He's Emily Lime.

"Emily?"

"What?"

"Let's go."

"I don't have any faith in this, Marcus."

"So what? Let's go anyway." He smiles. "Says Marcus, what do you do? You do what Marcus says."

"That is such an old one."

Still smiling, he holds out a hand. Emily sighs and—only because he is Marcus—lets him haul her up out of the chair. They walk over to Emily's, Otto tugging ahead on the leash as if he knows something good is waiting for him there.

16

He lived as a devil, eH?

He lived as a devil, eH?

(Late November 2002)

A week before Thanksgiving, Marcus takes the subway into Manhattan and rings the bell at Hart's place on Crosby Street. He hasn't been there since he first came to New York, when Hart gave him a place to sleep, an overcoat, and some rent money. Back then, Crosby was a sleepy little street off the beaten path between SoHo and Little Italy, where a couple of struggling antique shops wavered precariously between the remains of rows of tenements. Hart's upstairs neighbor used to hang her laundry from the front window, and it was not unusual to see a rat sneaking out of a Dumpster. Now the buildings on either side bear LUXURY LOFTS signs, with information about square footage, Euro kitchens, and wine cellars. Hart's building is a rotten tooth in a mouthful of glossy caps, hanging on by a thread, and it is obvious that the dentists are panting, ready to pounce.

Marcus doesn't expect Hart to be awake yet—his father was never the early rising type—so he is surprised when Hart answers the door promptly, and realizes he's probably been up all night. At least he looks like he has. He looks, in fact, even more than usual, as if he hasn't slept for a week.

Hart greets Marcus with a combination of disapproval and barely suppressed agitation. "What's this about, anyway?" All Marcus said on the phone was that he had some news for him.

"Let's walk up to Starbucks." Marcus figures a public place will be best for breaking the news. "I'll buy you a coffee."

Hart is immediately suspicious. "Why?"

"I'll tell you about it when we get there."

They walk the block to Starbucks in silence. Winter is in the air, and the city seems clean and fragile in the cold. Marcus knows he will miss New York with all its lofts and rats and crazies and dangers and comforts. But this is not something he can think about now; he has given notice to his landlord. Thanks to the booming Williamsburg rental market, his apartment has already been rented to a pierced young artist couple, starting December first. The Salvation Army, in the person of a hulking Pole who spoke no English and who carried everything out single-handed and usually one-armed, has removed all of his furniture but his bed. Marcus has packed one suitcase and seven boxes, and wrapped the double-dog *Daily News* in brown paper.

He is planning to leave on the day after Thanksgiving.

Beside him Hart shivers; he has come out in his shirtsleeves. Marcus—who has the provincial idea (for which he has been ridiculed by, among others, Lamont and Luther) that when you go to Manhattan you dress better than you do in Brooklyn— wears the old tweed overcoat he got from Hart two years ago. He is also wearing his brown hemp shirt, and real shoes, not sneakers. Hart occasionally glances down at his son, but Marcus refuses to meet his eyes, which he knows are puzzled and probably angry.

He is in no hurry to tell Hart what he has to tell him. His father is not a temperate man. Marcus sees himself frantically explaining the tangled legalities while Hart is trying to strangle him with his bare hands.

Marcus and Hart both order the Colombian special of the day, and they both add cream and lots of sugar. His father, Marcus knows, has always used caffeine and sugar to wake himself up; back in the Honesdale days, the coffee would be waiting, along with homemade raisin scones or a hot stack of buttermilk pancakes, when Hart stumbled downstairs at noon. Summer used to brew it in a special Italian machine with a row of buttons and dials that looked like a cockpit. Marcus has never been much of a coffee-drinker, and he only likes it if it's milky and sweet enough so it tastes like hot coffee ice cream. Their motives are different, but—like their eye color and food tastes—it annoys him that it comes down to the same thing, and that anyone observing them as they take their tall paper cups to the milk-and-sugar station would think *Like father, like son.*

Marcus waits until they have doctored their coffees, scoped out the tables, found one in the window, and are sitting at it, and then he says, "So I didn't do it."

Hart takes a sip of coffee. "You didn't do it," he says calmly. "Well, it's not Thanksgiving yet."

"And I'm not going to do it."

"Really."

"Really."

"Then give me back my ten thousand dollars, you little punk."

Marcus reaches into his pocket and brings out a wad of bills with a rubber band around it. "Nine thousand four hundred."

Hart sets down his cup and takes it. His olive green eyes burn into Marcus's. Time stops in Starbucks. Nothing breaks the sudden silence, not even the whoosh of the coffee machines or the tapping of laptops. Their coffees sit on the table between them, weird twins. Finally, Hart says, "You little twerp," and lets out a massive sigh that sounds like he's been holding his breath for a long time. The laptops start up again, the murmur of conversation. "You chickened out."

"You could say that. You could also say, if you knew anything about the law, that if you'd had Emily Lime murdered, the paintings would have gone to her next of kin. In this case, to her mother out in California."

Hart looks at him blankly. "What are you talking about?"

"She owns them. You gave them to her when you got divorced."

"I didn't give them to her! She was just storing them. We own them jointly!"

"Sorry." Marcus shakes his head. "Wrong."

"Give me a break. What are you, a lawyer or a fucking dog-walker? What about Joe Whack? He *wanted* us to own them together! He typed up a document, and we had the damn thing notarized! Don't a dead man's wishes mean anything?"

"Dad. You gave up your claim. It's all there in black and white, signed and witnessed."

"Shit." Hart frowns into his coffee, then pulls himself together and glares at Marcus. "Do you want to tell me where you get all this legal expertise all of a sudden?"

"I've seen the documents."

Hart pounds his fist on the table, but softly, and he lowers his voice. "I'm asking you how do you *know* all this? What the hell do you know about the legal issues involved?"

This is the hard part. Marcus pauses before he answers. "I went to the lawyer's office with her. The same guy who drew up the divorce agreement. Lenkiewicz. He confirmed it. The paintings belong to Emily."

"Lenkiewicz. Jesus. Joe's lawyer." Hart slumps back in his chair. "You *told* her?"

"I didn't tell her what you asked me to do."

"So what are we talking about here, Marcus? Or did you just subtract a week out of my life expectancy for the fun of it?"

"We're talking about Joe Whack, Dad. The paintings. I told her what I knew. That the paintings are worth some money." Marcus waits for Hart to attack him, or at least start swearing at him, but he just sits glaring, and after a minute even the glare isn't there any more.

"I haven't looked at that fucking agreement in years. I didn't think I gave her the paintings. I had no place to store them, and she did. She got the washer, the dryer, the car. My Trollopes! Now this." His eyes narrow. "How did you find out?"

"I did some research. What does it matter?"

"It matters because I want to know how you fit into all this."

"Dad, you asked me to kill her! That's how I fit in."

"Keep your voice down."

"There was *no way* I was going to kill her!"

"I knew that."

"What?"

"Give me a *break,* Marcus. What do you take me for?" Hart looks at him the way he used to when he saw that Marcus had finished the Saturday *Times* crossword puzzle: *If the kid is so smart, why doesn't he know anything?* "I didn't know what to do. I needed the money. I thought you'd probably figure it out and come up with something. You always were a bright kid."

"Is that true?"

"I can't imagine how it happened, since you hardly ever went to school, but somewhere there are tests that prove it. I'm sure Summer saved them all—"

"I don't mean that. I mean you really *didn't* want me to do it?"

Hart squeezes out something that passes for a smile. "That's what I said, isn't it?" There is a pause. Hart sits staring into space, shaking his head slowly from side to side.

Marcus sips his coffee, thinking: *Can it be true, that the whole thing was some sort of test? Like a fairy tale, or an opera. Or is Hart simply lying to him?* He says, "Hey, Dad?"

Wearily, Hart looks at him. "What?"

Marcus studies his father's face: putty-colored, morose, unshaven. His hair is, as usual, greasy and in need of a wash, and it occurs to Marcus that maybe Hart greases it up with some kind of gel in an attempt to make himself look younger and hipper. Actually, Hart looks older than he did a couple of weeks ago at the Botanic Garden. He seems to be aging rapidly, like a bad case of time-lapse photography.

"Why did you want the money so badly?"

Hart sighs and gazes out the window, where people in down

coats and woolen hats are hustling down Crosby Street. An occasional snowflake drifts in the air. "This weather," he says. "I've had it with the weather. My arthritis is no joke. It gets worse every day. And my fucking allergies. I've got a chance to relocate to Tucson. A guy I know is out there, selling cowboy art. He wants me to go in with him. I need money for that." Hart sips at his coffee. "It's big, Marcus. The cowboy stuff. That whole market is crazy, out of control. There's money to be made. This guy needs a partner, I need a change."

Marcus has no desire to know exactly what cowboy art is, but he wishes he knew where, on the spectrum of absolute fact/wishful thinking/blatant lie, Hart's plan should go. He finds himself hoping devoutly that, if there is a deal, his father doesn't blow it, whatever it is. Hart two thousand miles away in the desert sounds perfect.

"So you closed your gallery here?"

"You could put it that way." Hart exposes his canine. "Let's just say it closed. Over a year ago now. And some of my more recent endeavors haven't panned out. I do believe my long and checkered career in the New York art scene is officially over, Marcus."

"What exactly have you been doing in the art world, anyway?" It's a question Marcus has always sensed he shouldn't ask. Now, though, the issues between him and his father have subtly shifted, and he feels he can ask Hart anything—not caring if he answers or not, just enjoying his slight edge. "Like all that time in Honesdale. And before you opened the gallery."

"You really want to know?"

"Sure," Marcus says. "Don't I?"

"Maybe you don't, but I'll tell you anyway. What the fuck.

I'm out of here, one way or another." He sits back in his chair and laces his fingers together; immediately his face seems younger, smoothed out, less crabbed and gloomy. "Okay. I can put it pretty simply. For years, I was a fence. Back in Honesdale Pee Ay? Fence."

"You mean—"

"You know what I mean. Stolen goods, Marcus. Art. There was a guy in Allentown I used to work with. Buy and sell. I had a couple of collectors in Manhattan, plus one guy in Cincinnati. Fanatics. They didn't care where they got the stuff."

"What kind of stuff?"

"Not the big boys. Little stuff. I wasn't about to fence the fucking Mona Lisa. Drawings, watercolors, prints. Keep it low-key, that's my motto."

"Did Summer know?"

Hart gives him a look. "Be serious, son. Did Summer know who was president? Did Summer know it was Wednesday?"

Marcus ponders this.

The evening before, he had called Tamarind to tell her he was coming home. Tamarind has checked on the house every week or so since Summer died, mowing the lawn, having the driveway plowed. It will need a new roof one of these days, she said. And a paint job. And he might want to have the chimney pointed. Otherwise, it seems all right. "She's still there," Tamarind said before they hung up. "The whole place is Summer. You'll see. The little labels she printed for all the drawers? Not even faded. There's one in the kitchen that says: CORKSCREW, CAN OPENER, MELON BALLER, CHEESE KNIVES, MARCUS'S AVOCADO PITS.

"I was always going to plant them," Marcus said.

"Well, there's a couple dozen in there, Marcus. Labeled. In her beautiful fancy printing. It's going to break your heart."

It already has. Marcus wants to defend his mother to Hart—*a true innocent,* Tamarind called her—but he knows it's pointless. He also doesn't want to hear Hart's response. Even now that she's dead, when Hart says Summer's name there's always a little sneer behind it, as if he never loved her at all.

Or else can't face it that he did and she's gone.

Or something.

Marcus realizes he doesn't want to figure it out any more. All he feels for his father is a kind of wounded aversion, the same thing he felt when he was ten years old. Now, though, it is overlaid with something resembling pity. "So why did you quit fencing, Dad?"

"Because I'm not really a crook at heart," Hart says. "At least I don't think I am. Maybe I was for a while. I'll be frank with you, Marcus. I liked the life. The crazy rich guys, the risk—the art, for Christ's sake. I liked the art. And I liked having money."

"I think probably everybody does."

Hart looks dubious. "I mean, I *really* liked having money."

"There's a difference between *liked* and *really liked*?"

"You bet there is. I do not thrive on poverty," he says in an aggrieved voice, as if it's something he can't help, like an allergy. "I'm a *thing* person. I like *things*. I like *good* things. When I lost the old Volvo in the divorce settlement, I bought myself a Porsche. Used, but still—Jesus, what a car!" Hart looks off into the distance, smiling reminiscently. "Silver-gray 911 Carrera Coupe. And how long did I have it? Exactly two years. Christ. It damn near killed me to sell that sucker. But what the hell." Hart spreads his hands in a gesture meant to encompass his helplessness in trying to explain why he abandoned the life of crime that enabled him to drive a Porsche for two years. "Things were getting hot. It was a question of survival. I didn't want to end up in jail."

Marcus is reminded of the scene in murder mysteries where the hero, in the clutches of the killer, gets him to brag about his crimes. "So what did you do next?"

"I had some pretty good money, and so I opened the gallery. A big mistake. The art market was in free fall, but I thought I could beat it. I thought Selma was foolproof. Merlin Wolf. Harold Watkins. You know their stuff? People loved that shit. Blood, gore, internal organs, roadkill. But I made some bad decisions. Maybe I'm not that good a judge of character. Whatever. Anyway, since then, I've been a kind of consultant, handling a guy who specializes in the Fauvists. Dufy, Vlaminck, Derain."

"A guy who—what? Steals them? You're fencing again?"

For a moment, Hart looks affronted. Then he shakes his head. "No. That's over. These are fakes, basically. For collectors. Not copies. Fakes. Half the time these dingbat collectors know exactly what they're getting, and they don't care. We've done pretty well with the Fauvist guys. You don't want to mess with the really famous names, even in this game. Only a fool would work with Picasso or Matisse. And drawings. Not paintings. Drawings and prints."

"So what happened?"

"What? Oh. Alex. My artist. The Michelangelo of fakes."

"Your faux Fauvist."

"Ha ha! Very good! Well, unfortunately, he's getting married. His girlfriend thinks he's a designer or something. So he had to go get a design job. He works for some magazine, designing their website. And he likes it! Says he's making a lot more money as a Web designer than a real artist. Can you imagine? We made one last deal a couple of months ago, to finance the wedding. Honeymoon in Thailand. The whole bit. We made a killing, actually. That money I gave you was part of my cut. A series of late Dufy drawings." He almost chuckles. "Very late."

"And that's it?"

"Yeah, that's it, laddie. The game is over. It's back to the old drawing board. Out to the desert, far from the madding fucking crowd."

Marcus looks across the table at his father. He has never, really, known what to think of Hart. He wasn't a good father, he was mean to Summer, he was never there when they needed him, and God only knows what happened with Phoebe. What does his father enjoy? What makes him happy? He realizes with a jolt that, after this morning, he may never see Hart again, and he has no idea how he feels about this possibility. Marcus takes another sip of his coffee, lets a few more seconds go by, and then he says, "Emily's giving you half."

"Come again?"

"She's in the process of selling the paintings, and she thinks you're entitled to half—morally, not legally. She says Joe would have wanted you to have it. You wouldn't believe how many people have tried to talk her out of it. Lawyers, friends, relatives. But she insists. Fifty-fifty, Pop, right down the middle."

"You're fucking with me."

"I am not fucking with you."

Hart looks at Marcus for a long time, then transfers his gaze back to the window. In the harsh, wintry light, his father seems old again, tired, broken, and Marcus wonders if he is entirely well. The bags under his eyes make him look degenerate but also infinitely sorrowful. Slowly, Hart reaches into his pocket, brings out a grimy handkerchief, blows his nose, and slowly, as if he's an action toy that needs new batteries, puts the handkerchief back. Then he sighs and says, "Jesus."

"It's going to be a lot of money."

"Who's handling it?"

"A gallery on Madison. A place that specializes in twentieth-century Eastern European art."

"They think they can sell the stuff?"

"Are you serious? They're going crazy."

"It's the Polacks, right?"

"Partly. Not entirely. The Polish angle is driving up the value, of course, but the paintings are pretty valuable commodities in their own right. I think it's pretty generally accepted that Whack was a modern master."

Hart shows a canine again, the old familiar sneer. "Where did you learn to talk the talk? All of a sudden the kid's an expert." His teeth are so stained by years of cigarettes and coffee that they are almost beautiful—striated in ivory and ocher, like some semi-precious stone. Marcus has the feeling that his father could use the services of both Dr. Demand and Dr. Wrzeszczynski.

"I've spent some time with this gallery guy. Emily did the negotiating, but I went with her."

"What? Negotiating?"

"Yeah. She was pretty cool. She's into it."

"Emily? Jesus." Hart lapses back into his melancholy staring, then rouses himself. "So who's the guy?"

"Mr. Ptak. Charles Ptak. He'll be getting in touch. There's some stuff you need to sign. He'll tell you all about it."

Hart puts his elbows on the table and sinks his head into his hands. "There was a thing in *Art News* a couple of months ago. Little bitty two paragraphs, about how he's hot in Poland, and there are only a dozen or so known paintings."

"Now there's over seventy."

"Plus those self-portraits."

"And some notebooks."

"I forgot about the notebooks." He lets out another sigh. "We grew up together, you know. In Wisconsin. Me and Joe Wakowski."

"He was gassed in Poland."

"Yeah." Hart looks up at Marcus again. "He wasn't even eighteen when he went over there. It was some kind of poison gas, when he was rioting against the Commies in Warsaw. When he got back, he was sick. Nobody knew what it was—just me, I think. I don't think he had any family left in the states. And he never told Emily. He hated pity. Hated people fussing over him. He always tried to pretend he was okay. He used to ride his bike around the neighborhood. He'd bike up to Greenpoint for pierogies and borscht—I think it was the only food he could keep down. Every time he sold a painting, he sent most of the money to some second cousin of his in Poland. After a while, though, he didn't want to sell them. Didn't have the energy or something, I don't know. Lost interest. He just got sicker and sicker. But he kept painting. Those strange still lifes. I always liked them. I thought they were great. But hardly anybody else did." Hart shakes his head and takes a sip of his coffee. "Shit. I wish he was alive to see this money. He was my best friend."

"I know." *Your only friend,* Marcus thinks, and wonders

why Joe had liked Hart. Maybe the same reason Emily did, whatever that was.

"So—let me get this straight. She's selling the paintings."

"There's going to be a small exhibit after Christmas. A dozen of the paintings, to whet the appetite. That was Emily's idea, actually, but Ptak really went for it. Then, probably in the spring, a bigger one. I'd say by summertime you'll have some real cash."

"Real cash. What does that mean?"

"Talk to Ptak. What about this guy in Tucson? Can he wait a few months?"

"I don't know. I'll call him," Hart says, but he is clearly thinking about something else, frowning, pursing his lips, tapping his fingers on the table.

Marcus wonders why these things are the traditional signs of impatient thought. In more primitive periods of human existence, were they warnings to an enemy that those fingers might pick up a rock or a club? That those eyes were narrowed in order to focus in on someone's jugular?

"Hey, Marcus?" Hart says finally, and his tone is slightly belligerent. "Let me ask you a question. Were you one of the people who tried to talk her out of it?"

"No." Marcus is surprised that his father cares. He is also pretty certain that, if he had told Emily about Hart's evil intentions toward her, she wouldn't have changed her mind. She would have laughed and said that was ridiculous. "I agreed with her," he says. "That Joe would have wanted it."

"Do you get a cut or anything?"

"No."

Hart sighs. "Then here. Take this." He picks up the stack of money and counts out some bills. A woman at the next table glances over at them, wide-eyed. "Take half. And if I really do get some money out of this, I'll send you a check."

"You don't have to do that, Dad." Marcus takes the cash and stows it in his shirt pocket. He looks at the woman, and her gaze falls quickly back to her laptop.

"How is she, anyway?"

"Emily?"

"Yeah. She doing okay?"

"She is now. She was having a pretty tough time until this came along."

"Hah. Well." Marcus waits for more questions. He is reluctant to tell Hart anything much about Emily: The image has never left him of the innocent princess and the ravening beast. But Hart only says, "I'm glad it's working out for her," and after another moment, "Tell her I said that. Okay?"

"Sure," Marcus lies.

They sit for another minute in silence. Marcus can feel the lump of bills against his heart. For the second time since that fateful morning when Hart told him to keep the change from the ten, his father has given him money out of sheer niceness, no other reason—well, niceness and guilt, most likely. Still, it's a gesture Marcus appreciates. Suddenly he remembers that he has a dog at home who needs to be taken out, and he gets up and puts on his coat. "I gotta go."

"What?"

"I've got to get home."

"Hey, you don't have a piece of gum, do you, Marcus?"

"No."

"I'm trying to give up smoking."

"Oh. Good. That's great." Marcus sticks out his hand. "Well. Good luck, Dad. With everything."

"Thank you, son."

Marcus is tempted to tell his father he's leaving town, going back to the precise spot Hart advised him to get out of, when he has a sudden alarming premonition of Hart turning up on the doorstep, just as he used to, and so he keeps his mouth shut. What's the point? They shake hands. He half-expects his father to say something else, but Hart is still Hart and he doesn't, and finally Marcus goes out into the cold.

On his way to the subway, he looks back.

Through the window he can see his father, still sitting at the table, slowly dragging out his handkerchief, and slowly blowing his nose.

17

Mix a maxiM

Mix a maxiM

"The heel is a nice height," says the saleswoman. "Very becoming to your slender foot."

Emily is in a store on Bleecker Street trying to decide between the red shoes with black trim and the black shoes with red trim. The shoes cost more than she has spent on clothes in the last five years, and she wants both pairs. *Of course, the saleswoman would say that to anyone....* On the other hand, never have her feet—which though long are indeed slender—looked more fetching.

She puts a red and black shoe on her left foot and a black and red shoe on her right. If the next person who comes in the door is a man, the left foot will win, if it's a woman, the right. If it's a transvestite, she gets to buy both. If it's a nun, she can't have either.

No one comes in.

Emily walks awkwardly around the store admiring her mismatched feet in various mirrors. Besides the shoes, she is wearing her old green jacket over her red sweater and jeans. The shoes make her clothes look cheesy. She has nothing that could possibly live up to these shoes, which she intends to wear on Thanksgiving, three days away. She will have to go to trendy boutiques in SoHo and discount outlets on Sixth Avenue and vast department stores and boring chains. She will have to buy a black silk dress, or satin pants, or a white cashmere sweater like Anstice's.

Then she will need stockings or something. Tights? A coat. Gloves. Hat? Two hats? A bracelet? An ankle bracelet? A nose ring? A feather boa? A studded leather bustier? A mink coat? A diamond tiara?

She wonders where it will all end.

"How are you doing? Are they comfortable?"

The saleswoman has thick shiny brown hair that cascades down her back like something to eat—toffee, maybe, or barbecue sauce. She wears a dress that Emily suspects she herself could never afford, even with Dr. W's check. Emily wonders, not for the first time, where salespeople get their clothes. *Do designers donate clothes, just for the exposure? Is it only people with trust funds who work as clerks in stores?*

"Would you like me to get you the next size?"

"Oh—no, no, they're fine. I'm just trying to decide."

"Both styles look very well on you."

The door opens: A man and a woman are coming in together. Emily holds her breath. They stand at the door. The woman, who is young and hip and wearing a plaid miniskirt, a knit cap, leg-warmers, and white tights, says, "Are you, like, *totally* sure about this?"

"Positive," the man says, and gives her an affectionate little push. She enters the store ahead of him. Emily turns to the clerk, "I'll take the black," she says. But the clerk is already focused on the young couple. "Can we look at those fabulous satin shoes in the window? Size six." The clerk disappears into the back room. The young couple stands, arms entwined, gazing at a display of what looks like pastel bowling shoes. She puts her head on his shoulder. He pats her ass. The clerk returns. The woman marches around the store in the black satin sandals, which are composed of straps and rhinestones, with a few feathers.

"Very New Year's Eve," the clerk says.

"Oh, *totally!*"

"*Sans* tights, of course."

"I thought fishnet."

"Perfecto."

Emily feels old, dowdy, and insecure, but eventually she is allowed to buy her shoes. She pays in cash, a stack of twenties from the ATM that the salesclerk studies suspiciously before she rings up the sale. When the transaction is finished, Emily is demoralized. She feels she can't shop any more. Besides, what she really wants now is a miniskirt, tights, and leg-warmers.

Or maybe black satin sandals?

She is gathering her bags—in her odyssey down Bleecker Street she has also bought a desk lamp, a picture frame, and a purple silk scarf that she realized too late clashes with everything she owns—when the young woman in the legwarmers says, "I love your zipper."

"What? My—" Her wrist-zipper is visible where the sleeve of her sweater has hiked up. Her first impulse is to cover it, but she stops. *A compliment!* No one has complimented her on the zipper since she was in her twenties, much less a chic person who buys black satin pumps and does not even appear to be stoned. "Oh," she says. "Thank you."

"That is so cool."

"A youthful folly," Emily says airily.

"But so clever!" The woman's huge brown eyes beam on Emily. "Look, Jeremy, is that cute or what?"

"Totally."

Emily smiles at them and sails out of the store with her bundles, feeling so psyched that she stops at a boutique on the next block and buys a skirt and a pair of earrings. Emily is not used to shopping; mostly, she buys her clothes at the Salvation Army. Occasionally, when she has sold a TIME or a BREAD, she goes to Dee & Dee on Manhattan Avenue in search of something no human has worn before. Her green jacket is from there: $19.95. She has also, on her far-flung photography trips, stopped from time to time at a mall. She still has a strange pink fleece vest from the Target upstate on Route 17, and her red turtleneck sweater is from a Gap on Long Island.

But clothes are not a priority. This is not only because she rarely has any money; it also has to do with what she thinks is a sad, shameful, Proustian truth about human nature, or at least about herself: People crave what they can't have. As soon as the thing they crave is secure in their possession, they wonder why they ever wanted it.

She is already having doubts about the shoes.

On the other hand, Gene Rae once told her, "Emily, you're cute enough that you can wear any old thing. Trust me. Don't waste your time stressing out about clothes." Emily was twenty-three when Gene Rae said this, but she has never forgotten it.

Though it may no longer be true, she still calls it up like a magic spell on the days when she opens her closet door and teeters on the brink of despair.

She stops in a café on West Tenth Street for a cup of tea, to calm down. The thrill of buying retail has left her confused but elated, with a subtle overtone of sheer panic. The café is famous for its cupcakes, and she succumbs to a velvety chocolate one with a crown of pink frosting. It is another indulgence that, even as she eats it in three bites and orders a second one, she can't believe she is actually giving in to. She wishes Gene Rae were with her, or Lamont, someone who would pat her soothingly, tell her it's okay, people do this all the time, spend money on cupcakes and shoes. Someone who would tell her to chill when she remembers that Byron wrote in his diary one spring day in 1821, "I have added eating to my family of vices."

Or that Van Gogh's last words were, "What's the use?"

Emily does her deep breathing. It helps. The tea helps. She takes her new shoes out of their box: She still likes them, and that helps. She puts on the earrings, which dangle nicely. Her blood pressure declines, her heartbeat slows, her diaphragm unknots. She sits in the window of the café thinking happily about the craziness of an art market that can inflate the artistic talent of Joe Whack, a man she never liked, and make people compare him to Chardin and the late Manet. That and about what her mother calls the "staggering stupidity" of Tab Hartwell, who gave away seventy-four paintings because he didn't want to pay somebody to move them. A stupidity that Emily finds touching and rather sweet, in a way Hart in person never was. Then in a moment of truly amazing synchronicity she looks out the window and sees her ex-husband walking down West Tenth Street.

He is bare-headed and looks cold. His hands are thrust deep into the pockets of his jacket, and his hair, which seems thick with gray and badly in need of cutting, flies around his head. She hasn't seen Hart since divorce court, six years ago. He seems to be talking to himself, but as he gets closer she realizes he is chewing gum. She is poised between relief (that her ex-husband, with whom she is on the point of sharing many thousands of dollars, has not become so dotty that he talks to himself) and revulsion (her ex-husband is a man who chews gum with his mouth open).

Emily sits and watches him, almost willing him to glance in the window and see her, but he looks straight ahead, and his face is grim. His eyes seem sunken, his lips thinned out as if he has worn a perpetual look of disgust all these years. She considers rapping on the window, even dashing out after him, so she can admit, after all this time, that maybe Joe Whack wasn't such a bad guy after all and—by the way—isn't it great about the paintings. But she can see that Hart is no longer the man who went out for Thai food and never returned. Also, she is no longer the bereft wife weeping into his discarded shirt.

She has no idea who Hart is; maybe she never did. She realizes she has no connection with the man in the leather jacket, and suddenly, despite the cupcakes and the shopping bags, she feels light and unencumbered. Glimpsing her ex-husband striding down the street like any other person, just some aging guy in need of a haircut, reminds her that she needs to answer to no one but a dog and a bird. And that she's been thinking she might go over to the Pet Pound and pick out a kitten.

Because what Proust meant really applies only to people. Animals never disappoint, and, actually, she is pretty sure the shoes won't, either.

Emily finishes her tea and hauls her bundles out onto West Tenth Street. She stands there a moment breathing deeply. The sky is white, stark, wintry. Down the street a car engine struggles to start, like someone coughing. A pants-suited woman with a briefcase passes her, a mumbling man with a shopping cart, a black teenager in falling-down pants, a girl carrying a large plant, an Indian woman in a delicate pink sari and a sturdy wool hat, a pair of tourists with a guidebook. "Can you tell us where we can find West Eleventh Street?" they ask Emily, and when she explains to them that there are two streets between West Tenth and West Eleventh they chuckle affectionately. "What a city!"

Emily turns back down Bleecker, where there is a shop that sells Japanese pottery. She has always coveted a set of black Japanese dishes. She imagines serving Thanksgiving dinner to Marcus on a black plate.

This reminds her that Marcus is leaving.

He finally made his confession on the L train, when they were on their way back to Brooklyn after seeing Mr. Ptak at the gallery. "It's not that I don't like it here," he said. "I like it very much. I like everything. I even like this crummy train."

"You have so many friends, Marcus," Emily said. "Everyone is so fond of you. You'll leave a huge hole in the Trollope Group. Rumpy and Reba will miss you so much. And Elvis. And Otto. You know Otto thinks you're God."

Marcus smiled. "Dog saw I was god."

"Yes. He did."

"Nah. He thinks you're God. He thinks I'm St. Athanasius or somebody."

"The point is—oh, Marcus, everyone here loves you." The

word *love* almost made her cry, but she recovered. "And I'll bet you don't even know anyone in Honesdale any more."

"No, I don't. Not really." Marcus didn't look happy, but Emily knew he was, it was just that he knew she wasn't. "I don't really know how to explain it, Emily, the feeling that I'm in exile here. I never meant to be in New York forever. Honesdale, Pennsylvania is where I need to be. I always think of it as *Homesdale*. It's my home. My mother died there. My dog is buried there. I lived there all my life. It's my oldest friend, that house, that town. I lost a chunk of my life, and I need to get it back, and I feel that Honesdale can give it to me."

"But I lived in Berkeley all my life," Emily said. "My mother is out there. A lot of old friends. Those brown hills, everything new, the morning fog." The train stopped at First Avenue, people got off, people got on. A woman with a baby squeezed in next to Emily, so that she had to move closer to Marcus. She would have liked to clutch his arm, rest her head on his shoulder, stroke his overcoat—the funny, too-big tweed overcoat he'd had since she met him—make some gesture of affection, of bereavement. She did none of these things. She said, in her most reasonable voice—did she really think she'd talk him out of it?—"I still miss California, and I probably always will. But I don't want to go back."

"Well." Marcus paused. The train was always especially noisy as it raced through the tunnel under the river to Brooklyn, and it was hard to catch what he said, but it seemed to be, "You've had other things. I've only had Honesdale."

I've only had Honesdale.

Emily still doesn't understand what that could possibly mean. She knows he misses the country—woods, trees, animals.

There are eagles in that part of the state, he has told her. Many kinds of hawks. He even used to like the cows, he said, down the road at the dairy farm, even though they never did anything. He liked touching their pink snouts, feeling their warm breath on his hand. Occasionally one would let out a moo. Made my day, Marcus said.

She remembers Susan Skolnick, who has packed up and gone to Maine. And Luther and Lamont have flown to Italy to spend some time with their friend Silvio, who lives in a converted fourteenth-century convent. "It kills us both to miss the Trollope group," Luther told her. "But we need to do something drastic. We're pretty wrecked after all this." He meant Lamont, and Elliot C. "You know how there are places that can kind of fix you up? Bang you back together? That's Silvio's nunnery."

Emily knows—people might tell her she's wrong, but she knows it—that even if they write letters, send E-mails, talk on the phone, Marcus will be gone just as surely as her father is gone. Her old friend Jack who died in a car crash. Her dog Harry, and the cats of her childhood. People she has sat next to on the subway, on airplanes. Girls she went to kindergarten with. Her old boyfriends Peter, Kevin, Gil Harrison. Jeffrey and Neil from high school. The tourists who just asked her directions. Joe Whack, Crystal who used to wait tables at the Tragedy Club, the second-cousins in Tennessee she met at her father's funeral, the roommate she and Gene Rae didn't like, the clerk in the shoe store, Milo's friend Porter who moved to Australia, the blond waitress who brought her a cupcake on a blue plate, her grandma who died of cancer, her mother's old boyfriend Fred Campbell, her fourth-grade teacher whose name she has forgotten, the girl who got raped and went home to Poland . . .

Emily had gone out early that morning, before her shopping spree, with her camera. There was not much traffic, so she was able to get some pristine shots of the old houses on Berry Street, and, miraculously, she even found a DOG: specifically, LOST DOG on a hand-lettered flyer tacked to a post. It was illuminated by a patch of raw winter sunlight on North Fifth Street. She snapped her photo and then had a moment of panic: *Everything is slipping away*. Someone's dog was lost. The Japanese restaurant was going out of business. Mrs. Buzik was moving to Long Island. Overhead, geese in their strict formation were honking dismally, heading for the open ocean and the long flight south. . . . She thought of Marcus with his furry hair and funny smile. Then, because she was so close, she walked over to his place on North Sixth.

Ever since he told her he was leaving, she has wanted to take his photograph. She knows he would say okay if she asked, but she also knows he wouldn't like it, and that his reluctance would show in the photograph, and that's not the way she wants to remember him: looking trapped, with a fake grin. The only picture she'll ever have is Hart's old photo of Marcus, age ten, with the phone book and the front end of his dog. Then she got an idea: She zoomed in on Marcus's doorbell, where a little card still said MARCUS MEAD in his distinctive printing—each M with its flag, the S with its flourishes—and quickly, before he could come out and catch her, snapped a picture. *Everything is slipping away*, she thought. *Except what I can save.*

After Emily buys the Japanese dishes she splurges on a taxi back to Williamsburg because her packages are so unwieldy. When she gets home, she sits down to finish *Miss Mackenzie,* before the Trollope group meets the following night. She is particularly struck by the last sentence of the novel, in which Trollope assures his readers that his heroine Miss Mackenzie, now Lady Ball, accepts the life that comes her way "thankfully, quietly, and with an enduring satisfaction, as it became such a woman to do."

18

Now eve, we're here. we've woN

Now eve, we're here.
we've woN

It's Thanksgiving, and Emily is wearing her new shoes, her new skirt, her silver cuff bracelet, and a black silk shirt she has had since 1997. Marcus is wearing his one good shirt and his real shoes, not sneakers. He has walked two sets of dogs, fed a total of eight cats, and picked up two orders of vegetarian peanut curry at Thai Café on his way to Emily's loft. They have finished the curry and one bottle from Emily's brand-new case of champagne. They are now embarked on a second bottle, along with Grandma Mullen's cook's apple pie, baked by Anstice before she left for a clandestine weekend with Dr. Demand. The champagne has been poured into Emily's old champagne glasses, the thick and heavy ones from Dee & Dee on Manhattan Avenue. But the meal has been served on Emily's new black Japanese dishes.

When they first sat down to their Thanksgiving dinner, Emily told Marcus she had to make a terrible confession: She went shopping in Manhattan. She bought the Japanese dishes and the shoes and a desk lamp and a bunch of other stuff, and when she got home she had the champagne delivered from the liquor store in Greenpoint, and then she went on the Web and ordered four CDs and some books.

Marcus didn't tell her he knew all this. He had run into Gene Rae on Bedford Avenue, and she told him that when Emily got home from shopping she called her and said, quite seriously, "Help me, Gene Rae. I'm out of control."

Marcus is nursing his sixth glass of champagne. Emily sits across the table, touching the rim of the small squarish Japanese plate in front of her as if she still can't believe she owns it. Marcus is meditating on the bizarre fact that the champagne, the black dishes, Emily's chic new shoes, even Emily's crazy guilt, are all the direct result of his disreputable father's wish to get hold of some money so he can relocate to Arizona and sell cowboy art. *If Hart hadn't asked me to kill Emily, would any of this have happened?* In other words, is his father a very bad man but a very good wizard?

Out of evil, Marcus thinks tipsily, has come good. And since the evil is such a lame, shoddy kind of evil, arising out of bad judgment, cold New York winters, and a weak understanding of the intricacies of property law, maybe it's not evil at all when the good (and here he looks at Emily's face, where the slow smile comes and goes) is indisputably of such a high caliber.

During dinner, they have thoroughly discussed Emily's finances, and Marcus's flat refusal to take a cut for his role in the Whack drama, and her decision to give Hart half of everything she takes in. Marcus has given up trying to convince her that a third would be enough. She insists Joe Whack would have wanted them to split it, and Marcus has to admit this is probably true. "I want to be like Miss Mackenzie," she says, "who knew that the right thing to do was give half her fortune to her brother's widow."

Thanks to the payment from Dr. Wrzeszczynski for four Whacks—Emily gave him a deal, before the paintings hit the market—Emily's bank account is fat and happy. And when she had dinner with Wrzeszczyński and his wife on Java Street, they presented her, as part of the transaction, with an eight-by-ten view camera once owned by Stieglitz, who was a friend of Mrs. Wrzeszczynski's father. Emily thinks she might start collecting old cameras to use in her "Disappearing Brooklyn" series. One of Dr. Wrzeszczynski's patients is a prominent Manhattan editor, born in Greenpoint, who comes over twice a year on the L train to have his gums attended to, and Wrzeszczynski thinks he might be interested in doing a book. Emily has an appointment with him next week, right after she sees the financial planner Anstice recommended.

"Marcus, are you asleep?"

"No."

She pours more champagne for each of them and says, "Isn't it funny about the two thousands?"

"The two thousand whats?"

"Years." Her voice is dreamy, over-champagned, and slowly, as if in a trance, she cuts herself a third piece of pie and drops a spoonful of ice cream on top of it. "The twenty-first century is not really working, is it? I mean—we're about to hit 2003, and we're actually going to call it two thousand and three. It's as if we used to say *one thousand nine hundred and ninety nine.* Like when you write out the amount on a check in words."

"You mean it's time to just call it *three.*"

"Exactly. It is now *two.* In a little over a month it will be *three.* That is all we need."

"So simple."

"So economical. Even elegant." Emily almost eats a bite of ice cream and pie, but doesn't. "Let's make a pact," she says. "Maybe we can start a trend. Like everyone lighting just one little candle. You light one in Honesdale, I'll light one here."

They clink glasses. "To three."

"To three."

"What did you think of your last Trollope evening?" Emily asks.

"*Miss Mackenzie,* or the group?"

"Group. I feel the need for some gossip."

"It was funny without Luther and Lamont."

"Yeah. I hope Italy will help."

"The Elliot thing wasn't good."

"No. It wasn't good."

"I still don't know what to say about that. Maybe it's one of those things that there is no right way to think of, and the best way to deal with it is to forget it." Marcus smiles. "So here's another thing. Did you notice the way Pat insisted the next book has to be *Ralph the Heir?*"

"What?"

"Didn't she sound maternal? I think she's pregnant."

"Get outta here!"

"You wait."

"You're so full of it. The oracle of Honesdale." Emily props up her head in one hand and looks at Marcus through half-closed eyes. "Tell me about Honesdale, Marcus. Tell me a story. Tell me more about your dog."

"You already know about my dog."

"I know her name was Phoebe, she was killed when you weren't there, your father buried her in the woods."

"That's all there is to say."

"Is it?"

Marcus wants to say that he knows his father used to be her husband. He can't believe he hasn't said this yet, and he has a feeling she knows he knows. But does she know he knows she knows? During their long discussions about the Whacks, the legalities, and the amount of money Emily should share with Hart, she has never once called him by name: He is *him*, he is *my husband*, he is *my ex*. Mr. X, Marcus thinks. X marks the monster. Or does it?

"Yes," he says. "That's all there is."

"Then let me tell you about my dog Harry." Emily rouses herself and sits up straight in her chair. "Harry was my first dog. My parents always had cats. I love cats. But I told myself I wouldn't have any for a while. I had just come to New York. I saw myself as a solitary predator, sneaking up on the city and taking its picture. A woman with a camera, not a woman with a cat, much less a dog. No ties. Then I met Harry over at the Pet Pound, and I fell instantly in love with him. It was so strange—like Swann and Odette. He wasn't even my type. I was a cat person who looked into the eyes of that scruffy little mutt and became a dog person. Converted in an instant, like St. Paul on the road to Damascus. I became a Harryite." She sighs. "So. Then I got married. No—then I got Izzy. And *then* I got married. And one evening my husband had to walk Harry because I was sick in bed with the flu. Very bad. I had such a high fever Izzy refused to sit on my head. So my ex took Harry out. A rainy night. And when he came back he said Harry had been hit by a car, he was walking him off the leash, the dog ran into the road, he was dead. He took Harry over to the vet to be—you know. Cremated. He asked if we wanted the ashes, and he said no, that was okay, we didn't want the ashes, he thought it would be too upsetting for me."

Marcus doesn't say anything. While Emily talks, he has been sipping steadily at his champagne, and he has just passed quietly over into drunkenness. But he is listening, and he has no trouble sorting out the *he*'s in the story.

"I never saw him again. And I always—this will sound terrible—I always kind of wondered. My ex didn't like Harry, and Harry didn't like him. Harry bit him once. And he said I spoiled Harry, but what he meant was I paid more attention to Harry sometimes than I did to him. And that was true, I know, partly because—because that's sort of the way I am, and partly because Harry was more interesting. He was. He was a highly unusual dog. Marcus, are you asleep?"

"No."

"Good. So I wondered. And then one night, a couple of weeks later, we were in Kasia's, eating borscht. There was a couple at the next table, and the woman kept staring at my husband. Finally halfway through dinner, she said to him, 'You're the one whose dog was killed. You had him off the leash.' She turned to her husband. 'I told you about this guy—do you remember? Had that little dog running wild down Bedford Avenue? Big surprise he crosses against the light and a car gets him.' Her husband goes all apologetic, he says, 'Oh, my wife, this is her thing, dogs off the leash, she goes crazy,' and his wife goes, 'Hey! It's against the freakin' law, isn't it? And you see what happens? That dog was on a leash, he'd be alive today,' and so on. My husband gets upset, he says, 'That dog was always fine when he was off the leash, he was completely reliable, that was the only time.' He has tears in his eyes. But the woman wouldn't let up. Her husband was mortified. Finally we had to leave."

Marcus is gripping the stem of his glass much too tightly. He sets it down. "Is that true?"

"It's true."

"Thank you for telling me."

"It's a sad story. Isn't it?"

Marcus says it is, but he isn't feeling sad. He is feeling grateful that he has been given one more indication that maybe he is not, after all, the son of a heartless, psychopathic, murderous beast. That his father is not a sort of taller, older, differently disturbed Elliot C. He thinks of all the things he could tell Emily in return, things he feels sure she would like to know. About Summer, and the pies and cakes piling up on the kitchen counter, and the scary years after Grandma Mead died. The day he realized he had read nearly every book in the Honesdale Public Library; about Tamarind and the sonnets and Summer's blue mittens, and the time when through the window of his cabin he saw a hawk, in midair, snatch a smaller bird out of the sky and bear it away in its great claws.

But he doesn't say anything else, and after a minute, Emily says, "Can I tell you one more?"

"Sure. About what?"

"It's something I've never really talked about, and I don't know why I am now, except that—" Emily downs the rest of her champagne in a single gulp, like someone in a movie trying to gather the courage for a brave statement. "I'm drunk. And you're leaving."

"So what is it, Em?" Marcus asks gently.

"My husband," Emily says. "I think a lot of people wondered why I ever married him. I've wondered it myself. He was in some ways not a very nice man. He was cynical, and sarcastic, and sneaky. But, Marcus—" She smiles like someone smiling bravely through a bad case of flu. "I married him because I loved him. That's the simple truth. He was a rotter, but am I the first woman to love a rotter? It dwindled away after a while, of course. He did everything he could to kill it, and by the time he walked out on me, I think I was something like 78 percent over it, but I was still a wreck. He left an old shirt behind, and I slept with it every night for a month. I didn't give up the shirt until I got Otto."

The dog hears his name, and comes over to where they are sitting. Emily puts her dish of apple pie and melting ice cream on the floor for him.

"I'm not good at admitting it," she says. "I've never even said it to Gene Rae or Pat. It was too embarrassing. They thought he was such a jerk. And he was. I knew that. God, how he used to lie to me. About everything, anything. Just for the hell of it, I think. Or as if he just hated *clarity,* as if life were some peculiar experimental film. I almost had myself talked into the idea that I never loved the guy, but way back deep in my mind somewhere I knew that wasn't true. Like if you tell yourself, 'You know, you're not actually a human, you're a dog,' and you could come up with a bunch of doggish characteristics in yourself that you'd observed so that it kind of made sense? But you'd still fundamentally believe you're a human. So of course I knew he was a rat, but it didn't matter." Then she inhales deeply, as if she has just opened a window and leaned out. "And that's my second sad story, Marcus. And that's all I've got."

She knows I know she knows I know, he thinks, and he is aware this is the time to acknowledge that. He doesn't know what to say, but she is looking at him as if she expects an answer. He suddenly feels very young: This is his stepmother talking about his father. His stepmother is a glamorous photographer who is about to turn thirty-seven, wearing a black miniskirt and high heels. If it weren't for the divorce, the three of them might be sitting here eating Thanksgiving dinner together. There might even be a little kid at the end of the table calling Emily "Mommy." His half brother or sister. The imaginary sister he used to dream about when he was a kid, but years too late.

He looks at Emily, who has a sad, faraway look in her eyes, and wonders if she is thinking the same thing. Her eyes, he observes for the hundredth time, are very beautiful, even in the dim light where they have changed color like the river does, from blue to gray. As he stares at her, she turns her head and looks at him so intently that he begins to feel uncomfortable. It's a moment full of various nameless emotions he can't recognize—as if a piece of music has started up that seems familiar but that he can barely hear. Slowly, he arranges his face into what he hopes is a smile. He can't say what he knows he should say. Instead, he says, "But now you have Otto and

Izzy. Who are not rats." He knows it's dumb, but Emily doesn't seem to think so.

She looks down at Otto, who has licked the plate clean and is gazing up at them expectantly. He has ice cream on his whiskers. "It's true," Emily says. "I have Otto and Izzy. And did I tell you I'm adopting a kitten? You know how Otto loves cats. Gaby and Hattie said they have an adorable little tortoise shell."

"Sounds good."

"Actually, they have two. Siblings."

"So of course."

"Of course."

"Anna and Ada?"

"They're boys." She smiles at him. "I'm thinking maybe Leon and Noel."

"Excellent."

"And how is Willie?"

"He's doing better." Elliot Cobb's rottweiler ended up at the Pet Pound, and Marcus has been talked into adopting him. He has had him for a week, and he's not sorry, though Willie is difficult. *A challenge,* is how Hattie put it. *Obviously an abused dog.* Willie has mournful brown eyes that follow Marcus around the room. He stands next to Marcus looking up at him appealingly, but when Marcus tries to pet him he backs away. If Marcus approaches him too quickly, he snaps. He whines in the night. "When I took him to the park this morning with Rumpy and Elvis, he actually sort of romped a little, and he slept on the rug next to my bed last night."

"Those are good signs. The poor thing. He'll be all right."

"I think so."

"You know, I'm really drunk, Marcus."

"Yeah, me too."

"Maybe you should go."

"Yeah. But first I have to give you this present." He takes the bag he has stowed under his chair and hands it to her. "I'm sorry I didn't get around to wrapping it. Things have been sort of crazy, with Willie and everything."

"You shouldn't have."

"Should too."

"Well, maybe. And I have one for you." Emily gets up, wobbling a little in her high heels, and retrieves it from her desk.

His present to her is a copy of Thomas Trollope's memoir, *What I Remember*—a pretty little calfskin edition with marbled endpapers. "Wait," he says. "Get this." He opens it to page 137, and points, and Emily reads aloud: "Our mother's new puppy, Neptune, was a frisky Newfoundland." She gives a squeal of joy. "I knew it! And guess what, Marcus. I have a DOG for you. I figured now that you have a dog again, you might like it."

It's from the window of a groomer in midtown Manhattan, and under the word is a box full of petunias. Emily has put the photo into an antique frame she says was another fruit of her insane shopping spree.

"It's an excellent DOG. One of your best."

"I really wanted to buy you an iMac, but I figured you'd get mad. Or would you? If you won't, I will. It would make me so happy to do that. I could have it shipped to you in Honesdale."

He grins suddenly. "I wasn't going to tell you. I was going to *E-mail* you. I'm getting myself one, through Saul."

"Get outta here!"

"It's true. I had a little windfall."

The windfall is Summer's Whack, which Tamarind FedExed

to him. Wrzeszczynski says it's one of the best. "I think he was just starting when he painted this," Wrzeszczynski said. "Before he got so sick. I think this is a very early Whack. It has such freshness, such spontaneity. And it's funny, too—the burned toast."

Marcus has done his own deal with the periodontist—a Whack for a Mac, and then some. Marcus figures it was a dumb move—he should have waited for the right moment, sold it through Ptak or at Sotheby's and made a killing. But he likes Wrzeszczynski and wanted him to have it, and he wants the money now, not in a year. There will be the new roof, and he'd like to put a deck on the back of the house, overlooking the woods. When he told Wrzeszczynski all this, the periodontist looked at him curiously and said, "You seem so young for all this responsibility," and Marcus didn't know how to say he doesn't feel particularly young, and he doesn't feel particularly old either. He feels the way he has always felt.

In Honesdale, he thinks, he will live like a dog. The hand stretched out, or not. The romp on the lawn, or not. The walk in the rain or the nap by the stove. Present tense.

"Marcus?" Emily says. "Will you really E-mail me?"

"With annoying regularity."

"I suppose it's silly to say I'll miss you."

"No," Marcus says. "It isn't. But—hey, Em. Remember how I told you that if you walk in a straight line, you're really walking in a slight curve, so that if you go far enough you'll end up where you began?"

Emily smiles. "What goes around comes around?"

"Exactly."

"I hope that's true," she says.

"You will not hope in vain."

"Still, it sounds like a lot of walking."

"Get yourself a good pair of walking shoes. Don't try to do it in those heels."

She accompanies him to the door, where they look at each other for a minute, and then she leans over and kisses him on the forehead.

19

Are we not drawn onward, we few, drawn onward to new erA?

Are we not drawn onward,
we few, drawn onward
to new erA?

It's very late on the night after Thanksgiving. Emily Lime is sitting at her desk drinking a cup of tea. Earlier, she had dinner at Vera Cruz with Pat and Oliver, and over cheese burritos and guacamole they told her that Pat is indeed pregnant, the baby is due in June, they need more space, and would she consider trading her loft for Oliver's penthouse?

Emily is too excited to sleep.

She has been making lists.

She has figured out how she will arrange the penthouse, what furniture will go where, what she will have to get rid of, what she will try to palm off on Pat and Oliver. She has made a tentative list of the antique roses she will grow in pots on the roof: the Gallicas, damasks, albas, eglantines. She has balanced her checkbook and drawn up a budget for the year three, fast approaching. She has jotted down ideas for Christmas gifts for her family.

Now, at one in the morning, she can't think of any more lists to make.

The only thing left is to think about is Marcus, and she takes her tea over to the window to do so—*Marcus*—trying to picture him in Honesdale. His red truck is parked in the driveway of the gray farmhouse. The house will be dusty, spidery, and cold after being closed up all these years. Have he and the dog walked down Spring Hill Road to see the cows? And where did he have dinner? And is he asleep now, with Willie on the floor beside his bed?

Emily checked on the Web and found that the distance from North Third Street in Brooklyn to Spring Hill Road in Honesdale is exactly 111 miles, a fact she desperately wants to share with Marcus. Life, she fears, will now consist of things she wants to share with Marcus. And by the time she does they will be stale, boring, trivial—no longer fascinating little facts and numbers and what did you think of today's crossword puzzle, and the joke a little girl told her at the Pet Pound. *If you cross a cat with a parrot what do you get? A carrot.* She imagines Marcus's small down-turned smile, which will not come through in an E-mail.

Across the river, the city with its lights twinkles like Christmas, and the sky above it is a deep, dark blue. From the penthouse, she will be able to see the sun rise as well as set. The sun comes up in the kitchen, Oliver says, and the big thunderstorms start in the bathroom window, over Queens, and move west through the bedroom to the living room. How strange that she will be upstairs tending her roses and watching her kittens grow up while he and Pat raise a child here where she has lived so long. What she can't understand is how Marcus could bear to leave. Emily knows this odd little corner of the city is one of the things that sustains her, every bit as much as her friends do, and Otto and Izzy, and Noel and Leon, the new kittens, asleep in a tangle on her bed. How much will Marcus regret it all? How often will he think about her, and the park, and Rumpy and Reba and the Trollope group? "You guys were pretty tight," Oliver said at dinner. "You're really going to miss each other." The poignant thought has occurred to Emily that she and Marcus will miss each other a lot, and then after a while they'll only miss each other a little, and after a while they'll stop.

There could even come a day when she won't think of Marcus at all. Her SCARUM file will crash and die. The snapshot of little Marcus in his number 7 sweatshirt will fade away, and the photograph of his doorbell with MARCUS MEAD printed over it will be lost. She won't arrange his name at odd moments into inspirations like SCRAM, MAUDE. She will have forgotten who gave her Thomas Trollope's memoirs. She'll be a solitary old lady with a faded blue zipper around her wrist, wearing sensible cotton housedresses like they sell on Manhattan Avenue. "Remember Marcus?" Gene Rae will ask when she stops by with a bag of Polish cookies and pictures of her grandkids, and Emily will think: *Marcus. Marcus? Marcus who?*—and she'll have a vague memory of a boy with strange green eyes who used to walk her dog. Then she and Gene Rae will eat cookies and drink tea and talk about Proust, how maybe he was right, that we love only what we want and can't have.

But maybe after a while we stop wanting.

Thinking of cookies makes her hungry, and Emily gets up and looks in the fridge. There is a piece of Anstice's apple pie left. She sits down at the kitchen table to eat it. A postcard from Susan Skolnick is propped against the salt shaker. On one side is a picture of a pine forest with a patch of blue lake and GREET-INGS FROM THE LAND OF A THOUSAND LAKES. On the other side, it says: *Here I am. The lake hasn't changed. I'm trying to figure out how to do this. I'll let you know when I get settled. Thanks for your help. Happy Thanksgiving. Susan.*

Emily took the card with her to show to Oliver and Pat at dinner. "What kind of help?" Pat asked.

Emily shrugged. "I didn't tell her she was crazy to go."

"She was a strange bird."

"I ended up kind of liking her. I guess we're friends now. If she invites me up to Maine, I'll go and visit."

"You've heard about Luther and Lamont moving to Italy?"

"Yeah, but so far it's just a twinkle in their eye, I hope."

"Luther's eye, mostly. I think he thinks he can keep a lid on Lamont if they live someplace where he doesn't speak the language."

"Lamont will be fluent in Italian in about two weeks."

"Fiona's been cat-sitting at their place, and she wants to sublet. She's also interested in taking over the Tragedy. I hear they're trying to work out some kind of a deal."

"I can't think about this. It's too horrible. And I won't believe it until I hear *arrividerci* from Luther and Lamont's own lips."

"That would devastate the Trollope group. First Marcus, now the L's."

"Jeanette will be back in the spring. And Dr. Wrzeszczynski and his wife are interested in joining."

"Really? Maybe Anstice and Dr. Demand will join, too."

"They'll have to get out of bed first," Oliver said.

"Who knows how that will work out? It is fraught with difficulties."

"Speaking of difficulties," Oliver said, "get Anstice to repair the bathroom window. And frankly, at the rent you're probably going to be paying, I think she ought to put down some new tile. And fix up the kitchen a little."

"We'll see. I really like it the way it is." Emily knows she won't change anything: shabby linoleum, broken tile, leaky window. She has lusted after it for so long, it would be like marrying the man of your dreams and making him get a nose job.

"You're such a romantic."

"I'm not," Emily insisted. "I'm a stodgy stick-in-the-mud, probably well on my way to becoming an old fart. I hate it when things change. I'm so relieved you guys aren't moving to the suburbs or someplace after you have a kid."

"Raise little Kizette in the burbs? Be serious. We'll never leave."

"Kizette?"

"If it's a girl. Prague if it's a boy."

"Promise you won't move to Mineola or someplace? Larchmont? Fort Salonga?"

"Promise."

"I'm afraid for this neighborhood. Remember the old days? The pigeon flyers? The lace curtains? The Polish graffiti?"

"Em?" Pat put her hand over Emily's. "They're all still here."

"Yeah." Emily knows it's true. Just that afternoon, when the light was leaving, she watched two flocks of pigeons wheeling in the air, crossing each other, and as they angled down, the dying sun caught the underside of their wings, turning them to gold, like leaves swept up by the wind. The sight gave her such comfort she almost wept. "But they're going. You know they are."

"The crack vials all over the sidewalks are gone, too," Oliver reminded her. "And the boarded-up stores no one would rent. The garbage dump. And no one has been mugged around here in a long time."

"I know, I know."

"Things change, Em. They have to. And sometimes it's okay."

"I know. Like Anstice says, they used to treat migraines with powdered stag horn dissolved in mead. Now it's Lou Reed and sumatriptan."

"And Samuel Johnson used to crusade against the word *fun*. He thought it was vulgar."

"And they used to preach about Elvis in churches."

Emily turned her hand over to squeeze Pat's tiny hand, and reached out for Oliver's. They sat for a moment, connected—like a séance or a prayer group—before they returned to their chips and guacamole.

Before they left, she told them she's decided to go to Hugh Lang's poker game next Friday, and they looked at her—Pat with her little rabbity grin, Oliver with his big loose-lipped one—as if she had just given them a wonderful gift.

It has begun to snow, a few random flakes that, surprisingly quickly, become a thickening veil. Emily finishes her tea, yawns, and goes back to the window. The roof opposite, lit up all night, is covered, and the water tower has a white hat. One of the kittens—Noel, she's pretty sure—leaps off the bed and stalks over to the sofa where she is sitting. He jumps up and kneads her lap, then settles down, purring, and, together, they watch the snow fall on the city out of the deep blue of the night sky.

I cannot pretend that the reader shall know, as he ought to be made to know, the future fate and fortunes of our personages. They must be left still struggling. But then is not such always in truth the case . . .?

Solos

Discussion Questions

1. Marcus and Emily share an obsession with names, area codes, anagrams, crosswords, palindromes, and the like. Independently, they both play the "word worms" game to transform their last names—Mead to Lime and Lime to Mead. How do these interests reflect a desire to order the world, to find an inner logic in life's chaos? Can you see how they could give Marcus "a deep sense of peace and contentment that he achieved otherwise only in the company of animals" (p.68)?

2. How do the three words that Emily photographs—Time, Bread, and Dog—relate to her life? In the end, she gets money from someone else's art, instead of her own: but Joe Whack also worked in threes, and according to Wrzeszczynski, his paintings are "memorials to life. To what is around us. To the small nothings that are what our lives are made of. To the beauty of the insignificant" (p. 197). In what ways could that description apply to Emily's pictures as well?

3. Names are important to Marcus, and they're obviously important to author Kitty Burns Florey as well. As in Anthony Trollope's

novels (whose characters include Phineas Finn, Sir Marmaduke Morecombe, Lily Dale, and Quintus Slide), *Solos* is packed with unusual, evocative names, like Merlin Wolf, Tilda Ramsey, Summer Mead, Dr. Demand, and, of course, Emily Lime. How does Florey use names to suggest character and create atmosphere? What associations do you make with names like Tab Hartwell, Anstice Mullen, or Gene Rae Foster?

4. What do you think makes Marcus so attractive to Emily, and vice versa? Is age really the biggest barrier between them, or is it something else? Were you disappointed that they didn't end up together? Do you think that there are people, perhaps like Emily and Marcus, who were made to be alone—solos?

5. Why do you think Marcus feels more comfortable with animals than with people? The Trollope group discusses the dog in *Dr. Wortle's School*, including "his function in the scene as a way to demonstrate Peacocke's excellence" (p. 107). What do the pets in *Solos* demonstrate? For example, observing Elliot C. in the park with his rottweiler, Emily says, "He didn't even talk to his dog. He's probably one of those guys who buys cheap generic dog food and forgets to keep the water bowl filled" (p. 7). In this case, her distrust turns out to be justified; in general, do you think a person's interaction with their pet is revealing? After the Skolnicks' dog bites their daughter and they have it put down, Susan becomes a Williamsburg pariah, and even the mild-mannered Marcus says, "I don't care why or how, I just want her to suffer" (p. 10). Do you think this is justified?

6. "We love only what we want and can't have" is a bit of wisdom that Emily and Gene Rae ascribe to Proust (p. 266). Do you agree? Emily further refines the theory: "[W]hat Proust meant really applies only to people. Animals never disappoint, and, actually, she is pretty sure the shoes won't, either" (p. 242). Do you think Marcus's unattainability—because of his age, antecedents, and apparent asexuality—was part of his allure for Emily?

7. What role does Elliot Cobb, the Williamsburg rapist, serve in the narrative? Why do you think the author chose Susan Skolnick to vanquish him? Do you think it's significant that his death—falling off the roof—echoes the one that Marcus pretended to have planned for Emily?

8. During one of Hart's lectures, the young Marcus postulates to himself that "if you weren't happy, you were more inclined to think there was something wrong with almost everyone in the world, but if you were happy, then you figured other people were probably okay" (p. 81). Later in the book, we're given a more concrete example: What Emily sees as the "big jolly Hasidic families" (p. 200) in the Brooklyn Botanic Gardens are snidely described by Hart as "Eleven badly dressed kids, plus Mom in her tailored coat and sensible shoes" (p. 137). Can both views be correct? How do they reflect Emily and Hart's differing outlooks on life? Do you think Marcus is right?

9. Emily is struck by the last sentence of Trollope's *Miss Mackenzie*, in which Miss Mackenzie, now Lady Bell, accepts the life that comes her way "thankfully, quietly, and with an enduring satisfaction, as it became such a woman to do" (p. 247). Do you see parallels to Emily's own story? Do you see her as a passive character, or is her graceful, tranquil attitude toward life an action in itself? What do you think of Marcus's description of her as the last pigeon to fly from the sidewalk, determinedly pecking at a crumb (p. 192)? Emily herself wonders, "Is it okay that I'm distant? Removed? Oblivious? I mean, I like being the way I am, but I just wonder if it means there's something wrong with me" (p. 125). Do you think she's "oblivious," and if so, is it a bad thing? How might her obliviousness feed her optimism?

10. The Williamsburg presented here is, in many ways, like a small town—in the way everyone knows everyone else, the small shops, and even in the way Susan Skolnick is shunned. What is attractive about the community to you? What's not? Is Emily right to worry